Death in a Cold City

![logo] Buffalo Arts Publishing

Email: info@buffaloartspublishing.com

Cover design by Len Kagelmacher

ISBN 978-1-950006-01-4

Death in a Cold City

by

Joan Fitzgerald

Chapter One

Dennis Milvern crouched inside a small, domed ice fisherman's tent out on the frozen lake, waiting for his partner. He had never been so cold. He kept removing his gloves and rubbing his fingers together, trying to restore the circulation. Mike Stokes was supposed to meet him here for the drug transaction, and Mike had told him which tent to approach. The fisherman who owned it gladly accepted fifty dollars for a few hours use. Inside, a bucket of perch and walleye stood next to the fishing hole.

The weather was changing rapidly. In the morning, the sky had been a clear, electric blue, and the buildings of the Port City glistened in the light. A few hours later, gray smudges appeared on the horizon over the lake, and a fast-driven snow began to pit the surface of the ice beyond the break wall. By three in the afternoon, the storm had become a lake-effect blizzard. Visibility was reduced to almost zero as large drifts accumulated rapidly. Cars crept along the Lake Shore Road with their lights on, and all traffic slowed to under twenty miles an hour near the small boat harbor.

In front of the retaining wall, clumps of ice fishermen sat as motionless as statues inside the windbreaks they had erected over holes cut in the ice. Near the harbor, the ghostly outlines of abandoned grain elevators and a deserted cement plant faded as piles of snow changed from cobalt to a glacial white. A blackened sky hung over the harbor and obscured the thin arc of the recently reconstructed Shoreline Bridge.

The small boat harbor was a terrible place for a meeting, and now, because of the intensity of the storm, Mike was late.

Dennis had complained when the site was suggested. "I'm not driving out to the lake shore, for God's sake! There are plenty of places to meet in the city!"

His partner was insistent.

"We're too well-known on the West Side. All the places there are watched by the police or informants. You saw how the waiter acted suspiciously last month at Foschio's. I can't take any chances. These deals are important and have to be done in strict secrecy. No one will be expecting us to do a transaction at the small boat harbor. My brother-in-law will let us use his tent, and he doesn't want to know anything."

A heavy gust of wind blew snow under the bottom of the flimsy structure, almost uprooting it. Dennis was shaking. He felt that he would never be warm again. Why couldn't they have met at a bar in the suburbs?

He decided to think about his girlfriend, hoping to take his mind off the weather. She was really not his girlfriend, but a woman whom he dated when she let him, in return for gifts and money.

Black. That was how Katherine Denicia referred to herself, but that did not describe her. Her skin was a pale, smooth shade like a color of paint that his mother had spread on their living room walls when he was a kid. A pure, opaque beige. Sometimes, she wore blue contact lenses and the contrast between her complexion and the bright azure color made her look incredibly exotic.

Maybe he would buy her some expensive jewelry with the proceeds of today's deal, or perhaps another coat. He was always buying her coats. She never asked where the money came from. He didn't say much about his job, and she didn't know that he was married, had a kid. If it ever came to serious encouragement from her, he would leave his wife. The kid was too young to remember him.

He tried to conjure up Katherine's image in the frosty air, but it was as elusive as she was. She never seemed to be at her apartment. He would call and call, and finally jump into his car and cruise around the massive Gothic building downtown where she took a few college courses. Parked in a line of idling cars in front of the main door, he would examine the animals and birds carved into the facade, the lambs, eagles and a huge buffalo head. No one made buildings like that nowadays. He waited for her to trip down the front steps—propelled by that high-hipped walk of hers, and then she would feign surprise at seeing him in the caravan of boyfriends and parents waiting to pick up students.

Dennis pushed aside the tarp covering the entrance to the tent and scouted the frozen harbor. There was no sign of Mike. The wind was sandpapering the ice, blasting snow against the tent. He was going to wait ten more minutes and that would be it. They would have to set up another appointment.

He'd take Katherine out to dinner at a nice restaurant. God knows she ate like a student at times. Wings and pizza. Once, they had gone to a fast food place in the bus terminal across from the college.

"Not that dump!" he protested.

"But I am so starved! I want hot cherry pie and a hamburger," she pouted while slinging her books onto the back seat of the car.

He still argued, because he knew that there was going to be no reward for a quick lunch in the bus terminal. Just the chance to drive her home and watch her dash inside her building, calling over her shoulder about how her sister needed her or that her aunt was coming, and she would be sure to ask him up next week. She would vanish—her maroon-streaked hair caught up in a big bunch on the side of her head, suede coat open to the winter. She lived in a tall, crumbling mansion divided into apartments near the river on a street lined with ancient linden trees. It was a mixed neighborhood—blacks, Puerto Ricans, whites. The street was messy, always full of trash and old bricks. People seemed to be constantly tearing things down, throwing stuff out.

"I don't like this neighborhood," he told her. "It's not safe."

"Safer than the one you live in. Mine still has some elegance."

Dennis was becoming unbearably nervous. Five more minutes.

A gray pickup truck pushed its way through the drifts near the harbor entrance. The driver got out and braced himself against the vicious winds, plodded onto the harsh, rutted grooves of the ice.

Dennis looked up with relief as the tent flap was parted.

"Christ, Mike, I almost gave up hope that you were coming--" he started to say, but he was staring at a huge man with a large, round head, almost like a pumpkin, who filled the entrance, blocking out the murky light.

"What do you want? Who are you?" he demanded.

The man reached into his heavy, down jacket and brought his hand up in a deliberate arc.

The shot caught Dennis in the face, the wind muffling the sound of the report. As he fell, he knocked over the bucket of fish, their chilled, iridescent skin colliding with the packed snow. The stranger quickly searched him as he lay hunched over the ice hole, handled him roughly.

"What the hell! Where's the package?"

But there it was, tucked behind Dennis Milvern's belt, against his spine. The man pulled it out—opened it gently.

"It don't look right," he muttered.

He fingered the contents, brought a few grains to his lips.

"Definitely not product. This is bad, very bad. I got to get out of here." He removed Milvern's wallet and keys from his pocket, pawed at the coat once more to make sure that there wasn't another package.

"I've done my job," he rationalized. "If Jack is unhappy, tough shit."

He turned on the radio just as the weather reporter, Louetta Heatherton, was updating the news. Why did they hire a news broad who spoke as though her mouth was full of beans?

"There is a severe weather warning for the next twenty-four hours," she burbled. "At least eighteen inches of snow and possibly more are expected to fall over the city and the hills to the south. High winds are expected."

Good! More rotten weather! Exactly what he wanted. The body wouldn't be found for a while. Filled with elation, he switched to a country western station as he maneuvered the pickup around several stuck vehicles and turned onto an exit road. He bellowed out his own lyrics, obliterating the radio singer's voice, holding an imaginary mike in his right hand while steering with his left: "I got the bull rider blues. My broken bones ain't such good news." He wrote country western songs, expected to be a famous singer some day. In his apartment closet at home were three stetson hats and a floor full of cowboy boots. All he needed was the big chance.

His was the last vehicle to leave the Lake Shore Road before the police closed it, a patrol car parked crossways, red lights flashing in the thickened air. Officers were making an attempt to get the ice fishermen out of the harbor. The ones beyond the breakwall would have to be taken out by helicopter. Rescuing them was an annual headache which cost the city a bundle. But that would be much later—after the storm abated.

An unruly crowd shouted obscenities in English and Spanish as rocks, chunks of ice, and beer bottles were hurled indiscriminately at the two targets. The first was the dilapidated house where the shots had been heard. The second quarry was the two homicide detectives standing in the street behind their car, trying to ignore the catcalls and jeers, while being bombarded with trash. The bystanders were excited and angry, trying to dodge around other policemen who had cordoned off part of the neighborhood where the confrontation was taking place, hoping for a better view. The narrow snow-covered streets were filled with people, and more spectators stood in clusters on porches of the old, three-story houses, some of them drinking from cans of beer.

"Hey, Mister policeman. You gonna get the shooter?"

"I hope he kills you too! You guys beat up my brother down at the station."

"Why the hell don't they keep those idiots farther back?" Detective Leo Aronica muttered, ducking a pop bottle. Despite an insulating layer of fat, he was freezing cold.

"Most of them got here before we did. The neighbors called us after they heard shots, but the altercation had been going on for some time," his partner, Martin McCallister, explained. "The person who phoned it in said that the woman had a restraining order against the guy. He's been arrested for beating her up before."

"Now, he can be arrested for murder," Leo responded.

"Madre de Dios!" a woman screamed, as an Hispanic man threw open the front door of the house and walked onto the porch. He wore jeans and a filthy shirt that had one sleeve partly ripped away. Glaring wildly around, he raised a gun and fired at the police car, shattering the side window before ducking back inside.

The crowd yelled in appreciation. "Good shooting!"

The two detectives had instinctively dived into a snow bank.

"I really need this," muttered Aronica, shaking glass fragments and ice from his tousled, black hair as they stood up. "You O.K. Marty?"

"Yeah."

"He almost got you, policeman," someone called. Some children giggled nervously and a woman could be heard crying hysterically.

The fugitive slammed open the door again and flung an object at the two detectives. It hit Aronica on the shoulder before sliding off his coat into the snow. Leo peered at the mustard-colored smear on his jacket. "Oh, my God! It's a diaper! He hit me with some shit!" The crowd went wild with delight as he brushed frantically at his jacket. During the uproar, a patrolman standing back near the barricades took careful aim and shot the suspect neatly though the chest. The man fell in a contorted heap against the porch railing, and the crowd became instantly quiet.

"Well, that's it," Martin sighed. "Come on, Leo. We can go inside now. Just be glad that the TV crew hasn't arrived."

"I've got shit on my coat," Leo protested.

The detectives carefully skirted the body on the slushy porch and entered the cheerless house where a woman was sprawled on the cracked kitchen linoleum. She wore jeans and a blouse that was pulled up exposing green bruises on her chest. One hand pointed to the cupboards where a trail of blood mixed with the dirt on the floor. Two young children crouched near the refrigerator, their teeth chattering with fright. The girl was dressed in a ragged slip and the small boy wore only an undershirt. He clutched his tiny purple bud of a penis frantically. A smear of excrement ran down his leg.

"Marty! Kids! They can't be here! This is terrible. He shot their mother right in front of them." Picking up both children, he carried them into the living room where he deposited them on the torn couch and wrapped them in a filthy afghan.

Wrenching the front door open, he yelled to the patrolmen: "Get Child Protective Services fast! There are two kids in here!"

The crime scene team arrived shortly and, assisted by the patrolmen, started processing both shootings. An ambulance was expected any minute to remove the bodies. Martin and Leo took statements from several of the neighbors, most of whom were eager to give their opinions.

"He beat up the woman and terrorized the kids. I hear them fighting all the time."

"Was she his wife?" Leo asked.

"They live together, but they not married. Will I be on television?"

"I doubt it," Leo responded.

"There isn't anything else we can do here," Martin commented. The garage that the precinct utilized had been called to have the police car towed, the glass shards removed and the window replaced.

"We gotta stop at my house, Marty. Look at me! We have to take a taxi, so I can change out of this filthy jacket."

"Oh, I agree. You reek. There's a cab over there."

"I can't stand this smell, Marty," Leo complained as they headed for his house. The taxi driver was holding a Kleenex to his nose, and Martin pushed close to the open side window.

"We'll be there in a minute. Don't breathe deeply."

Leo and his family lived in an unpretentious gray two-story house not too far from the college. Martin waited in the living room while Leo went upstairs to change his clothes. The room was consistent with many others in a devout Catholic home. Leo and Maria's wedding picture hung on the wall, showing a much thinner Leo next to a smiling Maria in her long, white bridal gown, holding a bouquet of roses. Martin remembered rooms like this years ago in the houses of people of his parent's generation. A portrait of President Kennedy with an American flag unfurled behind him always decorated another wall. Few people hung pictures of presidents in their rooms anymore. This room was wallpapered with a pink floral motif, and the furniture was of some blue fabric. A large arrangement of family photos, the children at various ages and close relatives, adorned a chest under a window hung with stiff beige satin drapes. It was an ordinary room but pleasant.

He and Leo had been homicide partners for several years, and their temperaments were extremely different. His partner was married with three children and a wife who worked part-time in a drug store. Gregarious to the max, he had a huge extended family and belonged to all sorts of groups like the Knights of Columbus and the Port City Bowlers. Martin was divorced and somewhat of a loner. He had worked vice until it drove him crazy, and he transferred to homicide. Murder suited him more than pedophilia, and he was reasonably content. Leo, on the other hand, was prone to question his career choice. He had little appetite for human failings and hated twisted, involved cases. But they got along, and were even somewhat fond of each other, although neither one would ever admit it.

Leo appeared holding a black garbage bag.

"I took a shower and washed my hair, but I can still smell the crap. I don't know if a dry cleaner will touch this mess! I'm going to put it in the garage and ask Maria what she thinks. It's my uniform, but even so."

Back in the taxi, Martin noticed that the driver had sprayed a floral air-freshener lavishly, which was almost as bad as the diaper smell.

"Lets go to lunch, Marty. We can write up our reports after we get back to the precinct."

"All right. We'll take my car. It's in the lot at the station."

They went to a restaurant that they frequented a lot, Mama Cora's, where they had gotten to know the staff. The owner was a middle-aged man who wandered around the tables playing his harmonica, taking requests. He always wore T-shirts printed with the faces of popular musicians. The artwork today was Elton John, and he was rendering Rocket Man. Early American memorabilia crowded the walls and oddities hung from the fake ceiling rafters. Pictures of vintage fire trucks with their mustached crew members standing in front of them hung next to gold framed depictions of Victorian ladies. Rakes, buckets and other farm utensils competed with vases of artificial flowers, china dogs and blinking Christmas tree lights which were never turned off.

Leo had a pepperoni pizza and Martin ordered pasta broccoli, pretty substantial for lunch, but they were both very hungry after the morning's event.

"Marty, I got a lot of trouble with my youngest kid. She's driving us crazy!" Leo said between bites.

"What's the problem?"

"On Sunday, the whole family usually gets together for a big dinner. Maria spends the whole morning cooking and the relatives come over. Although, I tell you, it's not like the old days when eighteen people was nothing. Now, we're lucky if six attend, and it hurts Maria, because she goes to so much trouble. Anyway, our son, Rocco, was there, Gloria, the nine-year-old, Maria's mother and her Aunt Phyllis, along with the two of us. Not much of a turnout. Tina, my fifteen-year-old, went to a friend's house after church. She called us and said she was having dinner there. She didn't show up until ten o'clock in the evening. I could smell alcohol, and she was all rumpled. Her mother almost hit her. She had her hand raised. Now, the kid is grounded, but I'm afraid of what she's up to. Where did we go wrong, Marty?" Leo wiped pizza sauce off his chin.

"Leo, your oldest, Rocco, is a great kid. He's doing well at Saint Anthony's Academy, gives you no problems. You must be doing something right."

"But what kind of an example is Tina setting for Gloria? I tell you—I don't sleep nights."

"Just keep on with whatever you're doing. This might just be a phase. Is she into school clubs? Sports?"

"Just after-school girls' basketball. At least we think that's where she is. I'm not sure of anything anymore."

"Try to get her involved with other activities, so she doesn't have much time to get in trouble. Come on, time to go back to work."

After they got back at the precinct, the dispatcher sent them out to the small boat harbor to investigate a homicide. "The body was just discovered this morning by an ice fisherman. The road was closed yesterday because of the storm, so there's no way of knowing when it happened."

The snow had let up, and Lake Shore Road was plowed, though the driving was difficult because of the high drifts blown off the lake. They turned into a parking lot near a shuttered summer restaurant, parked the car and walked out onto the ice.

"I'm frozen already," Leo complained as they trudged through the deep snow. The fishing tents were occupied again, and men peered suspiciously out at the detectives. There was no mistaking the site of the crime. The dome-shaped tent had blown over, and the body was sprawled over a hole in the ice, both half-covered with snow. Martin carefully rolled the rigid form onto its back. The face was rank with solidified blood.

"Shot in the face," Leo commented.

Martin tried to pry the collapsed tent off the ice.

"Oh God, I hate the cold," his partner muttered through chattering teeth.

"Maybe you should move to Florida."

"When I retire, we are going to buy a nice Double Wide near a beach. What do you make of this?"

"Well, this is the perfect place for an assassination. We've retrieved at least six corpses in this same three-mile stretch in the past few years. Remember the Indian woman who was found back near the flats last September?"

"That was during warm weather. Why do they fish in the winter?" He gestured toward the fishermen motionless in their tents.

"They consider it a sport. Bring a couple of bottles of red wine, a few magazines, and they're out of the house for the afternoon, might even take home a few fish."

"I don't know. A lot of heavy industry used to be around here. This water is pretty polluted. I wouldn't want to eat those fish."

"Lets call the wagon, have the victim removed and get the team in here. I don't think we're going to learn anything."

"How did he get here, Marty? There's no vehicle."

"I imagine that somebody hot-wired it and sold it to a chop shop. We'll never see it. Three bodies in one week if you count the Spanish guy our patrolman shot. This month is off to a running start."

Chapter Two

Grace Milvern sat on the faded couch in her silent apartment watching snowflakes swirl against the darkened front window. The phone had rung continuously all evening, but each time that she answered, the caller had hung up. It gave her the creeps. She wished that Dennis would come home. Every fifteen minutes, she looked out the window at the street, but there was no sign of his car.

Her eyes strayed to the pile of bills and late notices on the end table—car payments, doctor bills for the baby. The phone bill was up to almost one hundred dollars. It was probably going to be shut off soon.

She jumped as the phone shrilled again, the sound piercing the gloomy room.

"Hello," she said, tentatively.

The man's voice was low and rough. "Is Dennis there?"

"No he's not home."

"He was supposed to meet me yesterday. Where is he?"

"Who is this?"

"Mike Stokes. If he comes in, tell him to call me. It's important. He knows the number." The man hung up abruptly.

"This is driving me crazy," Grace thought. "Where is Dennis?"

She went to rummage in the tiny kitchen to see if she could find some wine. Nothing. Half of the kitchen walls were white and the others were a dull, ugly mustard color. They had started to paint them, and then had run out of paint, and there was no money to buy more. The slanted attic walls made it impossible to stand up except in the center of the room, and it was always dark. The lights had to be kept on even during the day.

Their situation had been bad ever since Dennis was laid off from his job. Before that, they lived in a four-room apartment with large sunny windows over near the Science Museum. On Sunday afternoons, they went to the park behind the art gallery and listened to free jazz concerts, while the baby crawled around on a blanket. Afterward, they walked down to the Sweet Parlor for hot- fudge sundaes. Sometimes, they pushed the baby carriage down to the narrow walkway between the river and the canal where gulls swooped and dove. They never had much money, but they were happy enough.

Then, Dennis lost his job, and they were forced to move to these dilapidated rooms on the third floor of an apartment house on the West side. Dennis was never home. She hardly saw him.

"I'm trying to make contacts, look for work," he protested when she questioned him. His face was contorted. He looked as though he hated her.

She decided not to answer the phone if it rang again.

"I'm going out to buy some wine. He's not coming home, and I have to get through the evening somehow. I can have a glass of Chablis and watch TV, if it works well enough to see anything."

She went into the bedroom where the baby's crib was jammed against the sloping walls. He was on his back, dressed in layers of sweaters and heavy pajamas, breathing rhythmically, his arm around a Teddy bear.

He'll be asleep until morning, Grace decided. I'll only be gone for five minutes if I hurry. The liquor store closes at ten.

She locked the door of the apartment and went down the frigid stairway that was permeated with a musky smell like that of a dead animal. When they first moved here, she scrubbed the bare wood with Lysol, but the smell never went away. Opening the heavy front door with the dirty glass pane, she went out into the street. Outside, rows of dark, three-story houses sat close together. Some of them had snow-crusted fire escapes clinging to the upper stories like lacy skeletons. She passed one that had been the scene of a fire last month. There were charred areas on the outside walls, and plywood sheets were nailed over the windows. A sign nailed to the front said Palisano Emergency Enclosures.

The wind tore at her. She had forgotten to wear her ski hat, and her hair whipped across her face. It was snowing so hard that she could barely see the street. She trudged down to the main avenue where the businesses were located.

Garish blue light issued from the Soft and Clean Laundromat and flashed across her face, illuminating it with bars of color. A sign proclaimed Twenty-Four Hours. Open Twenty-Four Hours. There was no one inside.

The next store was Almada's Liquors, a small, cluttered place with standing shelves covered with rows of bottles. The front door chimed as she entered the store. Then, abruptly, a loud report obscured the sound of her labored breath. The bell still clanged as she was frozen in the doorway. Her startled eyes met those of a heavy-set man as he turned to face her. As he swung his arm around, she saw the gun in his hand. A violent surge of fear and adrenalin hit her, and she ran back into the street. Slipping in the snow, she passed the laundromat and turned, stumbling into the first alley she came to. It was terribly narrow, filled with garbage cans and stacks of cardboard boxes frozen into the mud. She blundered down the alley as far as she was able to go, fell, and then crawled behind a heap of cartons, pulled her coat over her head. She listened acutely, straining for any sound.

There was scuffling, the sound of garbage cans being kicked aside, turned over. Someone was in the alley. She drew further back and forced her way into an empty carton. The smell inside of rotten garbage and dog shit was disgusting. Another garbage can went over, toppling against her hiding place, flattening the box.

"Don't let him find me," she prayed. "Please."

There were sounds of harsh breathing as the man ripped the trash apart, threw junk around. Then, the steps receded and the alley became quiet. There were no more footsteps, just the sound of the wind lashing the snow about, but she didn't dare leave.

She remained in the dark carton for hours, her hands covering her frozen ears. Finally, she was so cold that she knew she had to get out. Pushing the boxes aside, she knocked over the garbage can imprisoning her and staggered down the alley on numb legs. She peered carefully around the corner of the building. There was no one on the street. Putting her head down, she limped home through the blowing snow.

When she got back to her apartment, she made sure that all the locks were set and went to check on the baby. He still slept just as she had left him. Dennis was not home. She yanked the blankets off her bed and lay down on the couch with them wrapped around her. All night, she shook uncontrollably.

The next morning, Grace lifted the baby from his crib, changed him, fed him and sponged the chubby face. It was too cold in the apartment to give him a bath. Then, she sat him on the kitchen floor where he rocked back and forth making singing noises and banging on some pots. Grace watched the locked door, nervously. The phone rang several times, but she didn't answer. She turned on the TV and stared at the game show in progress. As the day went on, there was no sign of Dennis. By late afternoon, her fear had given way to apathy, and she gazed dully out the tiny attic window. The news came on the TV at six o'clock in the evening. Outside, the darkened street was silent. The day had passed so quickly that she was unable to remember light at all. The baby's chaotic cries as he lurched about the kitchen were the only sounds. She picked him up and placed him in his playpen, as she turned up the volume on the set and adjusted the fuzzy picture on the screen. The face of John Bradford, the Channel 8 anchorman, materialized slowly.

He started his report, speaking in a very serious tone of voice. "Tonight we begin with two senseless acts of violence in the Port City. Two men died yesterday, alone and unaided. One death occurred on the west side of the city and the second in the freezing cold of the small boat harbor."

Pausing for dramatic effect, he continued. "Police discovered the body of Nathan Scortino, night clerk at Almada's Liquor store, on the floor of the establishment. He had been shot once at close range. There appears to be no motive for the shooting. Mr. Scortino was a student at the university by day and worked nights at the liquor store. At the moment, police tell us, there are no leads."

Grace abruptly came out of her dazed state. "Oh, my God," she whispered. "I was there."

"Miles away," Bradford continued, "In another incomprehensible act, an ice fisherman was gunned down in his tent at the small boat harbor."

Grace wasn't paying attention. She was still focused on the killing of the store clerk. "The murderer saw me. He could kill me too."

The anchorman was still discussing the other murder. "The body was not discovered until late morning due to high winds and drifting snow. The Lake Shore complex was closed by the police yesterday and only reopened at six this morning when highway crews were able to plow the area. The victim is an unidentified white male about thirty-years-old with brown hair and blue eyes, weighing about one hundred and sixty pounds. He was wearing jeans, and a gray jacket with a blue and yellow patch on the arm. No identification was found on the body, and there were no vehicles in the area. If any of our viewers have any information about either of these horrific crimes, call Channel 8 or the police at once. In other news— fire over night destroyed a building at—"

Grace screamed. "Dennis! That's Dennis! His gray jacket with the patch!" She twisted the dial on the TV to get another station.

"An unidentified man wearing jeans, a gray jacket with a blue and yellow patch on the arm—"

She turned the dial again.

"Mr. Scortino was studying economics at the university—"

She started to cry.

"He wouldn't be at the small boat harbor. Why would he be out on the lake? I don't understand. It can't be Dennis."

The baby started to howl in his playpen, and she picked him up and paced about the room. "I don't know what to do," she sobbed into

Denny's soft hair. "I don't know what to do. But what if it is Dennis? I have to call the police, tell them that it could be my husband. Dennis, what have you done?"

Sitting the baby on the floor, she pulled out the phone book. Her hands shook as she turned the pages until she located the number of the police station, and dialed.

"It's about the man who was shot out on the lake," she cried hysterically. "It might be my husband. Please help me!"

But then, after she had talked to a detective about Dennis, she remembered the other killing—the one she had witnessed at the liquor store.

"I can't tell the police about that. I won't tell anyone. The killer could come after me, kill me too. I don't know anything. I won't think about it."

Katherine Denicia Jordan was seated on her Victorian sofa in a living room crowded with hundreds of dolls, plant stands full of ferns, Indian pillows and framed drawings, while she watched the Channel 8 TV anchor report the evening news.

"The victim in the killing at the small boat harbor has been identified as Dennis Milvern. Mr. Milvern was unemployed at the time of his death," John Bradford intoned. "He formerly worked as a security guard at Greenberg Security Systems. Milvern is survived by his wife, Grace, and a young child, Dennis Junior."

"Unemployed?" Katherine mused. "Then where did Dennis get the money to buy me this?" She fingered an opal medallion with a gold filigree setting. "Or these?" She jangled several gold bracelets. "Unemployed, perhaps, but certainly working at something lucrative. Good heavens! Someone has eradicated Dennis!"

She couldn't care less about his wife and child, and she wasn't terribly surprised at his demise. He had always seemed to be a questionable person, and there were no feelings of remorse, just a slight regret that the gifts wouldn't be forthcoming any more. Dennis was always too demanding, trying to establish a relationship, and she definitely didn't want that—never! No, she wouldn't miss him.

Besides, he had crazy ideas, like the tattoo. He wanted her to get a butterfly or a rose or some stupid image inscribed on her hip.

"Black people don't go in for tattoos, unless they're athletes," she told him. "That's a lot of white sixties shit."

"Why not? I'm sure there are lots of blacks with tattoos."

"You mean designs that say 'Mother' or 'Dennis Forever?' You have got to be kidding."

"But didn't they used to cut scars into their bodies when they were running around naked in Africa? That's the same thing."

She hated him when he spoke disparagingly of black people.

"You are so dumb! Cicatrices. That's what they were! Scars were cut to enhance their appearance. Lovely patterns of decoration. Feel so nice when you run your fingers over them. The delicate ridges created beauty and stimulated sexual feeling."

"I think I like the idea. Let's try— "

"No! Answer this tattoo question. Why do you want me to mutilate myself?"

"For me," he said, burying his face in her hair between her neck and shoulders, burrowing into the creamy, beige warmth. "I want you to do it for me. They will be a part of you that's always mine."

"Honey, nothing of me will be yours, you or anyone else's. And I am not going to get no rose or no butterfly." She laughed at him, teeth gleaming in her mouth, strong as rocks.

They had been in her bedroom, lying on the bed—her very old, enameled bed with loops and sinuous shapes carved into the headboard. She had tied some waxy-looking artificial flowers to the post and hung a paisley shawl next to them. The sheets were patterned with purple and rose flowers, and a beige lace bedspread was folded on a bentwood rocker. A profusion of pillows was scattered on the bed in all sizes and colors: purple, pink, blue.

The thing that Dennis loved best about her bedroom was the mirrors—dozens of them covering the walls. Some were antique silver and others were edged in metal or fabric. Not that Dennis knew an antique from an apple, but whenever the two of them moved, they were reflected in the tiny panes of glass, fragmented a hundred times. Yes, he liked that. She had observed him sneaking looks over her shoulder when his eyes should have been closed.

However, he constantly expressed his hatred for her living room. He detested the dolls.

Katherine Denicia gazed fondly around at the dolls she collected. Her friend, Lakeisha Washington, was always puzzled by Katherine's attachment to her collection.

"I don't know why you spend so much money on dolls. Seems like a kid thing, not a grown-up interest."

Lakeisha had no idea how much she had spent. She would faint if she knew that a Shirley Temple doll had cost her five hundred dollars. She bought a lot of her dolls on line at eBay, and she had narrowed her focus to African American dolls, some of German manufacture, Native American dolls and certain white ones that interested her. No Japanese, Asian, or Eskimo. The mantle over her imitation fireplace held an exquisite, tall, plastic bride doll with a pale rose-beige face and blue eyes, dressed in a veil and full bridal attire. Two Naija Princess dolls from Nigeria, a Queen of Africa doll in traditional African dress, antique German dolls with porcelain heads and detailed, expressive faces were crowded near hand-carved wooden Hopi Kachina dolls. These were the stars of her collection.

Lakeisha viewed them derisively. "I just don't get it," she complained, glancing around at the black baby dolls piled to overflowing in an intricate wicker child's highchair, and rag dolls lying in heaps on the armchair. More dolls lined the windowsill, their button eyes staring at her.

"It's creepy."

"You don't like my coh-lection? Well, I don't care."

"I can relate to the black ones. They kinda celebrate our heritage, but the others? No way!"

Katherine laughed. "Everyone to their own thing!"

Dennis always had to move some of the dolls in order to sit down, picking them up gingerly, and then, nervously trying to figure out where to put them. The room made him feel stupid and she enjoyed that. He was stupid. Last summer, when the usual gifts had not granted him any special favors, he asked what he could buy to make her happy.

"You could buy me a doll," she pouted.

His blue eyes were full of bewilderment. "I wouldn't know where to get one. I don't know anything about dolls. That's women's stuff. Tell me something else."

"A doll," she insisted, liking his discomfort.

"How about a fancy handbag? Or a bottle of perfume?" He figured he could manage those.

"A doll." A week later, he had appeared with a large gaily-wrapped package and presented it to her. She had torn off the paper to reveal a funny, oversized South American doll dressed in gaudy clothes with a ridiculous smile on its face.

"Wherever did you get this?" she asked, studying it.

"That South American store on Lilac Street. Buenos something. Do you like it?"

"I adore it! Silly doll-- so peasant-looking." She carefully placed it on the mantle where its garish outfit clashed with the more beautifully detailed German and African ones. It never became one of her favorites, but it made him happy to see it there, and happy Dennis meant more gifts and cash.

She wasn't going to miss him. He took her out to dinner and bought her a lot of stuff, sometimes gave her money—three hundred dollars once. Not bad for an unemployed security guard. She always figured he was into something illegal. But what the hell was he doing at the small boat harbor in a fishing tent? Shit! That made no sense at all!

Martin McCallister watched the evening news dispassionately. He and Leo had been at the site of many of the crimes and outrages committed in the Port City that day, so there were few surprises. Their shift had been fairly busy. A bank teller had been shot during a hold-up at the Franklin Street Savings and Loan. The robber had been arrested three blocks away, trying to escape on foot. The teller had been transported to the County Medical Center, not expected to survive. There was a drive-by on Cherry Street, where a man had been shot by two juveniles on bicycles. What next? The roller skate bandits? Television showed the victim being carried down the steps of his house in a body bag, while the neighbors, mostly black, stood watching, some weeping. It was a quiet street, large old trees lined the curbs, their bare branches raking the sky. Another senseless crime.

"Such a nice man. Always willing to help anyone who needed a hand," one of spectators told the television reporter.

John Bradford continued the coverage of life and death in the Port City. "Police are urging anyone who has information about the shooting to contact them at once. We take you now to the Channel 8 action reporter, Harvey Gunnite, for a special interview with Inspector Battaglia about the increase in violent crime."

The action reporter's face under his salon-style haircut was set with a serious expression. He wore one of his expensive navy suits with a yellow-patterned tie.

Martin lowered the volume on his set when Battaglia appeared on the screen. He knew what the inspector would be saying. The same comments that he made during every interview. It was an occasion to complain about the lack of funds, to protest about how the mayor and the common council had cut the police budget. He would make a pitch for more men, additional patrol cars, and cite the youth gangs and out-of-town hoodlums operating crack houses in the inner city. The mayor hated Battaglia, and there was a nasty feud going on between them, but then, the mayor hated everyone.

Martin absentmindedly rubbed the area where his beard had been. He had grown it in last year on a whim and then shaved it when the weather became warm, but some days he felt as though it was still there.

Even with all the events in his crowded day, he had found time to attend the Milvern funeral that morning. Criminals frequently went to the final services to gloat and enjoy the excitement of being there undetected. They loved the power of being able to cause despair in people's lives. Martin hadn't spotted anyone unusual in the small group of mourners. Inside of the viewing room was a closed casket with a picture of Dennis on top. It was obviously taken for his high school graduation, but his widow apparently had no other formal picture. She trembled as she was led to a seat in the front row. A few people from the security firm that had employed her husband came up to express their sympathy. Mrs. Milvern looked totally defeated. After a brief reading by the funeral director, everyone had driven to the cemetery for another short service in the bitter cold. Martin remembered when his grandfather had passed away. In those days no attempt was made to dig a grave in the frozen earth, and his grandfather was placed in cold storage until spring when the ground thawed. He felt sorry for the widow. She looked so vulnerable at the cemetery. What kind of a life could she have now? No money and a kid to take care of. She had cried so terribly when the casket was lowered into the frozen earth.

Now, as Martin watched, Grace Milvern's face appeared on the TV screen, white and swollen as she went up the steps of the funeral parlor. The Channel 8 coverage was from earlier that day. The camera followed the slight body clad in a thin, black coat, lingered on her cracked shoes. Martin turned the sound back on.

"Mrs. Milvern. Did your husband have any enemies that you knew of?" the reporter asked.

Grace stared at the man, and then at the camera man, his shoulder twisting, trying to get a better shot of her. She knew that she didn't have to answer, but she was so confused. Nothing made any sense.

"No, no enemies," she stuttered.

"What was he doing out at the small boat harbor?" The reporter was insistent.

She shut her eyes and covered her mouth with her hand. Her

cousin, Jason, took her by the arm, shielding her. "Mrs. Milvern is very upset. No questions."

Jason was her only relative at the funeral. Her parents had come up from Cranston and taken little Denny back with them, refusing to attend the services.

"We'll keep the child for a while but no way is this permanent! Get a job and take him back."

After the funeral, Martin had talked to the undertaker, a pompous bastard named Samuel Harris, smug in his dark blue, pinstriped suit with a white carnation in the button hole. He was explicit with him.

"Contact me if anyone comes around asking questions about the Milverns. Are there any family members I could talk to?"

"A cousin made all the arrangements, a Jason Carmody. Mrs. Milvern's family lives out of town, and there was no one in attendance from the deceased's side of the family."

"Don't give the cousin's name to anyone. Remember, this is a murder investigation."

"I think I'm aware of that," Harris said, sarcastically.

Several days before, the police had taken Grace to identify the body, and until then, she had believed it was all a mistake, that Dennis would come home. The detective, Martin McCallister, had been careful with her.

"I'll be right next to you. I'm sorry that we have to do this. The man looks pretty bad—he was shot in the head. Just try to be sure that it was your husband."

They had gone into the morgue where the body lay on a stainless steel table. The detective motioned to the attendant who cautiously pulled back the sheet covering the man.

I won't look at the wound, she told herself. I have to protect myself, or I'll go to pieces. She sensed the blood, the carnage, but she did not view it. Instead, she averted her eyes and touched Dennis' hand, lifted the slightly spatulate fingers. She had never felt anything so cold. She supposed it was because there was no blood circulation.

This what dead is, she thought.

Then, she started to cry, hysterically. The detective took her into an outer room and brought coffee for her. When she calmed down, he asked her questions, but she knew nothing.

"I don't know who his friends are—he never came home when he should have."

"What about ice fishing? Did he do that often?"

"Dennis hated the cold! He would never sit in one of those huts and freeze, and he never mentioned ice fishing. I just don't understand."

Martin remembered when he was a junior in high school, wanting to be a doctor, mainly because his mother loved the idea. He belonged to the science club and their adviser had taken the group on a field trip to the city morgue. The kids had wandered around looking at the equipment until the attendant, in a very business-like way, pulled the drawers out slowly to show them the corpses that were chilling. He pointed out the people who had died of natural causes, vagrants for the most part. Martin was revolted. The lax, purple-streaked faces, mouths agape, the ugly grayness of the skin, had quickly dampened his interest in working with human bodies. Medicine was just a romantic notion. Now, he was a homicide detective who visited the morgue regularly. Strange how things work out.

In an expensive high-rise on the waterfront with a magnificent view of the lake from the living room windows, a heavy-set man paced up and down his living room. Gulls swirled through the air beyond the floor-to-ceiling windows, but he didn't notice them. He was engrossed in an interior monologue.

"We had everything," he muttered. "I gave her all that a woman could desire: money, clothes, gorgeous furniture. Did she want those things? No! Excitement, sleaze, sordid affairs—that's what appealed to her. And I never suspected. I loved her—trusted her. All I wanted was Jennifer, and now everything is destroyed. I don't care about my law practice, social life, nothing!"

The affair started when his wife signed up for a course in French at the local university last winter. French! What did she need another language for? He would have been glad to take her to Paris, and she could hear all the French she needed, but she wanted to develop her potential, fulfill herself. My God! Any other woman would kill for the chance to have the things Jennifer had. It wasn't enough.

That's where she met her paramour—at the university. There was a definite change in her when she started the damned course. She refused to go to Costa Rica for their annual vacation. She was absent from the apartment a lot, and came home with a sated, blurry-look on her face. The blunt edges of her personality had been filed down, smoothed out.

She convinced him that she was enrolled in other courses. He believed her, stupid ass that he was: thought that she was a student in Women's Empowerment, in Furniture of the Art Deco Period. She knew a lot about that: ask her anything and she'd have an answer. Finally, the absences were so frequent that even he—trusting old Frank—had to face facts and confront her.

"Oh, but I'm just so busy!" she explained, her hazel eyes as wide and innocent as a baby's. "I've joined this group—Women Against Nuclear power—and we have these meetings."

He refused to fall for her excuses. Almost berserk with jealousy, he opened her mail, listened in on the phone extension. She was too dumb to use her cell phone when she was home.

One afternoon, he left work early so that he could sneak back into the apartment. The dense carpet in the foyer muffled his footsteps, and he closed the door softly. She had romantic music playing on the tape deck. The voice of a popular singer crept in little ripples through the corners of the rooms. He walked carefully into the living room and picked up the extension.

Jennifer was talking on the phone in the bedroom, whispering seductively to the person on the other end. "Tomorrow, Nathan—two o'clock."

He stole quietly out of the apartment and drove down to the frozen marina where the river hurled huge chunks of ice against the bridge supports. He paced up and down near the deserted Snack Shack. Jennifer was slipping away from him, and he couldn't stand it. Something had to be done.

The next day he went to his office—the re-modeled Victorian on Mohawk Street festooned with gingerbread, painted in green, rose and navy: seven lawyers, two receptionists, four secretaries, three paralegals, two file clerks. Pearson, Bernstein, Harwood, Allesandro and White. The top firm in the Port City. At one-thirty, he borrowed one of the partner's cars, an Audi, and parked down the curved lane that led to his high-rise. Jennifer appeared shortly, and got in her Porsche. Nothing too good for his wife. She drove to an address on the west side, an old stucco house converted to apartments and rooms in the 'Charming' section of the city. Gentrification, high crime, prostitutes on every corner. She left the car and went rapidly inside.

Soon, a man arrived—a kid, really. It might have been another tenant, but there was something about this jerk in jeans and a fleece-lined jacket casually open to the weather, a long scarf. Frank knew instinctively that this was Jennifer's lover.

Snow drifted randomly around the house, but they were safe

inside. Frank got out of the Audi and walked down the side path. Leafless bushes near the walk were hung with icicles like static fingers. They shattered as he brushed by them.

Opening the door carefully, he scanned the tiny entry where the mailboxes hung on the wall. Names, all sorts of names: D. Felice, C. Polanski, M. Kapowitz, E. Kapowitz, N. Scortino, were on typed and hand-written tags. "D is for death, C is for cunt and N is for Nathan," he muttered. Shaking, he went back to the cart, drove to his office, insane with rage and jealousy.

That night, they had a terrific battle. He accused her of having an affair with Scortino. At first she denied it. He grabbed her, wrenched her arm behind her back and banged her head against the granite counter.

"I want a divorce!" she screamed.

"So you can run off with your boyfriend? Never!"

"I just want to get away from you!" Her hair hung wildly about her face.

"You'll never get a divorce! I know every judge in the city! Just try and get one!"

"Please, Frank." Her eyes were soft, pleading. "We've grown apart. I need space." She leaned against the imported Swedish stove, rubbing her arms.

Christ! He hated her then, but he would never let her go! Never!

"I like you, Frank, but I don't love you. Maybe it's the seventeen-year difference in our ages. I just don't want to spend my life with you. You'll get over me—find someone else."

He collapsed onto the kitchen chair. "You can't leave. You don't have any money."

"But I do. I've saved quiet a bit. You've always been generous."

"You've been planning this for a long time," he accused her.

"No, you're wrong. I always wanted to give our marriage a chance, but you don't want me to have a life of my own. I can't live this way."

He buried his face in his hands. When he looked up, she was not in the room.

"Jennifer!" he called.

Her voice floated from the bedroom. "I'm packing some clothes."

He waited, motionless, until she appeared, carrying a suitcase.

"I'll be back later in the week to pick up some more things." She had combed her hair, put on fresh makeup.

"Jennifer, please let's talk about this. Don't leave."

"We'll just be abusive to each other if I stay, Frank. Let's try and be friends."

"We are not going to be friends!" he shouted, getting out of the chair. "And you are getting nothing from me! Not a divorce, not money, nothing! You're just a whore!"

She picked up the suitcase and walked rapidly out the door.

He stood in the middle of the room, demolished. Then, he began to pace the floor, thinking of ways that she could be made to change her mind. If she gave up this Scortino jerk and apologized, they might still be happy. He could forgive her, pretend that nothing had happened, but had she been deceiving him all along? His mind ran like a train over the course of their marriage, trying to recollect any suspicious happenings.

Getting a bottle of scotch from the liquor cabinet, he started drinking. By dawn, he was exhausted and drunk. He stumbled down the hall to the bedroom, staggered and fell onto the carpeted floor. Pulling himself to his feet, he lurched into the bed and passed out.

The next morning, he opened his eyes to a bright, glaring winter sun. He was horrified to find himself fully dressed and stinking of booze. What had happened? Then, he remembered. Jennifer was gone. He sat up, put his feet over the edge of the bed and started to cry, tears staining his filthy shirt. Her loved her so much.

"It's all that bastard Scortino's fault. If she hadn't met him, things would be the same as they have always been. Scortino isn't going to get away with it. I'm a lawyer. I have lots of contacts." Picking up his cell phone, he dialed the number of a man who specialized in discrete, private investigations.

He didn't go to the law firm that day, but sat in the living room, the one that Jennifer had furnished so exquisitely, and drank steadily. About three in the afternoon, his wife returned to collect more of her belongings.

He followed her into the bedroom, where she was taking dresses out of the closet, slipping them off satin hangers. When she turned, he put his hands on her shoulders, tried to force her down on the bed, his eyes glittering, his mouth twisted into an obscene smile.

She pulled away from his grasp. "No, Frank. It's over. Let me pack."

He yelled at her. "You bitch!"

She scooped up the clothes, angrily, and stuffed them in a plastic bag. Then, she left the apartment.

Frank stayed away from work for three days, drinking and brooding. The private detective called and confirmed that Jennifer had been seeing Nathan Scortino, had met him at the university when she was taking a course in French. In a rage, he drove through the terrible storm, to the Fairfield Gun Shop, a place on the river that sold guns, archery supplies, live bait in the summer. There was a shooting range in a low cement room at the back of the place. It was easy to buy a gun. The pimply clerk didn't care who he was. He knew how to shoot, but it was years since he had been around a weapon.

White with anger, he drove through the densely falling snow over deserted streets, to Almada's Liquor store. Leaving his car in the street, he entered the garish light of the business. Scortino had been on the phone—perhaps he was talking to Jennifer. Frank approached the counter, staring at the clerk. This was the man who held Jennifer in his arms. His fleshy lips had probed her everywhere. The hands, fairly small, blunt, had touched her body. He was thin, young—very young.

"Can I help you find something?" His voice was high.

Frank shot him once. That was all he needed. He had carried the gun unnoticed at his side when he entered the liquor store.

Scortino fell against the counter, knocking over a display of miniature bottles, as he slumped down behind the counter. There was the sound of a bell tinkling. Frank wheeled around, the gun in his hand, to meet the startled eyes of a woman, her face as white as the swirling snow. Then, she vanished. He ran out after her, but she was gone. He searched the streets, the alleys, tramping through the piles of snow. but there was no sign of her. Then, tonight, he watched the late news on TV intently. The reporter was covering two murders in the Port City. One of them concerned a woman whose husband had been shot out at the harbor.

"Mrs. Milvern was interviewed this afternoon at Caskettis Funeral parlor—"

"Holy Christ!" he exclaimed. The woman on the screen was the same person that had surprised him in Almada's Liquor store when he shot Nathan Scortino. He remembered her coming through the door, and then running away. He was unable to find her in the storm that night. Now, he knew her name. Milvern. He could track her down and kill her so that she couldn't identify him. What was going on? How could she be involved in two shootings? It was bizarre. He thought that he had no hope of finding her, but now, thanks to Channel 8, he knew who she was. She could identify him to the police and ruin his life, what little life he had after Jennifer wrecked his existence. He would search for her and then it would be curtains. Caskettis Funeral Home. Easy. He would start there.

Chapter Three

Kathine Denicia Jordan cracked open the door of her apartment, but kept the security chain on. She didn't recognize the man standing outside.

"Katherine Jordan?" he said. "I'm Mike Stokes, Dennis Milvern's business partner. I know that you two were friends, and I wanted to stop by and tell you how sorry I am about the tragedy."

She looked at him, stonily, through the narrow opening.

"So, now you've told me." She started to shut the door.

"No, please wait. Dennis was in an extremely difficult business. He understood that dangerous things could happen."

"That's funny. I thought he was an unemployed security guard." Her eyebrows arched and the purplish mouth turned up sarcastically.

"Dennis and I were partners in an investment agency."

"Really? That sure sounds dangerous. I don't care what he did. He never discussed any of his occupations with me."

"He thought a lot of you, and he left me something to give you if anything did happen to him. Could I come in?" He smiled his most disarming smile.

"What did he leave me? Some halibut? I understand that he spent a lot of time ice fishing."

"I don't want to give it to you in the hall."

Katherine studied the man briefly. Brown eyes, brown hair, even a brown suit. Didn't look like an investment partner.

"All right. You can take me out to dinner. I'll meet you in forty minutes at the Prime Time. Know where that is?"

"Of course, but why can't you—?"

"Forty minutes. Get a table in the rear." She shut the door firmly.

"Now," she pondered. "What should I wear for my date with Brownie?'

Tellers Jewelry Store in the Downtown Mall displayed its wares in glass cases, and the merchandize looked expensive. One hundred and fifty dollars for a bracelet. No way! He looked for something cheaper. A tiny owl with amber eyes caught his attention.

He beckoned to the clerk. "How much is the bird?"

The clerk carefully lifted it out of the case. "The craftsmanship is very nice. Fifty dollars."

"Put it in a plain, white box and don't wrap it."

Pocketing the box, he rode the escalator to the second floor of the mall where it was quieter and took his cell phone out of his pocket. The place was full of school kids screeching at each other and mobbing the stores. He hated malls. Leaning against a pillar, he dialed.

"Jack? You there? Listen, this job is going to cost me a buck. The girl wouldn't talk to me at her apartment. Said I had to take her to dinner at the Prime Time, no less."

"You will be reimbursed. Just get the product."

"Is this going to be worth the trouble? Milvern was supposed to have the stuff with him."

"Well, he didn't."

"Are you sure George didn't cross you up?"

There was a cold silence at the other end. "I advise you never to suggest anything so stupid. Don't you think I know my own employees? Your job is to get into the Jordan woman's apartment. If the package was left with her, remove it. Do your own assignment and stop criticizing George."

The phone was slammed down.

Katherine Jordan was half an hour late for their dinner. She swept through the restaurant door, a cloud of snow following her, the long, suede coat open. She spoke to a waiter who led her to Mike's table.

"I was afraid that you weren't coming."

"Takes me a while to dress," she smiled, shrugging off her coat. She wore a very tight, low-cut black blouse with an impressive gold oriental brooch nestled between her large breasts. A gold metallic belt cinched her waist and black leather boots were covered by a full black skirt. A dozen filigree bracelets jangled on her wrist. A variety of rings covered her fingers. He hair was puffed out into a huge mass of curls.

How did Dennis ever meet her? Mike wondered.

"Cocktail?" he asked.

"Please. A White Russian."

While they waited for their drinks, Mike talked to her about Dennis.

"Did you know him long?"

"Oh, a while," she responded, noncommittally.

"He told me that he left a few things with you for safe keeping."

"Sounds like he told you a lot of things, mostly untrue."

He was dazzled by her beautiful white teeth. Blacks have more calcium in their bodies, just like Indians have an extra rib: gives them that barrel shape.

"We were partners."

"In the security guard business? So strange."

"No, no. Investments."

"Oh, I bet," she purred.

Mike was beginning to sweat. This was going badly. It had been a stupid idea of Jacks. If the package was stashed at her place, she was never going to tell him.

"Let's order."

She ordered lobster, and he asked for the house specialty, Prime Rib. After all, Jack was paying for the dinner.

While they ate, Mike tried again.

"Did Dennis leave anything with you that related to our business? I haven't been able to locate some securities."

"Now just a minute," she protested. "I thought he left something for me, not the other way around. Wasn't that the idea?"

"Oh, he did. Perhaps we could exchange packages."

"Got no packages to trade. Sorry." She speared a bit of tender, white meat, dripping with butter, and placed it in her ripe mouth.

"Maybe I misunderstood Dennis."

"I guess you did."

"I still have something he left for you." He rummaged in his pocket for the box. "Tell you what. Lets go back to your place after we finish eating, and I'll give it to you. Dennis told me you have a lovely apartment, and I'd really like to see it." He gazed into her eyes. By now, he really wanted to go back to the apartment with this gorgeous woman. He knew that she was a professional, although in a casual way. Forget the assignment, he thought, staring at those serious boobs.

"Ah, but I rarely invite men to my apartment. Only if I know then as well as I knew Dennis. So—"

She traced the design on the medallion between her breasts with a rosy, polished nail. "You had better give it to me here, or was that all a bunch of lies you were telling me?" She pouted, her full lips glistening.

"No, no. I just thought that we could get to be closer friends."

"I don't think so."

Mike handed her the box, reluctantly, knowing the he had failed, and that Jack wasn't going to be happy.

"A bird! He knew that I loved birds!" she exclaimed. "Now, this little owl is cute. I'm going to wear it a lot. Thank you for the lovely dinner. I must be off, but I will remember Dennis every time I wear the pin." Gathering her coat about her, she was gone.

"Damn!" Mike swore. "Damn, damn, damn!" Then, he took out his cell to give Jack the bad news.

Frank Pearson waited in the foyer of Caskettis Funeral parlor inhaling the hothouse odor from masses of flowers in the viewing rooms. It made him sick. He glanced disinterestedly at a notice on a stand in the plushly carpeted hall. Anthony Lombardo. Parlor Three. Finally, the director emerged from his office.

"How may I help you, sir?" His tone was subdued, unctuous, sympathetic.

"I'm trying to get in touch with the poor woman whose husband was murdered at the small boat harbor. My wife used to work with Mrs. Milvern a few years ago, and we wanted to express our sympathy. Do you have her address?"

Samuel Harris frowned at the man. He didn't like him. Certainly, he was well dressed—a pinstriped suit and a quiet tie, but there was an intangible air of something foul about him, something criminal.

"I am terribly sorry, but we are not a liberty to divulge information concerning our clients."

"My wife and I simply wanted to send a condolence card, offer our help." The man smiled, persuasively.

"I suggest that you leave your name and address, and if Mrs. Milvern calls, we will forward your message."

The man sighed. "I don't think so. Sorry to have troubled you. Good day."

"Shit!" he said, as he stood on the pavement outside of the establishment. "Another dead end." He had already been to the rat hole that Milvern and his wife had lived in, but she had given it up.

He must find that woman. She had seen him shoot Nathan Scortino. She was a threat and had to be removed. But where should he look?

After the funeral, Grace told her cousin that she had to find another apartment right away.

"What's the hurry? I can give you a little money for the rent. Why don't you take some time to recover?"

"Dennis was in some sort of trouble. I was getting a lot of strange phone calls. You have to help me! I'm scared!"

"I don't think that the shooting had anything to do with you, but if you're frightened, I can get a pickup truck and help you move. Go ahead and find another place."

After many tries, Grace found two rooms a few blocks away in a huge old house. Her parents had reluctantly given her a hundred dollars before they left with the baby, and she used the money for part of the rent. No security deposit was required because the building had a bad reputation, and the landlord was glad to get any tenant. A Hari Krishna Cult had lived there, and residents still remembered the disciples clad in saffron robes, their heads shaven, chanting and prancing about on the sidewalk. The yellow walls were re-painted green and the place cleaned up, but few people wanted to move in. Some students lived on the second floor, and an elderly couple on social security had taken up residence on the third.

There was no room for the baby, and she had no money to support him. She must get a job soon so that she could get him back from her parents. They acted as if this was all her fault. She couldn't think about Denny now. It was essential that she blot out all thoughts of the child or she would go crazy. Handing him over to them had almost killed her. All his clothes, his crib, were down in Cranston with them. When she called to find out how he was, her mother held the baby up to the phone.

"Talk to him," she insisted.

But Grace had shut down her mind and let him babble on. If she started talking to him, she would break down completely. She would be his mother again---later. After she saved some money, they would be together and could forget the time they were separated. She had to hold herself together until then.

She left no forwarding address with the landlord.

"I'll be staying with friends."

He didn't care. An Hispanic welfare family wanted the place.

She and Jason carried the battered bed down the flights of stairs and piled it in the truck with the old couch, dresser, the rest of her furniture. The front door banged in the wind, letting cold, fresh air into the rancid-smelling hallway. She was exhausted to the point of being nauseated when they finally drove away from the street,

At the new place, everything had to be carried up to the second floor and put inside. They set up the bed, but the rest of the furniture was piled in heaps wherever they could stack it.

She and Jason sat down on some boxes in the kitchen and finished off a bottle of cheap Cabernet, sweat dripping off their faces.

"What are you going to do next" her cousin asked.

"I'm going to get a job."

"If they ever find out who shot Dennis, you might have a basis for a law suit."

She laughed, bitterly. "Dennis was up to no good. More likely, I'd be sued myself."

"You think he was into drugs?"

She stared around at the cluttered room, wondering how she could ever feel at home here, "Who knows? I've been living with a stranger."

After Jason left, she fell into the unmade bed, fully clothed and slept for sixteen hours straight.

The greatest number of homicides in the city were committed in Precinct Eleven's district. Poor minorities, ex-cons, drug addicts inhabited the neighborhood around the station house. Nearby, the Palmer Heights Projects stood on a stark and treeless plain against the silhouette of the elevated section of the expressway. Marginally employed and welfare recipients lived anxiously next to crack houses and drug pushers. The station was over a hundred years old, and few improvements had been made during the years. It was an ugly, three-story building one block from Flowers Hospital, whose emergency room was always crowded with people wounded in domestic arguments, felled by drug overdoses or children suffering asthma attacks.

All the kids living in the eleventh had asthma. Their lungs were ruined by city air, the lead paint in their houses, and fumes from the now-closed photography plant. The only hospital that did more of this kind of business was County Medical.

Martin McCallister and Leo Aronica shared an office at the rear of the first floor of the station, a tiny cubicle with a huge smear of mold pointing like a finger down the eroded interior wall. The lone, filthy window was embedded with chicken wire and was barred.

Martin was at his desk, going over his notes on the latest homicide. A black kid had been shot on the rapid transit on his way home from school by a schoolmate. They were both fourteen, and had been arguing over a cell phone.

"He told me I could borrow it," the tearful kid protested.

But how did that explain the gun? What teenager takes a gun to school and where did he get it? It was insane.

He got up and poured a cup of coffee from the expensive machine that he kept on a file cabinet as the phone rang.

"Detective McCallister? This is Samuel Harris, Director of Casketti's Funeral Home. You told me to call you of anything suspicious occurred. A few minutes ago, a man was here, asking for Mrs. Milvern's address. I don't think he really knew her."

"You didn't give it to him?"

"You specifically told me not to," he sniffed, "and besides, it's not our policy."

"Did he leave his name?"

"No."

"I'll be over in half an hour with some photos for you to look at. Maybe he can be identified."

"I'm going over to Casketti's," he told Leo. "Do you want to come?"

"I've got too much to clear up here before lunch time. You want to meet me at Mama Cora's or The Spaghetti Cavern?"

"I thought it was my turn to pick."

"You made us go to the Juicery yesterday, " Leo scowled. "Did you forget?"

Martin sighed.

"Marty, why do most funeral parlors have names that make you think of death?" Leo asked. "There's Coffino's on the East Side and Bury's downtown? Also Carleton-Goners in the suburbs. It's weird. My Uncle Tony was laid out at Casketti's. It's an expensive place, but they do a good job. My aunt was satisfied with everything. I guess it helps with the grief. He's buried out at Park Lawn."

"If Casketti's is so expensive, I'm wondering how Grace Milvern was able to pay for her husband's funeral."

"Maybe his former friends at the security company chipped in, or maybe she took out a time plan payment."

"It's possible. The viewing was only one day and the coffin looked to be the cheapest one."

Samuel Harris put the phone down and shuddered. He hated crime, and he disliked doing anything with bodies damaged by gunshots. Some undertakers liked that sort of sensationalism, but he preferred dealing with natural deaths. Even accident victims upset him considerably. He considered his work to be an art form. Applying the makeup, padding the clothes discretely so that the deceased was improved upon, this was his challenge. It flattered him to have their relatives comment on his skill.

"You've made her look so wonderful! So youthful!"

He liked that.

It was a small benefit in a difficult business. He had to deal with the relatives of the deceased, plus his own employees, and they were a sorry lot. Just last week he had to sack a woman who had been hired to style hair. She possessed all the proper licenses and recommendations, but he had surprised her when he returned to the funeral home after a short lunch. Instead of working on the deceased's hair, she had her head under the sheet covering the man's body, examining his privates! She screamed when she saw him and tried to come up with some stupid story, but he fired her on the spot. Dignity must be maintained, at all costs. He styled the hair himself now, until a reputable cosmetologist could be found.

He wasn't looking forward to meeting with Detective McCallister. He had no wish to be reminded of Dennis Milvern. It had been a closed casket. The man had been beyond the exercise of his skill. He felt sorry for the widow when he mentioned the fee for the service, because she had obviously been practically destitute, but her cousin had insisted on covering the cost. He just wanted to forget the whole Milvern business.

When Grace woke up, cold winter sunlight was streaming into the disordered room. The couch was jammed against a wall across from the bed, its cushions piled with lamps and cardboard boxes. There was no way all of her furniture could fit into these two rooms. A lot of things had been put out at the curb in front of her former apartment: the remnants of marriage, most of it junk, garage sale and Goodwill furniture. More stuff would have to go.

She found her clothes in the disorder and changed. There was no food in the place, and the sight of the empty wine bottle made her stomach lurch. Pulling on her coat, she went down the stairs into the bright snow-packed street. There was a small restaurant on the corner, J J's Diner, and she went inside and ordered coffee and a donut before buying a paper. Sitting at a stool, she scanned the want ads while she drank her coffee.

A job would have to be on a bus route, because their car was still missing. The police had a description, but it hadn't been found. Just as well. The finance company would repossess it anyway.

She hadn't worked since she and Dennis were married, and before that there had been dead-end minimum wage jobs: clerking in a feed mill and cashiering at the local super market. She had no real training.

Until she met Dennis, she had gone through life in a trance, living within the framework of her nothing jobs and the dictates of her domineering parents.

She met Dennis when she and a girlfriend had gone to the fireman's carnival one summer. He bought her a few drinks at the beer tent, chatted with her for a while, but he hadn't taken her home. That fall, he called occasionally and they dated, but nothing special.

She knew he was seeing other girls. She liked him and hoped that he would get in touch with her.

One evening, after she hadn't heard from him in weeks, he picked her up after work and took her for a long drive through the hills south of the city. They talked about how much they disliked Cranston and about their problems with their families. He didn't speak to his parents and had moved out when he was twenty after a series of bitter arguments. Hers wanted to control her every move, as though she were fourteen. They parked near the river where she felt mesmerized by the blackness of the night, soft rushing of the water. She didn't think about what she was doing as Dennis led her out of the car to a near-by field. She wanted this to be romantic, and after she struggled out of her underwear and pulled her blouse up, she turned his face against hers so that she could gaze into his eyes. His face was distant as he pushed into her, his eyes tightly closed, so she looked at the moon over his shoulder, caught in the clouds.

After that, they met frequently. He was interested. She was sure that he loved her. When she told him that she was pregnant, she was nervous, afraid of what is reaction would be, but he surprised her with his reaction.

"I've been thinking about leaving Cranston for a long while, get out of this stupid town and go up to the Port City. There's nothing here. We can start a new life." He was working in a warehouse hauling boxes about, and he hated it. "A baby. That's great!"

The wedding took place in her parents living room, presided over by a local minister. She wore a beige suit, and her cousin Claudia was her only attendant. There was a brief reception afterward at an Italian restaurant, with family members and her disapproving parents. She and Dennis left for the city the next day. She wanted to love him, and she was so happy to get away from Cranston that she overlooked his many imperfections.

Her life had begun. Now, a few short years later everything had gone terribly wrong, and she was on her own.

She scrutinized the paper, lifting the heavy mug to her lips. She wasn't qualified for much, unless she wanted to clean houses or do telemarketing. The idea of waitress work had never appealed to her, but the tips were supposed to be good if you got hired at the right place. She circled a few listings to be checked out tomorrow. Today, she was going to try to make some sense out of her two rooms and get her sparse collection of clothes ready for job interviews.

Katherine Denicia stretched out on her bed in a peach silk nightgown studying for a political science test. Most of her friends thought she was crazy to take courses at the community college, but she really enjoyed them, especially this course, Politics of the Sixties, the most exciting time for black people. Angela Davis with her gorgeous huge bush of an Afro hairstyle, Stokely Carmichael. Blacks were militant and glamorous, like the old-time western outlaws.

She was totally absorbed in her reading when she glanced up and found a man standing in her bedroom doorway. He was large and ugly with a squashed, fighter's nose on his distorted, round face.

She screamed and jumped from the bed, scattering papers. The man moved quickly to her side, slapping her face and pinning her arms behind her.

"Where's the package Dennis left with you?" he growled, jerking her arms roughly.

"I don't have any package!" she shrieked. Her lip was split and blood ran into her mouth.

He kicked her viciously on the leg.

She howled and doubled over.

He punched her again and again. Katherine wailed in pain, a high, thin sound.

"The package, cunt—"

"Oh don't——OWWWWW!"

The man struck a heavy blow to her head, and she fell to the floor, unconscious.

He turned his attention away from her and began to tear the room apart. Dumping out the dresser drawers, he kicked through heaps of panties and teddies. He wrenched the mattress off the bed and ripped holes in it.

Nothing.

Now, he was really angry. When Jack sent him out on these stupid errands, he went into a rage. He was a hit man, not a damn burglar!

The wall of mirrors reflected his bulk. Fractured pieces of his image were caught in the reflective surfaces. Furious, he picked up a silver hairbrush and smashed them, mirror after mirror. Shards of glass flew across the room, and slivers fell in a splintered pile on the dresser. He kept swinging, hitting hard with the hairbrush.

"Not an errand boy!" he rasped. "Pansy job! Find the missing product! Shit!" he croaked, as he demolished an oval mirror with a spun gold frame. The carpet and his clothes were covered with chunks of glass.

"Craphead!" he yelped, obliterating his reflection from a square, velvet-trimmed mirror. The pieces cascaded to the floor like a jagged waterfall.

The girl was still out, sprawled on the floor. He shoved her away from the door with his foot and went into the living room.

Dolls! All around him were dolls staring blankly.

"Don't look at me!" he shouted. "Stupid! Stupid!"

He grabbed a china doll with yellow curls and wide, blue eyes and ripped its head off, shaking the truncated body upside down. Nothing fell out.

"I got to go through all these damn dolls! What does Jack think I am?"

Running his arms the length of the mantle, he sent fifteen of them crashing to the floor. Picking up a chocolate-colored doll by the leg, he smashed a lamp with it. Then, he kicked over a desk, the contents spilling onto the broken mass of china and ruffles.

There was a knock on the door.

The man froze, a doll still dangling from his hand.

"Katherine Denicia," a deep baritone voice called. "Open up sweetheart, Darnell's here."

The man standing in the wreckage stared around wildly.

"Turn off your TV, love. I'm coming in." There was the sound of the door opening.

A tall, black man stared at the intruder.

"What are you doing here, mister?" Then, his eyes widened as he took in the slaughter of the dolls.

"Where's Katherine?"

The interloper growled, threw down the doll, shoved the black man aside as he dashed out of the apartment and down the stairs.

Behind him, there was a tinkling crash as shards of glass fell off the bedroom wall.

Grace dressed the best that she could, not having many clothes to choose from. She put a safety pin in her navy skirt. She had lost weight. A beige sweater was pulled over it, and she covered the outfit with her old, green coat.

She left the house and went down the chilly streets. The morning was gray, dismal. Sidewalks were edged with frozen snow banks, and piles of dog droppings were smeared on the sidewalks, few of which were shoveled. She decided to walk a few blocks to warm up while she waited for a bus. Near the corner was a large reddish, soot-covered building as grim as a fortress. A line of people shivered on the front steps. In the ice-crusted yard was a sign that read Arms of Love Food Pantry. Open 12 to 2. 5 to 7. Monday through Saturday. An extremely varied group of people waited for the doors to open. A few defeated-looking mothers held small children in their arms, and a rough-looking bearded man wore a homemade badge 'Desert Storm Veteran.' Some of the people were obviously senior citizens. But the food pantry meant that she could have a decent meal. The donut hadn't been filling. She went over and stood on the fringe of the group next to an old woman who wore cumbersome men's shoes and a plaid overcoat with a frayed, velvet collar.

"On a freezing day like this, you'd think they would let us wait inside instead of out in the cold," she complained. "Wonder we don't all have pneumonia. I hope there's a good lunch today. Yesterday, it was so poor, you'd hardly want to eat it, but last Tuesday there was creamed chicken on rice. Maybe they'll serve that today."

A Channel 8 TV truck was parked in front of the building and a cameraman was filming the clients as they waited.

"What's the TV for?" Grace asked the woman.

"The director of this place, Jo-Jo, does a pitch every year at Christmas to get donations coming in. He's inside being interviewed. You'll see him later. Old guy—always wears carpet slippers."

Finally, the heavy door was opened and the line surged inside. Everyone filed over to a cafeteria-style counter and took trays and plastic silverware. Volunteers handed over plates of macaroni and cheese, two slices of bread and butter, a small paper cup of mixed salad greens and another of brownish fruit. Grace took her tray to a table and sat down. As she ate, she surveyed the crowd. Some of the people had friends that they chatted and joked with, but there were others who were alone. One man had a pronounced facial tic and a wild expression. A teenage boy pounded the table rhythmically with his fists as he jerked his head up and down.

The lunch wasn't half bad, and Grace wondered if she could come here every day until she got on her feet. Even if she landed a job today, there would be no paycheck for a few weeks.

A reporter emerged from a hall beyond two doors with hand-lettered signs *Rest Rooms*, followed by a cameraman and a rumpled-looking person who must be the director.

"We'll be on the six o'clock news today, Jo-Jo," the reporter announced, "and again at eleven. There will be plenty of coverage."

"We've got to have more donations," complained the director. "We're running low on supplies."

"Cheer up. You know that the TV appeal brings money in every year."

The director did not look convinced. "It had better," he rasped.

After stacking her tray, Grace went to the bread table and received a paper bag containing two loaves of day-old bread and a sweet roll. Then, she went out to find a bus stop and look for a job.

Chapter Four

The Hyacinth restaurant on the west side of the Port City was famous for elegance, superior food and criminal connections. Twenty years ago, a mobster was gunned down in the ornate wood-paneled bar in front of a room full of patrons who swore to the police that they had seen nothing. Even though it was February, there were boxes of fresh camellias on display in a case next to huge green plants whose foliage brushed the ceiling. The entry was covered with richly patterned carpet, wallpapered in mauve and silver stripes. Several antique benches held patrons awaiting admission.

"Welcome, welcome," the gray-faced octogenarian quavered as he pulled open the heavy inner door of the restaurant with his frail, uniformed arm. The old family retainer had been at his post forever.

"Uncle Gaetano, you're looking well."

The elderly man all but dropped to his knees to kiss Jack D'Angelo's hand.

"Such a pleasure," he purred. "Will you be dining with your friends?"

"We have the upstairs room reserved."

"You gotta come here more often," the old man urged. "Don't be a stranger."

Jack strode past huge pots of carnations, the air filled with their spicy, cool odor. He went up a staircase lined with oil paintings of landscapes and portraits supplied by a local gallery, down the hall to a private room. Inside, enormous vases of daffodils and tulips stood on polished tables. He paused to smooth his hair in a Rococo mirror. He looked like a lawyer. Black hair frosted with a little gray, compelling blue-green eyes, a dark tan from a recent vacation on the Mexican Riviera. He prided himself on looking professional.

It had not always been the way. The dark tan was preceded by prison pallor not too many years ago.

I was stupid once, he thought, but the mark of intelligence is the ability to learn from your mistakes. Back then, he had owned some small-time furniture and appliance stores, heavily mortgaged. He contracted to have them burned down by an arsonist who owed him some favors. There was no problem collecting from the insurance company, but he had gotten in trouble big time with the IRS. Knowing that he was about to be arrested, he put all his money in various large denominations into a paper bag and drove over to Canada with the bag on the passenger seat of the car. His earnest face and luminous eyes facilitated an easy trip through customs at the border. He placed the money in a Canadian bank for safekeeping.

As he had expected, he was indicted and spent some time in a downstate prison, where he used the time profitably, reading the classics and analyzing his past mistakes. Knowing that he had been a cheap third-rate crook, he resolved to elevate himself to a position of respect in the criminal element of the community. His vocabulary improved and with time-off for good behavior, he returned to the Port City. Retrieving his money from the Canadian bank, he bought slum property. After he owned a quarter of the ghetto, he went into the drug business. Slum Lord and Drug Czar. Not a bad title for the former owner of cut-rate appliance stores, and he meant to keep it.

He went to the bar at the far end of the room where the bartender handed him a Southern Comfort Old Fashioned, not muddled.

A table was set up in the center of the room for dinner with white linens, crystal glasses and English china. Four men were already in attendance. When he started to sip his drink, they went to the bar and ordered.

"Shall we sit down?"

He studied the men idly as they approached the table. Carlos Sanchez was from the west side, the predominately Puerto Rican neighborhood. He was a corpulent man, puffy-faced, with a thin mustache and dark, slow eyes. The second man, DeShaun Brown, who represented the inner city, was bedecked in gold. Gold chains, rings, watches, glittered against his ebony skin. He wore a green, suede jacket with a black handkerchief in the pocket. His brother was a councilman, a screamer, a rabble-rouser. Brown's tightly curled hair was like fleece, beginning to gray a little. Despite his gaudy appearance, he was an extremely dangerous man and had to be taken seriously. Jake McGill and Arnie Levenson completed the quartet. Although of different ancestry, they might have been twins. Balding, paunchy, wearing blue suits, their fleshy faces blank as pieces of pie, they reeked of cigar smoke. Jake was from the south side where the railroads wound around the lift bridges. The people who lived in his district used to work in the mills, but now the mills were silent. Arnie Levenson represented the affluent north district of the city, which included the university where the demand for drugs was especially high among college students.

"What are we meeting about?" Brown asked, sullenly.

Jack sipped his drink. It was perfect. Just the right combination of fruit and whiskey.

"You remember the man who was shot out at the small boat harbor?"

"Don't see why we have to discuss such an unimportant person or such an old issue," complained DeShaun.

"Well, it's the principal of the thing," Jack explained. "True, the man was an inept minor dealer, but somehow he held out on us. It's imperative that we find the missing merchandise and chastise whoever is concealing it, or other small-timers will think that they can renege on their commitments. There is also a question of monetary value."

"He didn't have the product when he was wasted?"

"My employee, George Shaunessy, you all know who I mean? George searched him thoroughly out at the harbor. The merchandise was not there. It had been arranged that Milvern's erstwhile partner, Mike Stokes, would meet with him and accept the goods. We advised Stokes not to appear. Milvern had become a problem. He held out on us before and was becoming too independent, but when George encountered him, there was fake product."

"So, where did he stash the real stuff?"

Jack coughed delicately. "George was sent to the apartment of a call girl that Milvern saw frequently, but he was interrupted while making a search. We shall probably have to return there."

"Wasn't Milvern married? What about his wife?" queried Jake.

Jack signaled the bartender, and another Old Fashioned appeared at once.

"We have been unable to locate her."

"It would seem that the primero thing would be to find the senora," Carlos Sanchez said. "George has not looked for her?"

"George is in Syracuse for a while. His last assignment upset him, and I sent him away for a little vacation. His father works in an OTB parlor there, and I thought some family togetherness would be beneficial."

"Should I loan you Gene Lempke? He's good," Arnie suggested.

"Perhaps. I don't maintain a large staff, and I have other things in mind for Mike Stokes."

"I'm curious about Stokes," said Samuelson. "Could he have been in on the deal?"

"No, he's too stupid. Milvern was a neurotic skirt chaser who became over-inflated with the idea of his own capabilities, but he was intelligent. Stokes is simple."

"Why are we bothering with this shit," Brown broke in, angrily. "I got gangs from California coming into my territory, shooting up my population! I don't give a fuck about no Milvern!"

"Easy, DeShaun, easy. I know that these gangs are operating out of a crack house on Magnolia Street, right? Tomorrow, I've planned that the house will suffer a mysterious explosion and vanish. That should be an object lesson for out-of-town interlopers. You see, one must look at the total picture. If small-timers like Milvern can rip us off, word gets around that we're weak. Those California gangs will be joined by ones from other states. You can't deal with that. It's a negligible amount of merchandise, but the lesson is the thing that counts."

"You take Gene. I guarantee that he will find the wife," urged Arnie.

"I may do just that. Shall we order, gentlemen? I feel like swordfish."

A black-coated waiter materialized to take their order.

"The grilled salmon is excellent tonight," he suggested. "Perhaps some Lobster Bisque to start?"

Martin lived in a large apartment on South Van Buren, an older section of the city, on a street lined with ancient oaks and lindens. The huge sycamore in front of his place had a plaque nailed to it's trunk attesting that it was the oldest tree in the Port City. Next door to his house was an American Legion hall, and more apartment houses were on either side of the Ceramic Center across the street, their architecture complicated and Victorian.

He owned the two-family house and lived on the second floor while renting out the lower flat. The reason he had purchased it was the attached two-car garage in the rear. The entire reinforced roof had been turned into a garden, and in the summer, he raised vegetables, even a few trees and miniature evergreens. Tomatoes were staked in buckets, and several varieties of squash wound their tendrils around the railings. Pots of bush beans clustered in the lush expanse. In the summer, a group of deck chairs and a patio table under a red and white striped umbrella invited his friends to sit and have a beer.

This was winter, however, and the summer landscape was a memory. Beyond the doors, bird feeders poked out of the drifted snow, scavenged by squirrels who could climb anywhere, jostling the winter birds for the seeds. He kept the feeders full of sunflower seeds and thistle. Goldfinches stayed around longer into the winter for the thistle, their yellow flame color softened to a dull olive.

Two years ago, he owned a rehabbed condo downtown and had a cabin in the country to satisfy his gardening desires. In the early fall, when he drove out to spend a weekend at his place, he found the garden trampled. Foraging deer had eaten all of his extensive garden. The corn stalks were chomped down to short sticks, tomatoes were reduced to pulpy mounds, and the bean plants ripped from the ground. He was staring, horrified, at the damage when the farmer who lived a mile down the road chugged up on his tractor.

"Deer got your tomatoes?" he asked, smiling maliciously, hawking a wad of mucus at the road.

"I fenced it off, but they must have jumped over."

"Deer can clear a seven-foot fence easy. You just here weekends?"

"I have a job in the city during the week." He didn't want to tell this rube that he was a cop.

"Can't keep tabs on the property from a distance. You some kind of country squire?"

"No, I just wanted a place away from the city. What do you do to prevent the deer from destroying your crops?

"Tried lots of stuff, but the one that works best is this: I go out into the fields late at night—you probably don't know it, but deer are nocturnal animals. Sometimes, when the weather changes, I go out in my long johns. Deer don't mind. And I fire off my shotgun a few times. Aim it up in the air. Don't have to kill them, at least not until hunting season. Every few nights. The noise scares them off, but you have to keep doing it. Try it." He hawked another green blob between splayed teeth before he rattled off on the tractor.

Martin had only been away from the property for two weeks, but the garden was a disaster, and the shed in the rear had been broken into. His shovels and rakes were missing. He went inside the cabin where the front door hung at an angle. It was in deplorable shape. Kids had gotten inside, and the interior was a mess of empty bottles, ground-out cigarette buts, used condoms and stained pizza boxes. They had damaged the furniture, shattered his dishes and wrecked the bed. It's a wonder they hadn't burned everything to the ground. Disconsolate, he spent hours cleaning the place up, threw everything that would fit into plastic trash bags, and hauled the broken furniture out to the curb. Then, he drove into Cranston and found a real estate dealer who would list it. The agent sold it for a ridiculously low price a couple of weeks later. It had been a pipe dream. Did he think he was a country gentleman, like the obnoxious farmer suggested? Talk about unreal.

There was no place at his condo for a garden, so he got rid of it at a substantial profit. City living was becoming very desirable. He bought this house in a charming, vintage neighborhood. The couple who lived on the first floor were quiet, interesting and sociable. The husband played the cello with the city philharmonic, and his wife worked as a guidance counselor at a local school.

He was excited by the attached two-car garage in the rear. He immediately had the roof reinforced so that he could put a lot of weight on it, and installed a fence around the perimeter. Then, he started his roof-top garden using rectangular raised bed structures. A line of tall evergreens shielded the garage from the view of neighboring houses. A few wooden benches positioned randomly around and a few birdbaths completed the outdoor area. There was no yard to speak of, except for a small one in front of the house where he ripped out all the grass and planted a lilac, some hydrangeas, and roses. No need for a lawn mower.

At one time, he wondered if he would be happy in the suburbs where he could have a real yard, but there was the job. He liked homicide, and there were not so many killings in affluent neighborhoods. He'd probably end up directing funerals. Solving a murder, watching the pieces fall into place, stimulated him intellectually. He was intrigued by the twisted motives that made people kill. The traditional labels were love, money, power, hate, but underneath all those were convoluted relationships, old childhood jealousies scarcely understood – a buried maze of infected emotions. Before he had joined the homicide division, he worked vice, and it had almost destroyed him emotionally. The horrible, sordid crimes that he encountered turned his stomach. Those involving child victims were the worst. He remembered finding a tiny child, three at the most, wandering naked near a deli, screaming, terribly mutilated. His relentless focus on the job, eclipsing everything else, had wrecked his marriage. Now, his ex-wife was married to a math teacher, and he had transferred to homicide.

After the first of January, his mailbox was full of gardening catalogs, and he made endless notes, evening after evening, scanning the photos of mouth-watering fruits and vegetables, sensational flowers, as he decided what he was going to grow next summer. Most of his jottings would become obsolete, as he changed his mind as soon as he saw what was offered at the local gardening centers. This year he was thinking beets and different types of greens. A picture of Purple Calabash Tomatoes was in the Spring Farm Catalog. These heirloom fruits dated from the 1700's, and the idea of growing them excited him. There also were miniature blueberry bushes available, and he was definitely getting into more flowers. Sun flowers, the taller the better-- eight-foot ones and maybe some angelica. He had a lot of sunlight.

Leo and Maria had their garden too. They grew nothing but

tomatoes for spaghetti sauce which they canned with a fervor each fall, putting up fifty or sixty jars. Their kitchen was full of steam and boiling caldrons, the two of them covered with perspiration, yelling at each other. Beyond that, they were not interested in plants.

"Marty, you can buy all that stuff at the supermarket!" Leo protested.

"This is therapy for me. It takes my mind of homicide."

Plus, due to his interest in gardening, he met his girlfriend, Elliot, last summer. She worked at the Plantasma Garden Center. *Landscaping, shrubs, annuals, perennials, hardscapes, pottery and water garden supplies. Visit us on Facebook. Everything for your gardening needs.*

Although her name was Elliot, he preferred to call her Ellie.

"Everybody asks about my name," she told him, when he was there purchasing bags of compost. Next year he would make his own. He had a sunny location in mind for the bin.

"My mother wanted me to be unusual, so she gave me a name that girls usually didn't have." He liked the look of her, her long black hair with a few threads of gray caught back in an arty leather holder. Her full, almost matronly body was clad in overalls, green garden clogs on her feet. A woman you could relax with. She was pretty, but not flashy.

"And are you unusual?" he asked her, flirting a little.

"I'm the most ordinary person you could meet," she laughed.

"Oh, I don't think so." But that was what he liked about her-- the down to earth quality. He had dated too many weird women in the past.

After a few visits to Plantasma, he asked her out and they had been seeing each other ever since.

The first time that she had come to his apartment, she was surprised to see his collection of photographs. He had purchased them at a photography shop in Downtown Mall one Sunday when he was on his way to the cinema. The exhibit featured black and white photos of the lake, taken during many seasons. One photo depicted the water with a storm coming in, another was of a tangle of driftwood and a third showed children cavorting on the municipal beach. He had bought six in all. Two large ones were over the sofa, one on the opposite wall, two more hung in the dining room, and a small photo of a gorgeous sunset graced the kitchen wall. He liked them because they were masculine and simple. Frills and cutesy objects bored him. "Of course," Ellie had commented. "The lake. Why am I not surprised? Seriously, Martin, they are wonderful. I've never heard of the photographer, but he is really good. I didn't realize that you were interested in art."

"I don't know much about art, but these seemed to be very competent, and you know how I feel about the lake."

"I think you've made a wise choice."

The white mats and slender black frames complimented the chocolate brown walls of the living room and dining room. He had hung cream-colored drapes and installed a red leather sofa and recliner. The kitchen was painted a soft cream shade. He hadn't been sure about the colors: his loft had been decorated in shades of blue with black accents, but once the photos were hung, it all came together. The rooms were severe and yet warm.

That evening he had cooked for her: a simple shrimp and rice dish with a tossed green salad. He didn't have too many specialties, but she had eaten the dinner enthusiastically.

"I adore shrimp, but most people ruin them with complicated sauces or fry them in breading, which destroys the delicate flavor. These are perfect."

After dinner, they listened to some of his CD collection. Neither of them was crazy about television, but they both liked music: jazz, classical and blues. They talked until it was time for her to leave, mostly about their jobs. He didn't want to rush things. He needed her simplicity and honesty. This could develop into a serious relationship.

He decided to go out and have a beer at a bar on Hemlock Street that he occasionally patronized. It was an old-fashioned place, quiet and dark. The restaurant section was in the rear, but the dining hour was over, and a handful of locals sat nursing draft beers and staring at the TV behind the bar. The wooden counter faced a mirror running most of its length that reflected glasses, bottles, displays of beer nuts and bacon rinds. Martin took a stool and ordered a Rolling Rock.

Sal Russo was bar tending and they exchanged a few words about the escalation of homicides in the city.

"It's weapons," Sal stated. "Domestics, also, but a big contributing factor is guns. The way I see it is that if weaponry wasn't available, you'd still have drugs and family altercations, but the results would be different. You'd have broken jaws, bashed wives, over-doses, but nobody would be lying dead in the gutter, full of holes."

"Tell that to the gun lobby," sighed Martin.

"You know the ones I feel sorry for? The poor shits who get wasted in a drive-by. Even young kids are getting hit. Thank God I don't have any."

Through the door to the dining room, Martin saw two waitresses cleaning up, changing tablecloths and filling bowls with wrapped cubes of sugar. He frowned. One of the girls turned toward him, holding an empty napkin dispenser in her hands, a slight figure with brown hair.

"For God's sake!" he exclaimed. It was Grace Milvern. He had tried to locate her since the funeral, but she had disappeared. Here she was. What a night for lucky breaks! Leaving his drink on the bar, he approached the back room.

"Grace," he said, intercepting her as she carried some trays to the kitchen. "It's Martin McCallister, the detective." Her light blue eyes looked blankly at him and then the emptiness was replaced by fear.

"How did you find me? I just got this job last week."

"I wasn't looking for you," he protested. "I stopped in to have a beer when I noticed you in the back room. We have been trying to locate you, but you didn't leave a forwarding address. Where are you living now?"

She appeared to be confused. "Why do you have to know? I don't have any information about Dennis!"

"We have to keep in touch in case something develops. Look, do you get off work soon? I could drive you home."

She considered his offer. "Could you keep my address confidential? Even from the other officers?"

"I suppose so, but why? Are you afraid that whoever killed your husband might be after you?"

"Yes, I'm afraid."

"I can provide some protection. It won't be twenty-four hours a day, but it would be something."

"I'm off in fifteen minutes. I'll meet you out in front."

Martin and Grace sat in her tiny apartment drinking coffee. Grace still wore her uniform from Russo's. She was exhausted. There were dark smudges under her eyes, and all she wanted to do was go to bed. She slept all the time when she wasn't working, but she didn't know why. She still ate at the Arms of Love so she could save every penny, but something seemed to be draining her energy. She lay back against the worn cushions of the couch. It made her nervous to have the detective here. He took up so much room in the small place, and the apartment was so awful. She had brought a menu home so that she could familiarize herself with the selections at Russo's, but she fell asleep each time that she tried to study it.

She scrutinized him as he drank the coffee she had made, instant powder in a cup. She had never seen him out of uniform, and he didn't look the way she thought a cop should look. He was lean, athletic, with a hawk nose and his brown eyes were sympathetic. He kept rubbing his chin as though he had grown a beard recently. He had large hands. She always noticed men's hands.

"Do you think Dennis was involved with drugs?" she asked him. "I never saw any signs of that sort of thing."

"I think that he was selling them. The trouble with these amateur dealers, and there are hundreds of them, is that they don't understand that they are competing with hard-core criminals, professional killers who don't give a damn. Eventually, the small fry decide to hold out on the big boys, and that's the end of them. I'm sorry, but I think that's what happened to your husband."

"Am I in danger?"

"Yes, it's possible. I think you should be very careful." He flipped open the menu lying on the table.

Grace started to cry.

"Look, I'm sorry that I upset you. Does anyone else have your address?"

"My cousin who lives downstate. He helped me move. My parents. I have a year-and-a-half-old baby who's staying with them in Cranston until I can get on my feet."

"I think I had better talk to your parents. It would be very easy for someone to find out who they are and contact them. I want you to call them and warn them not to give your address out under any circumstances. We just don't know what is liable to occur. I'll drive down to Cranston tomorrow and interview them."

"Why? They don't know anything about Dennis."

"Grace, I can't leave any loose ends open. Go to bed. I'll stop and see you when I get back. Just do not open your door to anyone. No one! Understand?"

She got up and took his cup. He hadn't drunk much. Not everyone liked instant. "I appreciate your help, but you have to understand that this is all so frightening."

"Just go on with your life. We'll get to the bottom of this." Inside, he was not so sure. Half the homicides in the city were never solved, and this one looked like a real dead end.

The expressway was clear of snow and traffic was light. Martin felt real pleasure driving through the countryside. Stands of spruce and fir appeared intermittently along with rest areas. A few farms with snow-covered barns broke up the landscape. He wished he could experience the area the way it was before settlers came. Pine forests had covered the hills and stretched into the state below. Now, there were small villages and a few suburbs, but no real forests until you approached the beginning of the mountains down in the southern corner of the state. He had grown up in a small hamlet a hundred miles west of the Port City, and sometimes he missed the rural atmosphere. He had looked forward to getting out of the city, but Leo didn't like anything that wasn't paved and was not happy about this trip.

"All this empty land," he commented. "A lot of houses could be built here, and stores. These rural spaces are depressing me."

"We'll only be here for a couple of hours so relax."

"I don't think the Milvern woman's parents are going to give us any useful information. We should be back at the station catching up on paper work."

"It's important that we follow all the angles."

Martin watched the city of Cranston gradually unfold. It was old, not much industry, an unexciting downtown. They stopped at a convenience store near the Allegheny River to ask for directions to the street where Grace's parents lived. Leo bought a chocolate-covered donut and a bottle of soda to console himself.

The house was in an older neighborhood—quiet, nothing fancy. A sidewalk bisected the center of the yard, surrounded by aged shrubs that needed pruning. The street trees were locusts and they stood out starkly in the winter light. A fire hydrant in front of the Buell home was painted red, white and blue in honor of some celebration, probably the Fourth of July. It looked tacky and pathetic.

The Buell house had a large porch across the front with skeletons of vines clinging to one side. In the summer their leaves would block out the light. He wished he could remember the name of the vine—you only saw them in older neighborhoods. A rocker dusted with snow sat near the front door.

Leo rang the bell.

The plump woman who answered the door was middle-aged and held no claims to youth or beauty: the kind of woman whose husband called her 'Mother.' She wore no makeup and her hair was gray.

"Yes?" she said.

"Mrs. Buell? I'm Detective McCallister and this is Detective Aronica. We're from the Port City police force. There is still an open investigation of your son-in-law's murder, and we'd like to ask you a some questions." He handed her his identification.

"I don't know," she fretted. "I'd be happier if my husband were here, but he's at work. You can come in, I suppose, but I don't think I know anything that will help you."

She led them down a hall into the living room and indicated a brown overstuffed couch. The room was sparse and incongruous. It had been years since he had seen doilies on the arms of furniture. A massive, permanently attached TV covered one wall, and a painting of Venice, the sort purchased at a starving artist, nothing over twenty-five dollars sale, hung above the sofa. The coffee table held an ugly ceramic box.

"Were you close to Dennis?" She had not taken their coats, and the room was over-heated.

"I despised him. Grace was a fool. She got herself in trouble, and they had to get married."

Martin noted the old-fashioned way of indicating pregnancy.

"We forbade her to see him, so of course she sneaked around, meeting him wherever she could."

"But wasn't she twenty? Twenty-one?"

"She lived here. Our rules were to be obeyed. We thought that we were through with her after the wedding, but it didn't work out that way, did it?" She made a motion of disgust.

Martin could sense the poisonous atmosphere that Grace had to endure before escaping with such a poor excuse for a future as Dennis Milvern. Probably anything seemed better than this.

"They moved to the city, and now he's dead because he was some kind of a shady crook, and we're stuck with the baby. If she had listened to us, none of this would have happened. It's not fair to expect us to take on a child!"

As a punctuation mark to her anger, a baby's cry came from an upstairs room.

"He's awake now. I have to get him some juice, change him and watch him tear my house apart." She started to get up from her chair.

"Just a minute, Mrs. Buell. Look. I think that your daughter may be in some danger. We still haven't much of an idea about what happened. You have her address and phone number. Please don't give it out to anyone! This is very important! We are providing her with some police protection, but whoever killed the husband might want to harm her."

"We don't mean to alarm you," Leo interjected, "but this is urgent!"

The woman looked nervous.

"Oh, I wouldn't tell anyone where she is." A thoughtful look crossed her face. "Except--"

"Except for who?" Leo insisted.

"Just the insurance man."

The back of Martin's neck prickled. He and Leo stared at each other.

"What insurance man?" he demanded.

"The man who was here yesterday. He said that Dennis had some insurance with the security company, and that Grace had money coming to her from the policy. She'll need all she can get. Dennis never gave her much of anything."

"So you told him where she lived?" He was agitated, knowing that things were horribly wrong.

"If she's entitled to insurance money, I want her to have it. The sooner she gets on her feet, the quicker she can take the boy back. We're too old to raise a child," she whined.

Martin and Leo stared at each other. The miles between Cranston and Grace's tiny apartment rose up against them like a wall. The man could have gotten to her already.

Martin went out into the hall and pulled out his cell phone.

"Who are you calling?" she demanded, suspiciously. "I don't understand."

Kevin Polarski answered the call immediately.

"Get a car over to thirty-eight Georgia Street as fast as you can. Apartment three on the second floor. Grace Milvern. She's in danger! She should be there—doesn't go to work until four."

"Got it. Where does she work? Just in case."

"Russo's. A bar on the west side—you know it?"

"Oh, yeah. We'll get right on it."

Mrs. Buell had come into the hall and was watching him.

"I still don't know what's wrong."

"Would you please describe the man who told you he was an insurance agent?" Martin wanted to choke her. She was so stupid.

"He was tall, somewhat heavyset, dark hair."

"What kind of identification did he show you?" Leo queried.

"Well, nothing. He said that he represented Minnesota Indemnity, the company that handled claims for the security firm. I believed him. Why would he lie?"

She was anxious now, afraid that she had made a mistake.

"I don't know, Martin said. "I just don't know."

Martin drove as fast as possible, sometimes breaking the speed limit, on the way back to the Port City.

"Marty, that woman is an idiot. Do you think we'll be too late?"

"I told Grace not to open her door to anyone, but all I can hope is that she's smarter than her mother."

"I hate cases like this," Leo complained. "They're too complicated."

Grace froze. There was a knock on the door of her apartment. She had been cleaning, straightening up a few things when she heard it.

"Who's there?" she called, tentatively.

She could hear loud rock music coming from the hall.

"Mrs. Milvern?" A man's voice cut through the sound. "I'm from the Minnesota Indemnity Insurance Company. Your late husband's policy is being honored, and I'd like to present you with a check. May I come in?"

Grace knew that something was wrong. Only her parents, her cousin Jason, and Detective McCallister knew where she lived.

The man outside sensed her concern. "We obtained your address from your parents in Cranston. Your mother can vouch for our authenticity. Call her if you have doubts."

She hesitated. Dennis did have some insurance, but she thought it had lapsed when he was laid-off. Maybe not. She reached for the doorknob.

The man waited. He had the gun in the pocket of his overcoat, ready to shoot her when she opened the door. Cautiously, he drew it out.

"Mrs. Milvern?" he inquired, unctuously.

She was torn. Her mother had given him her address, so it should be alright. She stared at the worn, brown paint on the door.

No! The detective had told her not to open the door to anyone. He was a policeman and must know. She took her hand off the doorknob. She was very afraid. What if the man broke into the place? She had to get out of here.

"Mrs. Milvern?" the man asked again, softly.

She tiptoed carefully across the kitchen and soundlessly opened the window, climbing onto the sink. The window looked out onto a tiny back yard where garbage cans were kept. There was a shed beneath the window. She gingerly climbed out and dropped onto the roof. She was only wearing sneakers, a sweater and slacks, and it was a frigid day. She panicked. The man in the hall could see her if he got into the apartment. Terrified, she scanned the snow-covered ground beyond the shed. She could jump onto the drifts left by the snowplow. Squatting on the slippery ledge, she forced her legs over the roof and dropped onto the mounds of piled snow.

Out in the hall, Frank shot the lock off the door with a gun equipped with a silencer.

Once inside, he looked around quickly. The woman wasn't here. What the devil? He went into the miniscule kitchen where a window was open. He stuck his head out. Christ! The shed roof was covered with footprints, but there was no sign of the Milvern woman. One last quick look around. He spotted the menu on the living room table: Russo's written in gold block letters on the cover. Pocketing it, he hurried out into the hall.

Over the railing, he saw two cops starting up the stairs. Shit! How did they know he was here? He ran down the hall to the apartment where the loud music was coming from and tried the door. It was open, a lucky break. Inside of the room, several kids were sitting in a haze of marijuana smoke, nodding in time to the cacophonous sound.

"Is Professor Akeem here?" he shouted over the racket, as he closed the door.

"Don't know that professor," one of the boys replied, complacently.

"Would you please turn down the music just a bit?"

One of the smokers, who was shirtless, reached over and gave the dial a brief turn.

"Professor Akeem is the chair of the Political Science Department at the university. I understood that I was to meet him here."

"We go to Port City Community," the other boy said. He was sitting barefoot on a filthy rug, surrounded by a disorder of beer cans and candy wrappers. There was a torn and sagging sofa where a mess of clothes was strewn.

"I am Professor Goddard from the Sociology Department. If he shows up, would you tell him that I stopped by?"

"Can't think why he'd stop, man. We don't know him."

There was a knock at the door.

"Must be our day for visitors," the barefoot boy commented.

"Excuse me," Frank said. "What if it's the police?"

The boys looked nervously at each other, at their cigarettes. They started brushing the smoke around ineffectually with their hands.

"We can't get busted," the shirtless one whispered. "My dad would kill me."

"Don't let anybody in," Frank advised. "Just go to the door and tell them that you are alone. Walk out into the hall."

"Yeah. They can't come in without a warrant, can they, professor?"

"Absolutely not, but tell them you are alone, or they might try to."

The boy opened the door. Two officers stood there. He ducked quickly into the hall.

Frank strained to hear what was being said, but he was unable to catch anything over the intense sound still pouring into the smoke-filled air of the apartment.

A few minutes later, the boy re-entered the room.

"They wanted to know if I had seen anything suspicious at number three. I told them I was busy studying and had the music turned up loud. I guess they believed me. They didn't ask to come in or anything." He sank nervously onto the couch.

"I thought you handled that well," Frank said.

"I was really shaking," the boy confessed.

"Say, Professor Goddard," said his friend. "You're from the university. Can you tell us anything about how to transfer there? I hate Port City. It sucks."

Frank pushed aside some dirty jockey shorts and settled down at the far end of the sofa.

"Tell me which department you're interested in, and what current courses you're taking. We at the university are always looking for motivated transfer students like yourselves."

Chapter Five

Grace shivered uncontrollably, as she waited on the worn bench in the hall of the police station. She had run desperately through the snow-clogged streets in her thin clothes, and then sat for an hour in the dreary area next to the public phones and the pop machines. She refused to speak to anyone but Detective McCallister. Uniformed officers walked by accompanied by violent-looking prisoners. A man wearing handcuffs had been dragged in by two policemen, as he kicked and screamed obscenities within inches of the bench where she was sitting. The room was full of people, of noise.

Martin and Leo came through the front door.

"Grace!" Martin called as he spotted her. "I was so afraid that something had happened to you! Your mother told us she gave your address to an insurance man."

"He found me, but I went out the kitchen window and came here. You told me not to let anyone in," she stuttered, cold and terrified.

"You're frozen. Come back into the office, and I'll get you some hot coffee." He took her arm and guided her past the switchboard down the hall into his small room.

"We went to your house," Leo explained. "Someone had blown the lock off the door to your apartment. Two policemen were there. They questioned the other tenants, but no one had heard anything."

"What happened?" Martin asked.

She kept shivering. "He said that he was an insurance man. My mother had given him my address." She was shaking violently. "The man was outside in the hall."

Leo went to the closet and got an old sweater that he kept there and draped it around her shoulders.

"I don't understand. How did he know who I was? Where my parents lived? Why did she give him my address?"

"Probably from the death notice in the paper. It listed your maiden name. It wouldn't be hard to track down the information. She was able to give us a description. A heavy-set man with black hair."

Grace put the coffee cup down and started to sob. Martin grabbed her arms and held them tightly.

"Easy, easy."

"I saw him!" she cried. "That's why he's after me!"

"What do you mean?"

In an almost incoherent stream of words, she told him about the shooting at the liquor store.

"You're sure that it is the same man?"

"Who else would be trying to find me?" she cried. "He'll kill me!"

"Not if he can't find you. We'll provide protection."

Martin was trying to calm Grace down when the dispatcher's voice came over the speaker.

"We've got a reported assault over on Broughton Street. It's not a homicide, because the guy was interrupted before the victim was finished off. The reason I called you is that there were letters in the apartment from a Dennis Milvern. I know that's your case."

"Who was the victim?" He reached across the desk for his notebook.

"A Katherine Jordan. She may have been a student— some textbooks were found, although the officers on the scene said the apartment looks more like she was a call girl. The Jordan woman was taken to County Medical."

"When did it happen?"

"Sometime last evening."

"I'll get right out to the hospital."

Grace looked questioningly at the detective.

"This seems like a new development in your husband's case. Did he ever mention a Katherine Jordan to you?"

"Never. What is going on? What does this have to do with Dennis?"

"I don't know. Someone assaulted this woman. It could be the man who shot your husband." He rubbed his chin. "Look, Grace, I'm going to have Detective Aronica drive you home while I go see Katherine Jordan."

"But I have to go to work!"

"Leo will take you to Russo's, and we'll have someone take you home when your shift is over. I want you to call a locksmith. There are some that operate twenty-four hours a day. Have him meet you at your apartment and install deadbolts. I'll stop tomorrow. Be as careful as possible until we can re-locate you."

"Can that man find me at Russo's?"

"I don't think so."

"I'm afraid. He knows where I live."

"We'll do our best to protect you, move you to a different location if we have to."

"I don't know how much more I can take," she protested, her shoulders slumped with defeat.

Martin stopped at the Jordan woman's wrecked apartment on his way to the hospital. The letters from Milvern were in the bedroom under piles of broken mirrors. The place was a disaster with ravaged dolls everywhere in the living room. Whoever trashed the place had been enraged. He flipped through the correspondence, not too surprised that they described what Milvern was going to do sexually to the woman.

County Medical stood at the fringe of the inner-city. It's clients were victims of stabbings, accident cases and the dying poor. It was as bad as Flowers Hospital was in the Eleventh Precinct. Getting off the elevator at the seventh floor, he proceeded to a station and showed his identification. Then, preceded by a nurse, he followed her down a long corridor where despondent-looking people in bathrobes sat in chairs hooked up to devices that dripped medication into their arms. One elderly man in a hospital gown and tattered bedroom slippers clutched a Teddy bear. A few patients hung onto walkers. An orderly was vacuuming the carpet, moving gingerly around them.

"We have orders not to let anyone see her but the police. She may not be able to talk to you, so don't press her. She has a fractured skull and other injuries," the nurse admonished him.

Katherine Jordan lay on the bed, her head swaddled in bandages, her dark skin yellow against the white sheets.

"Has she been conscious at all?" he asked.

"She came to briefly when she was in intensive care, but now she's unconscious again."

"Miss Jordan, can you hear me?" Martin spoke softly as he bent over the motionless form.

"Miss Jordan?"

The woman's eyes opened slightly, swollen to mere slits.

"Who are you?" she whispered.

"I'm Detective McCallister. You were severely beaten at your apartment, and the place was torn apart. Do you have any idea who did this to you?"

She started to cry, tears running down her bruised cheeks.

"I never saw him before. He broke in. My beautiful place—ruined."

"Can you describe him?"

"He was huge, and he had a big, fat head with a broken nose. That's all I remember. He kept hitting me and shouting something about a missing product. I don't understand. Leave me alone. I can't talk!"

"You have to go now, she's upset," the nurse insisted.

"I'll be back when she's more coherent."

Martin was very tired but still wound up when he let himself into his apartment. He wondered if he had consumed too much coffee earlier in the evening. He hated the decaf that Grace had given him. Months ago, he bought an expensive coffee- maker and kept it in his office. He tried to limit himself, but when the precinct went crazy, he automatically reached for another cup. He rubbed his chin. Winter was so damn long in the Port City. He was tempted to grow his beard in again, no matter what Commissioner Battaglia thought. It had been late in the evening when he left the hospital, and then he checked out some inexpensive hotels downtown hoping to find a place where he could hide Grace. The department had no contingency for such things. He probably would have to pay for it out of is own pocket. He turned on his answering machine to see if there were any calls.

"Martin? Vince Czerwinski here. There was another attempt to break into the Jordan woman's apartment tonight. The landlord lives downstairs, and he heard strange noises and called us. Arnecki picked up the call and investigated. He surprised a man, but the guy got out. Arnecki took a shot at him."

Martin turned the machine off. There must be something in the place that they hadn't found, he mused. I'll go over first thing in the morning and check it out. God! What a long day!

Mike Stokes felt the blood running down his leg into his sock. The injury hurt a lot. He had gotten out the door of the apartment and jumped over the side railing of the front porch, when the cop got off a shot at him! He landed in a jumble of trash and broken bottles, and one of them cut him sharply. Thank God he had gotten a tetanus shot recently when he was bitten by a cat. The bullet winged off the porch rail, and he ran down the street, wincing with pain and scared shitless. Christ! He had been frightened!

He was furious with Jack D'Angelo for sending him over there. He was sure that the Jordan woman didn't have the stuff. Dennis wasn't that stupid. He hid it someplace totally inaccessible, and they would never find it. Either that or the wife had it.

There was no problem getting into the place. The idiot of a landlord had put a flimsy lock on the door, and it was a snap to break it. George had made a real mess of the apartment. That damned psycho had been incredibly destructive, breaking dolls all over the living room, wrecking lamps. The bedroom was the worst—a sea of broken glass. The place looked like a war zone.

He gave everything a cursory search and then rummaged through her books. She had a notebook that said Port City Community on the cover. This seemed to be the home of a hooker, rather than a college student. He went into the kitchen and was dumping out a canister of flour when the cop came through the living room door. Mike heard him crunch on a broken doll. He dashed past the guy and plunged down the stairs onto the porch, leaping over the rail, as the cop fired at him. Running fast, he made it to his car and burned rubber. He had escaped after finding nothing, hurting his leg and being shot at. Enough was enough! Jack had better give up the idea of the product being in the apartment. It wasn't there!

Russo's was very busy. There were more diners than usual. The crisp air made people seek companionship and warmth. Grace dreaded going outside into the cold at the end of her shift to the unmarked car where a policeman would be waiting for her.

"The special tonight is Veal Marsala," she recited to the patrons. "It's very good. I recommend it."

The tips were excellent here. The customers were mainly from the neighborhood, and she was getting to recognize some of the regulars. Sal Russo was a decent employer, and the other waitresses easy to work with. She had hopes of getting out of the financial hole she was caught in. She was exhausted all the time, and when she wasn't working, she slept continuously. Maybe she should buy some vitamin pills. Doggedly, she placed salad bowls in front of her customers.

Frank watched her reflection in the mirror that ran the length of the bar. He was seated on a stool surrounded by a crowd of people waiting for tables, so he knew he wouldn't be noticed, not that anyone but Grace knew who he was. He covertly checked Grace's image reflected in the glass as she slipped into view and then disappeared while serving customers. When she left the restaurant, he would be waiting. This time she wasn't going to escape by going down any roof. He planned to force her into his car and drive her to the river where it snaked around abandoned cement plants. The flats--that's what the area was called. Environmentalists were always trying to clean it up. Tours were conducted on the water in the summer to view the empty grain elevators. She wouldn't be the first person to vanish in the flats. Last spring, police found the body of an Indian woman rotting in the underbrush. It had lain there all winter, unnoticed. He fingered the folded menu in his pocket, the one he had taken from her apartment, glanced at his heavy, gold watch. A few more hours, and he'd get rid of her.

Gene Lempke sat on a stool a ways down the bar from the heavy-set man. He had followed Grace Milvern from her apartment when she left for work. Jack's snitch at Precinct Eleven had come up with her address. She was the cleaning person and had access to all the offices. It had been easy for her to go through the papers on McCallister's desk after he left for the night. The woman was one of a network of Jack's informers spread throughout the police department. In his business, you had to keep ahead of things.

Gene had watched the cop in the unmarked deliver Grace to Russo's at the beginning of her shift. He figured that she'd be picked up by the same man later and driven home. Jack told Gene to talk to her, find out what she knew. She was Milvern's wife and must know something. Jack didn't want her hurt, not yet, anyway. Gene was just supposed to scare her into telling him some important details. If that didn't work, then they would have to get more serious.

He gestured at the bartender for another Black Velvet and water. The local hockey game was on the TV and he watched it idly. He planned on intercepting her before she got to the unmarked when the cop picked her up.

No one was picking Grace up tonight. The cop assigned to her had received an urgent message to proceed at once to the Seminole Expressway. Some teenage thugs had dropped chunks of concrete off the walkway over the highway, and a car's window had been smashed. When the concrete struck the vehicle, it veered into the side of an SUV and a third car plowed into them. The road was a disaster area, and there were probably fatalities. The expressway was closed and traffic was backed up for three miles to the Onandaga exit ramp. Ambulances were on the way to the scene, and all patrol cars were ordered to the scene of the accident. The policeman who was to escort Grace turned on his siren and headed for the disaster.

At the end of her shift, Grace put on her coat and gloves and prepared to leave. The unmarked would arrive soon, and she planned on waiting in the doorway until she saw it appear.

"Good night, Sal," she called.

Gene Lempke put his change in his pocket and got to his feet. He was going to make small talk with her and then muscle the woman into his car. They would drive to a quiet place and converse until he found out all that she knew.

The heavy-set man went through the door immediately after

Gene. Gene stopped next to Grace.

"Mrs. Milvern?" he inquired. "I used to work with your late husband, and I want to tell you that it's a terrible shame what happened to him. It's getting so the average citizen just isn't safe anymore."

"I don't know you!" Grace protested.

Lempke gripped her arm and pushed her out the door to where his car was parked. As he did, he pressed his hand over her mouth so that she couldn't call out. The cop car was nowhere to be seen.

Frank watched with amazement. Someone else was trying to abduct her! What the hell was going on?

Grace tripped on the icy sidewalk and fell to her knees as Gene opened the car door and prepared to shove her inside. Frank dashed out of the building and grabbed him, spun the man around, and slammed him against the side of the car. Freed of his hand, Grace screamed and screamed. She attempted to get up, but her new assailant caught her and wrenched her arm behind her back. Grace kicked at him, ineffectively. Hearing the noise, Sal Russo burst through the door of the restaurant, waving a gun.

"Let her go, you bastard!" he shouted.

The man dropped Grace and took off across the street. Gene jumped into his car and careened down away as fast as possible, skidding on the icy pavement.

"Two of them, eh. Muggers. Probably wanted your purse. This isn't the first time I've chased scum away from here. You okay, Grace?"

Grace was so shaken that she couldn't answer.

"Come into the bar, you're wobbly."

She stumbled into the bar and fell into a chair.

"I'm pouring you a shot. You're white as a ghost."

She drank it in one gulp, shuddering as it brought tears to her eyes.

"I have to make a phone call," she quavered.

Sal pushed the house phone over to her as she got Martin's card out of her purse and dialed. She knew he wouldn't be at the station, but maybe they could forward the call.

An hour later, she was sitting on the faded beige bedspread in a modest hotel near city hall. It wasn't luxurious, but the room was clean, and the lobby had been quiet and deserted.

Martin sat in the only chair.

"You'll be safe here. Whoever those men are, they won't look for you in a hotel."

"But I recognized the big one!" she protested. "He's the man that I saw shoot the liquor store clerk! And now he knows I work at Russo's.

How did he find me?" She was distraught.

"I don't know. I wish I knew his name."

"How am I going to get to work?" She rubbed her raw knee with her hand. "And as soon as I leave Russo's, they'll follow me here!"

"You're not going back to Russo's. It's too dangerous."

"I have to work! I can't lose my job!"

"Look, Grace, don't be a fool. You know you're in grave danger. Two men are after you. The other guy may be the one who murdered your husband. We don't know what they want from you."

"But wouldn't they be afraid to try something at the restaurant because the police might be watching? Please---" she pleaded.

"We can't take any chances. For God's sake, Grace, your husband was murdered! These people are serious! I should put you in a cell for your own protection."

She looked around at the dull, depersonalized room.

"I can't stay here all day! I'll go crazy! And I don't have any clothes. I have to go to my apartment right now and get some things."

"I'll go over there. You're not leaving this hotel until we figure out what to do."

He stood up and rubbed his chin. She was so obstinate. He felt affronted. He was paying for this room out of his own money. By the time the police department processed the paperwork to get her in a protection program, she'd be dead. He had to hide her. He wished he knew who these people were, but he had no leads. Christ! What a case!

Grace stared at him. She was very frightened—she could be killed—but she was damned if she was going into hiding. She had enough of that sort of thing. All those days in the other apartment waiting for Dennis to come home, the empty hours with just the baby. No, no more. She had to earn money so she could get her child back. She had changed. Working had made her stronger, more confident. When Dennis was alive, she depended on him for everything, had no personality of her own. Now, she understood that he hadn't been good for her at all. She could take care of Denny by herself, but she had to make money—and that meant a job.

"When will you bring my things?" she asked.

"I'd better get them right away before the place is broken into again. I'll be back in an hour. Will you be all right?" He touched her shoulder.

She nodded, "There are some pictures of my son in the left hand drawer of the dresser. Make sure that you get those."

Martin found a battered suitcase at her apartment and emptied the contents of the dresser drawers into it. In the tiny, windowless bathroom, he surveyed the pathetic collection of makeup, toothpaste, Band-Aids and swept it all into a paper bag. Her jumbled furniture would have to remain. It would be stolen—not that it mattered—junk, that's all it was. He found the baby's pictures. They showed a chubby child with dark hair and serious eyes standing in a playpen, one of him rolling on a rug, another of him clapping his hands. There was a photo of Dennis at the bottom of the stack. Brown hair starting to thin already, blue eyes, a boney face. Martin stared at it for a while. This was the man who had caused all the trouble. He looked harmless. Martin left it in the drawer.

He returned to the hotel with Grace's belongings. She had been napping on the bed, and her cheek bore the imprint of a crease in the pillow. She looked incredibly young and vulnerable.

"Try to get a good night's sleep," he told her. "You've been through a lot. I'll call you in the morning from the station."

"I appreciate all you've done."

"Just stay in your room. That's all I ask."

"I find it very unfortunate, Gene, that you were less than successful in your meeting with the Milvern woman." Jack D'Angelo's voice was soft. He wore a taupe silk suit with a pale cream shirt and a dull lavender tie. He was seated at his desk in the Highland Commons Office Building, a towering, graceful structure that spanned the lower section of Main Street. The office, located on the ninth floor, below the Ambassador restaurant, was a suite of three large, richly furnished rooms. Prints and photographs of old Port City landmarks, long since demolished, lined the walls, interspersed with original paintings of local scenes. The window behind his desk presented a panoramic view of the waterfront. The opposite wall was covered with floor to ceiling bookcases, and there was a conversational grouping of a sofa, chairs, a coffee table.

Gene stood before the desk. He had not been invited to sit down.

"Jack!" he protested. "Who would have expected someone else to be tailing her? And to try and grab her! What's going on here? Who else is interested in that woman?"

"It seems as though you could have been more prepared, or somewhat prudent." Jack stared quietly at Gene.

"Hey, I did my best! It was just that----"

"Let's forget Mrs. Milvern for a while. I don't like the complications we are running into. I may require your services at a later date, but not at the moment. See my secretary on the way out, and she will reimburse you for your efforts."

"Jack, are you mad at me?"

"No, a little disappointed. I was told that you were good at what you do. That doesn't seem to be the case." Jack stared quietly at Gene.

After Gene left, Jack swung his chair around to study the lake. It was a frozen expanse under an iron-colored sky. The ice boom was visible beyond the mouth of the harbor. Every year it was constructed to protect the power plants down the river from a surge of ice. Critics said that the boom delayed the growing season by preventing the lake from warming. They were probably right.

Jack mulled the problem. There were only two avenues to follow, Mrs. Milvern and Katherine Jordan. If Dennis hadn't bragged to Mike Stokes about Katherine, they would have never known of her existence. Now that surveillance on the Milvern woman was temporarily blocked, it might be auspicious to resume operations concerning Jordan. Unfortunately, she had disappeared. Well, we will just have to find her. What did Mike Stokes say? He had found textbooks when he searched her apartment. Maybe he will remember which college the erstwhile intellectually gifted Miss Jordan was attending. Perhaps she would be reachable that way. Yes. He pressed the phone button, and when his secretary answered, requested the number for the OTB parlor in Syracuse. It only took a few minutes to reach his employee.

"George!" he cried heartily when the man was summoned to the phone. "How are you? Refreshed and rested? Good! You have a new assignment waiting, and I guarantee that you will like it better than the last one. Come back Friday and I'll elaborate. And be sure to give my best wishes to your father."

He was smiling when he hung up.

"We'll retrieve the merchandise yet." He buzzed his secretary.

"I'll be playing squash at my club and then lunch. Back at two."

Chapter Six

Frank was staring out the window, watching the sunny horizon when the phone rang. He picked it up after a few rings. His estranged wife, Jennifer, was on the line. His heart started pounding. He loved her so much.

"Frank, I know that you did it," she stated, flatly.

"Did what?" God! Talking to her hurt.

"You killed Nathan."

"I did not shoot that scum!"

"You shot him because I was involved with him, and you couldn't stand to see me have a life of my own. I'm going to the police and tell them."

Frank felt a surge of rage. "How are you going to prove that I shot him? It's only your stupid imagination! You are a sick and unhappy woman, and no one will believe you. Listen to an unfaithful wife? A slut who screws college students? I think not!"

"I'm not sick, and I have been more relaxed since I left you! You didn't have to kill him. You did it because he made me feel like a new person. Frank, you are so rotten!"

Up until this moment, Frank had wanted Jennifer back at any cost. He had been crazy with missing her. If she returned, he would forgive her, and they could start again, provided that she was repentant, sorry for her lapse. He dreamed of her at night—the touch of her loose, blond hair, the rosy skin, her exciting underwear. He slept with his head buried in her pillow, because it retained the special scent that she wore.

But now, hearing her berate him, he suddenly didn't want her anymore. He felt repelled by her. She had gotten him into this mess with her wanton fucking. He bet that Scortino wasn't the only one. She probably had banged half of the campus. For her, he had killed that idiot, Scortino, and now he was going to have to eliminate Grace Milvern. How deluded he had been. She was nothing but a bitch.

"Listen to me carefully, Jennifer. You are not getting anything out of me. No money and not one stick of the furniture that you love so much. Do you hear me?"

"I'm entitled to half of our assets under the law, and I intend to get them!"

"You'll never get a divorce."

"I will. I'm filing soon. You'll hear from my lawyer."

"What are the charges going to be, sweetheart? Come on—tell me what you've dreamed up."

"Cruel and inhuman treatment!" She spat out the words.

"I'd love to see you prove that, Miss Flatback."

"I'll prove it. Just you wait. But first I'm going to the police and telling them that you shot Nathan Scortino!"

"You have as much chance of proving that as you have of getting the furniture."

"Why don't you divorce me? Do it and I won't go to the police. You can charge me with infidelity."

"Because I don't want a divorce, bitch. I want you to suffer for a long time. You're not going to get a damn thing! Don't forget – I'm a lawyer!" He slammed down the phone.

Frank paced about the apartment for a few minutes, and then went into the kitchen and poured some Kentucky Bourbon into a glass. He looked around at the bleached-oak cupboards, the granite-topped counter, the chopping-block island with an overhead rack hung with French cooking utensils, wicker baskets, gleaming pans. Potted trees stretched up to the skylight. Impulsively, he picked up a blue and white fourteenth-century plate and hurled it against the wall where it shattered.

"Nothing! She's getting nothing!"

He groped for his binoculars near the kitchen table. Watching the gulls always calmed him down, but his hands were shaking so badly that he was unable to focus on the birds. He must find Grace Milvern soon! If he didn't, it would be all over, and Jennifer would have everything that she wanted.

Katherine Jordan was released from the hospital on a dark, depressing afternoon, an afternoon that made light-sensitive people want to end it all. One side of her head was still bandaged, and there were yellow and purple bruises around her eyes. Stitches held the inside of her mouth together where her lips had been split.

The detective-- McCallister-- had been to see her several times during her stay, bringing pictures of known burglars, but she hadn't been able to identify her attacker from them.

"No. None of them. I'd know him at once. He was so weird looking."

Her friend, Lakeisha, picked her up in the lobby, ready to take her to her place in the Palmer Heights Projects, but Katherine insisted on going to her old apartment first.

"I don't think that's a good idea," Lakeisha protested. "You're still too rocky. Rest a few days at my house. We can go next weekend."

"I have to see if there is anything salvageable."

"It's going to hurt like hell being back there."

"I know."

Katherine went cautiously up the stairs to the apartment she had loved so well. She made Lakeisha stay in the car.

"I don't want anyone to see you."

When she opened the apartment door, her head started to throb painfully. Neither the police nor the landlord had cleaned anything up, and smashed and broken dolls were still strewn over the living room. She sank into a chair that had slits cut into the sides.

"I want my life back," she sobbed, viewing the destruction, all her beautiful things ruined. Her collections tossed about as they were trash. Wiping her face, she went into the bedroom where there was a sea of broken glass. Her vandalized suitcases lay open on the floor, and she began to pack them with anything that hadn't been torn to shreds. Picking her clothes up from the closet floor, she piled them on the bed, along with a stack of sheets and pillowcases. There were towels and cosmetics in the bathroom. She needed boxes. All this stuff would never fit into the suitcases. Carrying some dresses, she went down to the car and asked Lakeisha to go over to the corner deli and get some cardboard containers.

Lakeisha brought them upstairs and silently helped Katherine sort through the terrible mess and disorder. They walked carefully on the shattered glass littering the floor.

"What kind of a perverted creep would do something like this?" Lakeisha asked. "What could he gain by breaking all these mirrors?"

"I don't know. Why would he beat me up? I never saw the man before."

"I'll carry the stuff down to the car," her friend told Katherine. "You're still sick."

"I don't want that man to see you," she protested.

"It's all right. No one's watching."

Katherine's head hurt so much that she thought she was going to pass out. She lay down on the exposed mattress and shut her eyes.

Except for Lakeisha and a few other friends, she was all alone in the Port City. No children and no family. She came from the inner city in Palmerton, a place several hundred miles away, where she lived with her mother and three younger brothers in a disintegrating row house owned by a man who resided in another state and let the place go to hell. She and her mother lined one wall of the kitchen with plastic to keep the rain from pouring into the room. They stapled cardboard over a broken window. The house was never warm.

When she turned eighteen, she quit high school with a year still to go and got a job as a model for drawing and painting classes at the university. She loved the work. Her nude body tingled all over as the students drew her, their pencils and charcoal moving slowly transferring the image of her body to paper or canvas. Seated on a chair or reclining on a platform under the skylights in the art studio, she watched the instructor in his tan lab coat moving slowly around the class—correcting, advising. Illumination from the skylight fell like pollen onto her creamy beige skin.

But the pay was terrible.

She could hardly give her mother any help with the household expenses. She quit modeling and got a job in a downtown department store, where she was assigned to the perfume counter. Except for the money she gave her mother, her salary was spent on clothes, cosmetics, fancy hairdos, while using her store discount. Men continually stopped at her counter, looking to buy perfume for their girlfriends. Many of them asked her out—to dinner, shows, whatever. All kinds of men: black, white, Asian. She dated a lot of them.

One man talked her into a weekend in a fancy hotel at the Port City, where he had a real estate business.

"You're too attractive to be working as a clerk in a department store," he told her.

She realized that he was right, and that she could make a lot more money another way. She moved to the Port City, because she didn't want her mother to know what she was doing. The woman sang alto in the church choir, for God's sake.

Katherine began living a wonderful, lazy life, having profitable dates, taking a few classes.

But one of the men that she met was Dennis Milvern.

Now, she was in the worst possible position. She didn't even have a place to live, thanks to Dennis. But it was also her own fault, she realized when she lay in the hospital bed, hurting. She decided that she would only have real freedom if she had a profession or a career. She talked to the nurses, asked them questions about their jobs, the tasks that they liked best, the ones that they hated. They assured her that there were lots of jobs in health care on many levels.

"You could be a nurse, or a Medical Office Manager, X-Ray Technician, Dental Hygienist. Go back to school. There's a lot of jobs out there."

I've got some money saved, enough to pay Lakeisha rent, she thought. I think I'll apply to Port City Community as a full-time student. There's financial aid available. I can get my GED while I'm taking classes. Go into the health care field. My old way of life was too dangerous. I'm lucky that getting beat up was the worst thing that happened. I'm through with men and dates. Someday, I'll have another apartment, even nicer than the one I had. Maybe I will even have enough money to buy a house! Why not?

She got up off the bed and went to sort through the torn and broken dolls thrown around the living room. Most of them were trashed beyond help, heads yanked off, stuffing hanging out. She managed to salvage eight that weren't too bad. Most of her favorites had been destroyed. A black baby doll was missing an arm, but two of the German ones were intact. The beautiful, blond bride doll's satin dress was torn to shreds, her hair ripped out of her head. Most of her furniture was demolished.

Lakeisha helped her cram everything into the car.

"Look," Katherine told her friend, "if anyone comes looking for me, especially that dude Darnell, tell them I moved back to Palmerton. You haven't seen me."

"I don't know nothin."

"You know, you're taking an awful chance having me at your place. What if that man comes after me again?"

"Shit, sugar. He don't know me at all. Everything will be fine."

John Bradford's serious face appeared on the TV screen.

"We begin tonight with coverage of the court appearance of well-known Port City slum lord. Jack D'Angelo was in court today to answer charges that some of the properties that he owns are unsafe to live in. Building inspectors have cited numerous violations on these properties. Mr. D'Angelo owns thirty-one houses in the inner city and the West side, and he has been to court twelve times in the last three years to respond to charges. We take you now to city court where our action reporter, Harvey Gunnite, is standing by.

The reporter stood ready as the camera zoomed in on an extremely well-dressed man, accompanied by two assistants and three lawyers.

"Mr. D'Angelo," the action reporter called. "Can you tell the viewers why you have had to appear in court so many times for building violations?"

Rather than being affronted or marching silently past the reporter, D'Angelo turned to the camera with an expansive smile.

"Nice to see you, Harvey. My best to John Bradford. I'll explain the situation. It's becoming more and more difficult to teach people the basic aspects of tenancy. I have conferred repeatedly with my renters and pointed out that the best way to deter rat infestation is to replace the garbage can covers. To insure that the furnace remains in working order, it is essential that the doors and windows of the house be closed when it is running. Some of them prefer not to learn."

"But haven't some of the charges been that there wasn't any hot water available in the house? One tenant had no electricity and was forced to run an extension cord from the home next door: that the ceiling collapsed in a renter's bedroom."

"My plumbers and electricians visit the premises constantly to remedy problems. Unfortunately, the crux of the matter still remains renter education. If you bang on a ceiling with a broom handle repeatedly, chances are that it will eventually fall. It's prudent to pay your electric bill on time. Nice to have talked to you, Harvey." With a wave, as though he were bidding adieu to a horde of admirers, he and his entourage swept down the courthouse steps.

"You heard the man, John. It's all a matter of education!"

"Thanks, Harvey," laughed John Bradford. "To continue— the city's ninth homicide happened today on the west side—"

Martin turned off his set. He knew all about the latest homicide.

His mind stayed on Jack D'Angelo. The man was certainly a drug czar, and the brains behind much of the crime in the city. He was an enigma. He spoke like a lawyer and dressed like an ad in Gentleman's Quarterly. Martin could not understand him. It was easy to relate to some poverty-stricken kid from the inner city turning to crime, in order to afford the things that he would never have a chance at any other way. Martin might detest what he was doing, but he could understand. D'Angelo was something else. He was obviously intelligent. Wouldn't it have made more sense if he had become a lawyer, instead of a crook who talked like one? The police hadn't been able to connect him to any of the drug activity in the city, but they knew he was involved.

Opening the French doors that led to his roof garden, Martin stepped out onto the drifted snow. It was hard to imagine that this frozen scene would be lush and green in not too many months. The empty plant containers were almost buried, and the sky was full of remote, cold stars. He filled the bird feeders with sunflower seeds. In the morning, juncos and chickadees would be twittering at the feeder.

Spring comes, he thought, and with it an influx of increased gang-related activity and a new wave of homicides. He wanted to get the Milvern case wrapped up soon. He couldn't afford to keep Grace in that hotel forever.

Back inside, he decided to make a tossed salad for dinner with some fettuccine and tomatoes. Opening the refrigerator, he took out lettuce, olives, cucumbers and green peppers. He had been a vegetarian for almost five years and had lost ten pounds and slept better. One or two beers in the evening, minimal dairy. His vice was still coffee, pots and pots of it, but nobody's perfect. He and Leo took turns picking the restaurant where they decided to lunch each day. Leo hated the vegetarian ones.

"Marty! You need meat to get all the vitamins! This stuff is rabbit food! How can you pass up a nice, tasty steak?"

In response, Martin just stared at Leo's portly figure with its protruding stomach.

He tossed the salad with oil and vinegar. Ellie was a vegetarian also, and she was coming to dinner tomorrow night and would spend the weekend. Food was one of the many things they had in common. Her son, Mathew, was going to stay with his grandmother.

Sometimes they stayed at her apartment. It was like her, earthy and artistic. Her sister was a weaver, and the walls displayed many woven hangings in bright colors. The living room had a built-in bookcase and a working fireplace with a large basket of logs nearby. There was an outsized poster from a seventies movie on one wall along with several black and white drawings. She always lit candles on the mantle, and the air was sweet with the smells of apples and spices.

The weekend before he had taken her out for a rare treat-- skiing on the frozen lake. They skied at night because Martin didn't want any of the shore residents seeing them and becoming alarmed, even calling the police. He didn't think that it was illegal, but who knew the laws in these small lakefront villages? Elliot was a good skier, probably better than he was. She and her son skied regularly at the resorts south of the city. They put the equipment into the rack on the top of his car and drove out to the lake shore. He knew of a tiny sliver of beach that was close to the road where he once rented a trailer for six months. They could park the car and get out onto the lake. There were no houses nearby, so they wouldn't be observed. It was easy to traverse the brittle grass and push out beyond the ice-covered beach. Then, they were moving farther and farther away from land, their skis making soft, whooshing sounds. The vast purple-black horizon swept far off to the left. Minute distant lights from the far shore were barely visible.

The night was clear, as they skied in the chill air.

"Martin! This is wonderful!" Ellie exclaimed. "It's a magic spot. You've must have done this many times."

"I wouldn't take anyone but an experienced person out here because it can be dangerous. Just watch for sounds of cracking. If you hear that, turn and head for shore right away. That means the ice is unstable in that area."

"I feel so free!"

The land had receded, and they were alone moving through the darkness. The lake was very quiet. All the traffic sounds were muted and distant. Martin loved the lake. Safe or dangerous, calm or disturbed, it answered something in him. He canoed or kayaked in the summer, swam at a public beach, hiked along its perimeter. It pleased him to see how much Ellie enjoyed the experience. Her no-nonsense winter gear was warm and practical. A blue ski jacket and navy pants, a wool cap pulled low over the long black hair bundled inside. He hated trendy clothes for sports—fashion statements.

"Time to head back," he stated after a half-hour. They were quite far out on the lake, but there was still a slight chance that they could be spotted if they stayed too long. They turned and poled back toward the shore.

"I'm going to remember this for a long time."

"I knew you would like it. We'll do it again some calm night."

As he ate, he thought about Grace Milvern again, and his stomach tightened. There were no leads to her husband's murder and no evidence. It wasn't falling into place. Everyone involved seemed to be rapidly moving, swinging around Grace, their prey, circling her, pulling ropes tighter and tighter, while he stood off to the side wondering what to do, feeling stupid.

Chapter Seven

Everybody had problems. He and Leo were eating at the Spaghetti Cavern, a huge four-story place crowded with lunchtime diners. It was Leo's turn to choose, and he loved Italian food.

During the meal he complained. "I'm having so much trouble with our fifteen-year-old! I can't stand it! I'm sure I'm getting an ulcer!"

"What's the problem?" Martin asked, working on his Cesar salad.

"Saturday night, she wanted to go out and meet her friends. We were going to say yes, and then a call came on her cell, and we overheard her mention a boy's name, tell him she would meet him in an hour."

"Maria and I do not want her sneaking out to meet boys. If they are respectable, they will come to the house."

He sighed, pushing his plate of lasagna away.

"We all ended up in a shouting match, and her mother made her go to her room and locked her inside. Sometime later that evening, after we all went to bed, Tina jumped out of her bedroom window! This is on the second floor! We heard her scream when she hit the ground! Maria and I ran down and there she was laying on the ground, sobbing. She landed on her leg and fractured her ankle. The neighbors must have thought that we were insane. All the yelling and crying, and then we had to get dressed and take her to the emergency room in the middle of the night!"

"Is she all right?" Martin frowned.

"Well, she's in a cast and she's storming around the house screeching at us, telling us she's moving out as soon as she's sixteen and going to live with this punk! She can't do that, can she Marty? She's got to be a legal adult to leave."

"You don't want her to be a runaway, Leo. That's the road to big trouble."

"What should I do?" he begged, impatiently. "We're at the end of our rope!"

"Why don't you go talk to your parish priest. He's probably seen cases like that of your daughter. And maybe if you invited the boy over, Tina could see him with your family and he won't seem so romantic. She might not even like him anymore."

"Invite him to the house?" Leo screamed. "That little punk is not crossing my doorstep!"

"Well, try the priest angle anyway. It's a start."

"You're lucky you don't have kids, Marty."

"I agree. But now, we do have some cases to solve. Didn't you tell me your mother used to say 'Eat as though every meal were your last?' Finish your lasagna and we'll go back to the precinct."

"My mother had kids who obeyed her, never gave her trouble." He put down his fork. "I can't eat. I'm too nervous. After work, I have to go home to an upset wife, a crying kid, my mother-in-law who will be there by now to put her two cents in, and maybe a few aunts. I can't stand it."

When Grace woke up, the only sound she heard was that of bird's chirping. She listened for a moment, imagining them in the stark branches, swooping down to pick up things from the snowy sidewalks. There were always abundant winter birds in February. She remembered them clustering at the feeder behind her parents house in Cranston.

Then, she opened her eyes.

The dawn light was muffled and gray in the stuffy room. Her bed was only a foot away from the next one, where a woman lay with her broken arm cradled stiffly on top of the blanket. Another bed was pushed against the frayed wallpaper, where a third woman slept. There was also a crib in the room, occupied by a large, pale baby who breathed asthmatically. The child's face bore purple and green bruises.

Grace sighed as she remembered where she was.

Women's Haven—a temporary lodging for abused women and children and an escape hatch from terrorizing husbands. Two days ago, she had taken a suitcase packed with her meager belongings and quietly left the hotel. There was no way she could stay there. She must get a job or else she would never get Denny back. She had taken a bus to the Arms of Love dining hall, in order to see one of the volunteers that she had become friendly with. The woman was attentive as she explained her problem.

"My husband beats me. I've run away from him and I have no place to go. Do you know of a shelter?"

The woman looked critically at Grace's pale skin. There were no visible marks, but that didn't mean that there was no abuse. Her body could be covered with bruises and lacerations.

"There is a director over at Spirit of Hope dining hall, Sister Dominski, who assists battered women. You might try talking to her."

"How do I get there?"

"It's on the East side. I'll give you directions."

The nun wore street clothes, a dark skirt and sweater with low, sensible shoes. Grace hadn't patronized this soup kitchen before because it was out of her way, closer to the abandoned train station. She was struck by the quiet atmosphere, unlike the sense of commotion always about to erupt that characterized the Arms of Love.

"We do referrals if they seem to be legitimate. Tell me about your problem."

Grace repeated the story that she had related to the volunteer at the Arms."

"Do you have children?"

"One. A year-old boy."

"Where is he now?"

"Downstate. My parents are taking care of him. I just need a place to tide me over until I can work and make enough money to support him."

"You are not going to contact your husband, are you? Some of the mistreated women eventually try to mend their relationships. Then, they show up at Spirit of Hope six months later in worse condition then they were originally."

"I'm terrified of him." She felt guilty about lying to this nun.

"Why so you think your husband abused you?"

"He's a drug addict," Grace lied. "He beat me because I wouldn't become a prostitute to get him money for drugs."

Sister Dominski pondered for a moment as she studied the woman. Then she made a decision. "I'll give you a card for Women's Haven. They may take you in for a short period, although they prefer to aid families. It will depend on how crowded they are. It's over near the river."

It took Grace several hours to find the place after walking around the West Side through street after crumbling street. There was no sign in front of the anonymous-appearing dark-green house, just a street number. A cheerful, young black woman admitted her after scrutinizing her through the peephole in the door as Grace shivered on the porch, stamping her feet to keep them from becoming numb.

"I'm Tawanna, the day manager. Come into the office."

The office was right next to the front door, a small room not much larger than a closet, with a cluttered desk, file cabinets, several distressed chairs, one of which the young woman indicated.

"Who sent you?"

"Sister Dominski."

"I'm not surprised. We get lots of referrals from Spirit of Hope. Have you told anyone where you were coming?"

"No one."

"Make sure that you don't. We have to protect the safety of all our clients. Tell me about what brought you here."

Grace repeated the story she had made up for the nun, and Tawanna seemed to accept it, although she had a lot of other questions concerning Grace's prior living arrangements, and the extent of her neediness. Finally, she said:

"You can stay for two weeks unless we become crowded and need the bed for a woman with children. Do not, under any circumstance, attempt to contact your husband while you are here. We aren't able to do much, but we offer job counseling and a free physical exam."

Grace was not interested in those things. She needed a place to sleep until she found a job.

"If you have any valuables, you can put them in our office safe."

Grace shook her head.

Tawanna led her up a battered staircase to a dimly lit hallway.

The room that she was shown to was not large, but it already contained the woman with the broken arm and blackened eyes sitting on a bed staring into space. Another woman was mumbling obsessively to herself, alternately picking up her baby, putting the child in the crib and then taking it out and transferring it to her bed. She never stopped rambling, recounting how her husband had struck her, kicked her little girl, thrown the baby against a wall. Over and over, she described his viciousness.

"He twisted my arm, hit me in the mouth with a heavy pan, kicked the baby—"

Grace stared at the baby with longing, and then pushed all thoughts of her own child out of her mind. She lay down on the bed and closed her eyes. She had to plan, figure out what she was going to do. The next thing she knew, it was morning.

She took off the clothes she had slept in and dressed quickly from the items in her suitcase, turning her back away from the other woman. Then, she used the bathroom down the hall. Leaving the house, she walked down the ice-clogged streets trying to find a phone. There were a lot of bars and small grocery stores in this part of town, not far from the Kleiber Street entrance to the expressway. Signs in Spanish and some languages she didn't recognize, studded the storefronts. She found a drug store that was quiet and empty and had a pay phone. Fishing some change from her pocket, she dialed the number of Russo's Restaurant. She knew that Sal came in early to check the dining room supplies.

"Sal? This is Grace Milvern. I won't be able to work for you anymore. After that episode the other night, I realized that it was too dangerous. I just wanted you to know that I appreciate all you did for me. You're a good person."

"Well, I took a chance hiring you because of what happened to your husband, but what the hell. Listen, I'll give you some advice. If you go to get another job, don't use your real name. Somebody's out to get you."

Katherine waited in one of the rows of chairs filled with perspective students hoping to register for courses. In her hand, she clutched the number that the General Studies secretary had handed her.

Thirty-seven. She was exhausted and weak. The bruises had disappeared, and her hair had grown out some, but she wore a wig to cover the uneven shortness, and she felt sick all the time.

Tables were set up in the college atrium, an area that served as a student lounge and cafeteria. Sunlight flooded down from a skylight four stories overhead onto a scene resembling a madhouse. Tired students waited for hours and then went from table to table getting instructors to check course availability on their computers. A lot of them had children in tow or pushed crying babies in strollers. She could have registered online and saved herself all this trouble, but she needed advice and didn't want to enroll in the wrong courses.

She put her head back and studied the walls above. The top floors were ringed with offices and classrooms. The magnificent Flemish Gothic building was originally designed as a post office, and the city wanted to tear it down and turn the site into a parking lot for the auditorium. The City Preservation Committee had fought the common council and persuaded the administration to convert it into Port City Community College.

Finally, number thirty-seven came up and she was seated across from an advisor.

"I see that you are interested in the nursing program. You have to take prerequisite courses before you can be accepted into the program," he explained.

"But I want to get started on nursing courses," she complained.

"You can't do that until you've finished the General Studies courses. I have to tell you that the competition for the nursing program is fierce because only seventy students are accepted each semester."

"I have some credits already."

"I can see that," he said, referring to the computer screen. "You've gotten good grades and your placement tests scores were high."

"So what do I enroll in?" she asked. Her head itched under the wig where the hair was still growing in, and her heavy gold earrings dragged her head down. She shouldn't have dressed so formally. Everyone else wore jeans.

"Your prior courses can be used as electives. You must take the required English, Math and Biology. You can take Anatomy and Physiology, however, which will give you a start on the Nursing requirements. Add one elective and you will have a full schedule."

"Seems like I'm going to have an awful lot of electives."

"Unfortunately more than you need. Try to take some that relate to your field, like Medical Ethics or Nutrition."

"Whatever you can fit into the schedule," Katherine replied, wearily.

The adviser scanned the computer listings. "Oh-oh. We have a problem. All the Anatomy and Physiology courses have just closed."

"Closed! What can I do? I have to get started on my nursing degree."

"Let me check at the Biology table."

He went over to the Science Department where he conferred with the other advisers.

"Good news!" he told Katherine. "They are going to open up an evening section on Thursdays with the lab immediately following. If you don't mind attending school until nine-thirty at night, I can register you for it."

"I don't know if I want to be downtown that late in the evening," she protested.

"There is an escort service after five-thirty. A guard will walk you to your car or to the bus stop."

"I guess I don't have any choice," she moaned. "Sign me up for it."

"I can fit a Spanish elective in right before Anatomy."

Katherine was utterly exhausted now. She wished that she had a car. The thought of waiting for the transit drained her. Too bad she hadn't made that bastard Milvern buy her a car. She was going to make this work, no matter what. That was the only good thing he had done for her—forced her to think of the future.

A little boy was seated in a highchair between his parents in the Chinese restaurant. He was a beautiful child, golden hair, smooth, downy cheeks. Grace thought that she would break into tears at the sight of him. She missed Denny so much. Every night, she took out his pictures, laid them on the bed and picked them up one at a time to study them. Then, she fantasized what their life would be like when she had enough money saved to collect him from her parents.

The golden-haired child's mother and father fussed over him, feeding him bits of food, wiping his face. Sighing, Grace went over to take their order. She had gotten the job without any trouble using her maiden name, Buell, and asking that the owner call her Sally. Her social security card was in her maiden name. It would have been easy no matter what, because the place paid below the minimum wage and made the waitresses split their tips with the owner's son, who was the manager. He did nothing but sit behind the cash register all day. The register was kept locked, and he opened it importantly with a key each time someone paid his or her bill. But, terrible as the Red Dragon was, it was still a job, and she could save money. Finding another place to stay was paramount because her two weeks at the women's shelter were almost up. She planned on renting a furnished room near work and saving on bus fare. Her parents had to be called, even though she didn't trust them. They had given her name to the man who was trying to kill her. She also didn't want Detective McCallister to know where she was. He would try to make her stop working for her own protection. Easy to see that he didn't have any kids. She'd take any risk to save enough money to get Denny back.

"Sally," hissed the manager. "Table flee."

"Coming," she answered quickly.

The Red Dragon was a cheap place with unbelievable filth and commotion behind the kitchen doors. If the patrons could see the cooking scene, they would run out in a panic. Chinese shrieks and screams—Chinese dirtiness. She was afraid of the cook, a murderous man who yelled expletives at her in Chinese when she picked up her orders. It was an awful job, but no one knew where she was, and that was good.

When Grace vanished from the hotel, Martin called the Buells and asked when they had last heard from their daughter.

"Is there something wrong?" the mother whined. "No, we haven't heard from her recently. She's going to dump the child on us, isn't she? Expect us to raise him."

"I don't think she'd do that, Mrs. Buell. She's probably working long hours and hasn't had time to get in touch with you. I'm sure that she'll call soon, and when she does, please inform me. Call anytime, either at home or the precinct. You have the numbers."

Martin leaned back against the wall behind his desk. No leads. The case had evaporated into thin air. He could put a picture of Grace on TV, but if he did, the heavy-set man would see it and intensify his search. He just didn't know what to do. When he found that she had fled the hotel, he was angry. It was a stupid thing to do. She had no concept of the sort of danger she was in. All he could do was hope that when she contacted her parents, they would share her address with him.

Well, there were plenty of other cases to work on. The homicide rate in the Port City was escalating. He had to be in court in an hour concerning one that happened two years ago. Drugs again, so often drugs. He hated going to court, testifying. The old court had been awful. There was only one elevator, and the prisoners—in handcuffs or sometimes chains—rode up to the courts, pressed against lawyers, judges, witnesses. It was overcrowded, hot and miserable, not to mention dangerous, but it had a certain excitement. The proximity of the criminals lent an air of reality that the new court lacked. The new one was an ugly building, two years old, built directly across the street from the old structure that was now a refurbished legal office. The building had sealed windows with the air conditioning set to frigid. Prisoners were whisked up into the respective courtrooms in a private elevator well to the rear of the building. The edifice projected straight up for seven stories of gray, featureless concrete with some sort of a fluted design at the bottom, making it look as though it had feet. It was as cold and impersonal as possible. The front steps of the nearby jail were crowded with the wives, boyfriends and girlfriends, some with small children in buggies, of those awaiting trial or already jailed until they could be sent to larger institutions. It was sad.

He put on his boots for the half-mile walk from the precinct to the court. The weather had warmed a bit, and there was a lot of slush in the streets.

When he came back, he'd try to figure out an angle on the Milvern case.

Jack had beautiful eyes that he never tired of admiring in his hall mirror: very light blue-green with a dark rim around the iris under important eyebrows, black hair, an upright bearing. Tall, in great physical condition, he attracted multitudes of women. He looked like a successful banker or a top-notch attorney, even a professor. He did not look like a drug lord. It irritated him, mildly, when people commented on that Channel 8 action reporter, Harvey Gunnite's intense green eyes. He was absolutely sure that the reporter wore contacts. Anyway, the man was insignificant, second rate.

He was dressing for a date with his latest girlfriend, Raven Saint Claire.

"What kind of a name is that?" he asked her when they were introduced at a cocktail party given by a well-known contractor.

"A stage name, obviously. I'm an actress. What's your game?"

"Property Management. I don't need an alias for that."

"That's funny. I heard you were a drug dealer."

"Would you rather go out with a property manager or a drug dealer?"

"Oh, a drug dealer, absolutely!" She was exotic looking: long wild, curly black hair, sapphire eyes, an incredible figure with outstanding breasts that were obvious in a very low-cut shimmering purple dress.

"And where do you act?"

She looked incredulous, amazed that anyone didn't recognize her fame.

"I'm currently starring in Letter to the World with the Madhouse Productions Group which is being presented at the Harmony Theater.

"I've never been interested in theater---until now."

"We will have to change that." Her smile was sultry.

"Tell me when your next performance is, and if I'm free, I'll catch it. Then, I'll take you out to dinner."

"Saturday would be fine. The last performance is at eight."

"Saturday it is."

The play had been a boring mess, and he understood why she was not a top-ranked actress even in the Port City. Her part in the play had been nebulous, sketchy, and she was no Sarah Bernhardt, but she was gorgeous, and her acting ability didn't really concern him.

"Where do you want to go for dinner?" he asked her when her stint on stage was over. "I thought Hyacinths."

"Hyacinths? You must be joking! That place is for elderly gangsters or tourists! No! I want to go to Cinematricity!"

"What is that?"

"It's where all the theater people congregate."

"Oh, you want to be seen, maybe network. Well, I can go along with that."

He waited in the lobby while she changed out of her stage clothes and makeup. When she appeared, she was dressed all in coral: dress with plunging décolletage, shoes, lipstick, nail polish. The color contrasted beautifully with her dark curly hair. He helped her into her floor-length fur coat, and took her arm. She didn't seem too impressed with his Jaguar, but they didn't have any trouble getting into the restaurant without reservations.

Cinimatricity, located on a street behind one of the major theaters, was collapsing under the weight of theatrical posing, false hilarity, egotism and mini-performances. Second-rate hams were emoting all over the place. The walls were covered with blown-up photos of celebrities interspersed with cutouts of stars and balloons. The lights were brighter than usual restaurant lighting. Jack figured that was because everybody wanted to be seen. No one cared about the menu, the service or the outlandish prices. They were more interested in waving and air kissing. He wanted to check Raven's coat, but she kept it and draped it carefully over the back of her chair. A violinist near a small stage soldiered on, sawing away over the hubbub. God knows what music he was playing.

"Isn't this a great place?" Raven asked Jack, but her eyes were patrolling the crowd, as she blessed several people with a huge fake smile.

"Darling!" she cried to a woman who hurried over to peck her cheek.

"Wonderful performance! I loved the second act."

"Were you there tonight?"

"Last night." She looked curiously at Jack who had not been introduced. He was highly amused by all this.

"I'm sorry," Raven confessed. "You haven't met my date. Mitzi Tolbeck-- Jack D'Angelo."

"Are you related to the photographer, Chuck D'Angelo, who does the glamor photos?" Mitzi wanted to know.

"He's my cousin," Jack lied.

"Is he terribly expensive? I have to update my portfolio, and I want some terrific shots."

"Terribly. He has a huge waiting list. You'd be lucky to get an appointment by July."

"I'd better call him right away." Mitzi was obviously concerned. "Nice to meet you."

As she scurried off, Raven commented. "He's not really your cousin, is he?"

"No."

"You are so bad! I love it."

"You have no idea how bad."

"I think I'm going to find out soon."

"Then lets order dinner, so we can get out of here."

Their overdone filet mignon was served by an aspiring actor, who plopped down the platters accompanied by sighs and attitude. Jack wished that he were an aspiring waiter.

After they dined, there was the gauntlet to be negotiated as Raven bade farewell to most of the patrons with kisses and hugs, much laughter and a few artificially shed tears.

Her third floor apartment was in the North side of the city, in a quiet building near the university. It was spacious and eclectic, the living room dominated by a large, plaster statue of a woman with outspread wings. A collection of fans was nailed to the wall above a green velvet love seat. A church pew piled with cushions served as a sofa, and the marble coffee table held a collection of theatrical magazines and some bird's nests and pottery. It was just as pretentious as Raven.

She offered him an Appletini, and they sat on the unbelievably uncomfortable pew, while she gave him a run-down on her acting accomplishments—sort of an oral resume. When she finished her litany, he took her in his arms and kissed her, and they proceeded to her bedroom. After he had divested her of her dress, bikini underwear and pushup bra, they started to grapple on the bed. It was more like an all- out war than a seduction. Raven kicked, scratched, bit, socked him, yanked his hair, wrenched his head around, yelled and screamed. When he finally rolled off her, his back and his face were bleeding, and he knew that bruises would appear in the morning. Those coral nails were vicious. He wondered what the people in the neighboring apartments thought about the noise.

She pulled the comforter around her demurely. "We must do this again," she murmured.

He dressed quickly. Gave her a long contemplative look and left, glad to escape without serious damage.

The next day, he was as sore as if he had engaged in hand-to-hand combat, which, in a way, he had. His face stung where he had applied after-shave and the scratches were still visible. What a night! He got to his office later than usual, ducked any conversation with his secretary and went straight to his desk. There were problems to solve, including the search for the Jordan woman. Jack knew all kinds of people in the Port City. He made it a practice to have lunch with the bankers who authorized his loans, the lawyers in the firm that handles his real estate transactions, the well-known names of men and women who chaired fundraisers to which he donated large sums of money. After Mike Stokes told him about the college textbooks he had seen in Katherine Jordan's apartment, he decided that the question of whether or not the woman knew about the merchandize must be pursued further. There was no information as to where she was living, but she might still be a student at Port City Community. This could be a productive lead, he thought. Accordingly. He called his friend, Daniel Meyerhoff, who was on the board of trustees at the college.

"Daniel, do you realize that I've never set foot in that architectural triumph where you're a board member? Could you show me around? Maybe do lunch?"

Daniel was delighted and agreed to pick him up at his office the following Wednesday. He was actively seeking donations for a scholarship fund, and Jack was always good for a substantial contribution.

They drove to the college and parked in an area reserved for trustees near the back door.

"We'll walk around to the front so that you can get a good look at the exterior details," Daniel told him.

Jack murmured appreciatively as his attention was brought to stone carvings of gargoyles, lambs, bears, and a huge sculpted eagle next to a buffalo that loomed over the main door, frosted with snow.

Entering the spacious lobby with its high ceilings, they joined a throng of students, their heels clicking on the terrazzo floors as they walked between tall columns.

"Do you want to meet the president? He may be in his office."

Jack demurred. "Not at this time. I'm interested in the architecture, but I also have a personal reason for visiting. My sister's only son will be starting life as a college student next year. He's a good student, but he's had a lot of emotional problems, and they've made him timid. I'm trying to get the feel of the campus atmosphere in order to see if I think he can handle it. Perhaps I can bring him over for a walk-through."

"So, you would like to see the student areas, the book store, things like that."

"Everything. Classrooms, the registrar's office, the library. Then I will be able to answer any questions that he comes up with."

Daniel escorted Jack through the entire campus. They visited the auditorium where a drama class was rehearsing a one-act Russian play, the student government offices, the counseling center, where he was introduced to several counselors. They walked through the noisy combination food service, student lounge area under the high glass windows of the atrium, and rode the elevators packed with students.

The elevators were old and rickety.

"Do you have any problems with these things breaking down?" Jack asked, nervously, sandwiched against the wall next to a boy carrying a tray of food. Daniel wiped his forehead. "They break down constantly. Unfortunately, these are the building's original elevators, and they were never designed to carry such huge amounts of people. We have a contract with a repair company. They are on call twenty-four hours a day year-round, and a week doesn't go by that at least one elevator is out of commission."

"Why haven't they been replaced?"

"Expense, Jack. Five-story elevators cost a fortune. Don't forget that we're funded by the county. It's not a high priority in the county budget."

"I'll tell my nephew that he can get good exercise climbing the stairs."

When Daniel was satisfied that Jack had been shown everything of interest, he took him to lunch in the small elegant dining room run by the Culinary Arts students.

"Open to the public and absolutely the best food in town. The service is a little slow, after all, they're students, but wait until you try the deserts! We're very proud of this little restaurant."

"I like the nice variety of artwork on the walls."

"All student work!"

The food was indeed delicious. Jack had a cold consommé with a seafood risotto and a cherry tart. As he ate, he thought about the next step of his plan. It would be easy to find Katherine Jordan if she still attended classes here. Very easy.

"How is the security in the building? What happens if an intruder come in to cause trouble?"

"We have a small but effective security force. They monitor the premises constantly to make sure that no one is here who shouldn't be,"

"Are they armed?" Jack asked, nonchalantly, as he sipped his coffee.

"Oh, no. Just the night escort service people carry guns. Those men are all guards from city court who moonlight here. The regular campus security is unarmed, but I'll tell you—the students pay attention to that uniform! We've had very few problems!"

"I'm glad to hear that. I want my nephew to feel safe."

When Jack left the campus, he called Gene Lempke on his cell phone and asked him to come to the office.

"I've been told that you have computer skills, and I would like to have you put them to use. I need information about Katherine Jordan. Specifically, is she a student at Port City Community and what is her address? Can you break into their system and find that out?"

Gene was not happy. He hedged a bit. "I can try, but there's no guarantee."

"Oh, come on."

"I'll see what I can do. When do you need this information?"

"Tomorrow."

"I'll go home and start working on it," Gene replied, wearily. He was not happy working for Jack.

"Call me. Don't bother to come over to the office."

Martin and Leo had a visitor waiting in their office. The late afternoon light cast a few gray streaks through the filthy window, making the office look grimier than it was. Leo went to his desk to do paper work or to fixate on his problems, and Martin was left to talk to the woman had taken a seat across from him. She was extremely attractive and looked out of place in the station house where the sound of phones ringing, shouts, and the general disorder could be heard beyond the door. Her hair hung down below her shoulder blades, longer than most women wore theirs. It was reddish-blond and looked natural, but who could tell these days. Her hazel eyes were wide and friendly and her mouth was a bit oversized, giving it a lush look. She wore a green leather coat and fur boots. Everything about her spelled expensive.

"I was told at the desk that you were a homicide detective, Officer McCallister, and I wish to give information concerning a homicide."

Martin decided to be brusque. Her appearance might sway him. He opened his notebook.

"What is your name?"

"Jennifer Pearson." She brushed her hair back and crossed her legs.

"And—Miss Pearson?"

"Mrs. The information concerns my husband, Frank Pearson."

Martin's eyebrows shot up. "The name sounds familiar."

"It should. Frank is a partner in Pearson, Bernstein, Harwood, Allesandro and White." She undid the buttons on her coat and gently shrugged it off. Under the green coat, she wore a tight, rust-colored dress.

Martin tried not to stare at her substantial breasts. He coughed slightly.

"That's a well-known law firm. They have been council to some of the biggest property deals in the city, including the transfer of the Spring Gardens Hotel."

"Oh, you are so right." She moistened her lips with the tip of her tongue.

"So, who did he shoot?" Martin smiled, leaning back in his chair. It was rare to have such an attractive woman sitting in the office.

"I'll tell you. Do I call you detective or officer?"

"Call me Martin."

"Let me give you a little background. My husband and I have been married for six years. Frank is considerably older than I am. Our marriage was fairly happy for a while, but then I became bored with not having any life of my own. He's a very controlling person, and wanted me to be at home or busy with volunteer work all the time. I was simply as an ornament." She made an expression of distaste.

"I decided to broaden my horizons, take some classes, join interesting discussion groups. Frank resented this. He started to give me a hard time. One of the courses that I enrolled in was Conversational French at the university."

"He didn't like that?"

"No! Not at all! He insisted that I withdraw from the course. By this time, I had lost all interest in the marriage. I wanted out."

Martin chewed the end of his pencil, thoughtfully. "Your husband didn't want you to leave?"

"He was very bitter about the situation. To be truthful, I met a man in the class, and we became friends. For a while, we compared assignments, went out for coffee. Then, he asked me to come over to his place to do homework together, and we became more than friends. Do you understand what I am saying?"

"Perfectly."

Frank found out about the affair and started to make threats. I refused to be intimidated and moved out."

"Did you file for divorce?"

"No." She examined a slight mark on her handbag. "He told me that I would get nothing if I divorced him."

"And that didn't make you too happy."

"At first, all I wanted was my half of the furniture. I spent a lot of time decorating the apartment. He has his fingers in many pies and makes a lot of money. Why should I be left penniless?"

She gazed at him, her rosy mouth trembling slightly.

"No reason, but what has all this to do with homicide? Shouldn't you be consulting a divorce lawyer instead of seeing the police?"

She stared at him for a minute, and then, in a voice so low that he could hardly hear it, said:

"Because he killed the man I was seeing."

Martin's mouth fell open. "His name was--?"

"Nathan Scortino. The man who was shot in the liquor store."

He fell back against the wall. "Can you prove any of this?"

"No. Nothing. That's why I came to you. I know positively that he did it. He was so violently jealous! He enjoyed killing Nathan!"

Martin whistled in disbelief. "Do you have any evidence? Anything that would connect your husband with the crime."

"I did bring you a picture of Frank Pearson. Maybe someone saw him shoot Nathan."

She opened her handbag and drew out an 8 x 10 glossy photo.

"This was taken for the paper when he was chair of the United Charities drive two years ago."

Martin took the picture and almost jumped out of his seat.

The man in the photo had a dark, swarthy face, slicked-back hair. This was the face that Grace Milvern had described, the man that Mrs. Buell said was an insurance agent. The man who was trying to kill Grace.

"Good God!" he exclaimed. "I've finally got a lead! Oh, yes, Mrs. Pearson, I'll get your husband! You can bank on it, because someone did see him kill Scortino! Now, tell me everything that you can about him; his schedule, friends, where he eats lunch, the clubs he belongs to."

Jennifer smiled triumphantly. "I'll tell you everything!"

Chapter Eight

"You're looking rested, George," Jack D'Angelo commented. "How was Syracuse?" George did indeed seem to have gained ten pounds and lost some of the bizarre facial expressions that he displayed when he felt pressured. His orange and purple cowboy shirt bulged across his stomach. His waist was circled by a belt with a huge, silver buckle, and he wore a Bolo tie. Western attire gone berserk, Jack thought.

The pseudo-cowboy was happy. The night before, he had visited a country western bar called Dudes. The band, Ridin' Double, played on a small stage set up in the rear of the restaurant. George danced to three tunes, knocking the other line dancers about like toothpicks. People seated at the periphery of the dance floor moved their chairs back to avoid his flying feet. He wore cowboy boots with three-inch heels and a Stetson hat that made him almost seven feet tall. The dancers tried to avoid him, because he looked so weird and frightening as he galumphed around the floor. Several patrons went to the bartender to complain.

"Who is that nut? Get him off the dance floor! He's kicking people!'

"He hit my wife on the shoulder with his elbow. She's in the ladies room, crying."

"There's going to be an open-mike session soon. That will end the dancing for a while," the bartender consoled them.

Just then, the restaurant manager stepped to the stage and announced that the open-mike session was about to begin. "Four people have signed up for tonight's slots. Our first singer will be Carrie Lou Pularski, who will sing *Watermelon Crawl*."

A smiling young girl carrying a banjo, wearing a beige cowboy hat, a suede vest and hand-tooled red boots stepped up to the mike.

George elbowed his way to the front, shoved her aside and grabbed the mike. As she stumbled awkwardly back into the audience, she protested loudly.

"It was my turn! Get that creep off the stage!"

The bar manager stepped up. He tried to get the huge man to leave, but George had launched into his first song, *I'm Hoarse From Singing to my Horse*, drowning out the manager's protests. One of his boots connected with a drum, blasting a hole in it. The drummer fled. When he started yowling *Saddle Sore Blues*, the rest of the band silently packed up their instruments before sneaking out the side door, abandoning their mike. One by one, all of the patrons left, some muttering "We're never coming back here" to the bartender. George sang on, alone in front of the stage, totally absorbed in his performance, while the owner went to the bar and gulped down several large whiskeys, knowing that his business was ruined for sure.

Now, George had been summoned to Jack's office.

"I wrote some new songs," he confided to Jack. "I'm going to sing them to you. You want to hear *These Boots are Made for Stalking* or *Bullets and Blood?*

Jack suppressed a shudder. "All in good time, George, when I am able to really concentrate on your inimitable lyrics. Before we have music appreciation, I want to tell you about your next job. It is essential that we discover where Katherine Jordan is living. She has vanished from her apartment without a forwarding address. Do you remember the place?"

"Fuckin' dolls," the huge man muttered.

"What did you say?"

"The place was full of fucking dolls."

"Well, George, you know how women collect unusual objects. This new job is quite straightforward, though. I had Mike Stokes search her apartment while you were in Syracuse, and although he found no product, he did discover that she had been attending classes at Port City Community College. I believe that we can obtain her address from the registrar's office."

George was beginning to perspire. His clothes felt tight. School! He hated school worse than he hated dolls. He had dropped out in the eighth grade when he turned sixteen.

"Couldn't Stokes have grabbed the product when he tossed the apartment?" he wondered.

"Hmm. I never thought of that. I'll keep it in the back of my mind. Now," he continued, "I know that if I call the college and ask if they have a Katherine Jordan registered, they will inform me that this information is confidential and not available. What I propose is that you break into the registrar's office and locate her address in the student records."

George brightened at the thought of a break-in. He adored break-ins. He could smash some stuff.

"Gene Lempke will accompany you. He was able to access their computer system from his house, but could not get onto the main server and search for the records. Your job is to gain admittance to the building. This is how I propose that you do it. Pay careful attention. I will facilitate a drive-by shooting at the rear of the college so that you and Gene can break in unobserved. The security guards will be investigating the ruckus. An unarmed skeleton crew is on duty at night. Remember that. You do not have to shoot anyone. I repeat. No gun play! And try not to make a lot of noise. The drive-by may be reported, but I doubt if the city police will respond until the next day. I have a diagram of the location of the registrar's office. Do not lose it. Do you have the idea?"

"Piece of cake," George responded. "Break in, stay cool. Be quiet with any inside damage." He was happy now. Revenge on a school! What could be better?

"Good. You will do it next Thursday."

George was good at break-ins. He had lots of practice. It was a snap for him to jimmy the window in the first floor office. That side of the building was dark and no one was walking down these streets at this hour. It was too cold even for the homeless who frequently huddled against the building's stone wall. George had brought a stepladder, and after he forced the window, he and Gene climbed inside, stepping carefully onto an employee's desk. They dropped to the floor, pulling the stepladder in after them. The building was eerily quiet except for the distant murmur of a radio, probably from a cleaning woman's cart. The room contained cabinets, desks, computer terminals, all briefly illuminated by Gene's flashlight. Holding the light close to his side, he scanned the rows and rows of cabinets lining the walls. He tried one, experimentally. It was locked. They were all locked. He motioned George over, and the man bent down to jimmy the locks. He soon had one open. The drawer contained computer printouts of course grades. Not what they wanted.

"All the information is in the computers," Gene whispered. "I'll see if I can gain access."

"We could take the computers," George suggested.

Oh, God! Why am I working with this idiot, Gene wondered.

"How about checking out what some of the other drawers hold before we take it a step higher." Breaking and entering was one thing. Major theft more complicated. "These grades are all for past semesters. The recent stuff must all be computerized. Good thing I know how to get around passwords."

George pointed to a rack of drawers that had alphabetical listings on the front. Gene indicated that George open the one that said 'J', while he sat down at one of the computers and booted it up. His fingers flew rapidly as he surfed the system.

He was hoping to access computerized addresses and pertinent information on students whose last name began with J.

Gene entered the system easily and called up the Jordan listings. There was a Jordan, Eleanor, and a Jordan, Regis, but that was it. He scanned the Regis papers. It appeared that Regis had been a student for about three semester five years ago. That meant that none of these students were current. He opened another file.

There wasn't much more time. When they entered the room, there had been sounds of gunshots in the distance, followed by the reverberation of the guard's feet clicking on the terrazzo floors as they raced to the rear of the college. Now, each moment brought them closer to being discovered. George was forcing cabinets open randomly, throwing papers to the floor.

There was a Katherine Jordan in this file. He printed the whole file out, the printer humming softly, it's tiny light glowing in a corner of the darkened room. The address and phone number were for a place on Broughton Street. He shoved it at George, highlighting it with the flashlight.

"One forty-eight Broughton Street," he whispered.

"Nah. That's the old apartment. The one I broke into."

"Oh, shit! What do we do now?" He pointed randomly to other cabinets and George set about breaking into them, his face gleaming, maniacally. Gene was frantic. What if she doesn't attend the college anymore? They would have nothing to report to Jack. His fingers flew as he opened more files. George dropped the papers on the floor in untidy heaps and kicked them aside as he forced more drawers. The room was being destroyed.

Gene opened a file that bore the heading 'Matriculated students-recent.' He scrolled through the pages. The name Jordan, Katherine, Denicia. Palmer Heights leaped out at him.

He printed this file out.

At that moment, the door to the room was violently thrust open and the overhead lights were switched on.

A Spanish-looking man stood framed in the doorway.

"What are you doing in here," he yelled.

George felt a cold thrill run through his chest as he reached in his pocket for his gun. Jack had said no shooting, but he would be crazy to go on a job without a piece. The guy had spotted them—could identify them. There was only one thing to do. He was very excited, sensing the blood pump into his trigger finger.

The security guard reached for his mobile phone, his eyes wild. Then he saw the gun emerge from the huge man's pocket.

"No," he cried. "Dios--"

George blasted the guard in the chest, the bullet tearing into the dark blue uniform. The man buckled, slid slowly down the doorframe.

"You asshole!" Gene whispered, hoarsely. "Why the fuck did you do that? Christ! I'm getting out of here! Fast!"

He stuffed the Jordan printout in his pocket, leaving the printer and the computer humming. Sprinting to the opened window, he dropped through, landing on the snowy sidewalk.

George stood there for a minute, wondering if he should plug the guy again. Then, he lumbered to the window and climbed out, knocking a vase of artificial flowers off the desk.

"Damn!" he muttered. "I forgot the ladder!"

Martin watched the eleven o'clock news while seated in his red leather recliner across from the TV set as he contemplated one of his beloved photos. It depicted a row of summer cottages taken in the early dawn light. Morning sun glistened on the water, and the lake was silent, mysterious. He was waiting for the sports to come on so he could find out how the local hockey team was doing. John Bradford's owlish face filled the screen with late-breaking news. "A third young woman has been attacked by a rapist in the area surrounding Tyler Park. During the past two weeks, neighbors in the quiet park neighborhood have been shocked to learn that a predator has been stalking young women. His latest victim was found, unconscious, near the statue of the Peace Dove. She is unable to identify her assailant. He apparently struck her from behind and attacked her while she was unconscious. A passer-by called the police and she was taken by ambulance to Flowers Hospital. The other victims were attacked in a similar manner. Our action reporter, Harvey Gunnite, interviewed Commissioner Battaglia earlier today.

The familiar figure of Harvey Gunnite, wearing his winter trademark, a trench coat, but one with fur lining, over an expensive navy suit, appeared on camera. He looked as though he had watched too many detective series on TV. "The Commissioner was interviewed about these crimes this afternoon. He sends a strong message to the residents of the park community, where he has stationed a large police presence."

The commissioner stood at the snow-covered park entrance as he spoke to the camera. His face was weary, gray, a man past retirement age.

"I urge all women to stay out of the park! We have officers patrolling, but you are still not safe. Do not go there for any reason, and if you must be out at night, always have a friend with you and carry your cell phone. If anyone has seen any suspicious activity in the area, call police headquarters at once!"

"Do you think the same person is responsible for all three attacks?" the reporter questioned, earnestly.

"We don't know at this point. But I repeat-- take extra precaution if you are in that general area."

"Now, back to you, John."

Martin turned off the set. Why didn't these women learn? The park was a well-known pick-up spot, and the victims were probably prostitutes looking for johns. There must be other areas nearby to find customers. He knew from his vice days that hooking was an awful occupation, but it was made worse by the frigid weather. A lot of drug buys went on in that park, even in broad daylight. All those statues placed randomly, providing some cover for the deals, didn't help. The area had originally been envisioned as a sculpture park, a place to provide the citizens with a little culture, and the common council had appropriated a chunk of money for public art and park benches, even a few flowerbeds. However, the location deterred much art appreciation. Situated near the lower section of the West side, not far from the Arms of Love soup kitchen, it immediately attracted all sorts of scum. He turned off the set and took his empty beer bottle to the kitchen. Thank God he was in the homicide division.

Grace had left the women's shelter and found a single room in a ravaged mansion on Decker Street, near a tiny patch of trampled snow where drunks and addicts were strewn on the ground like fallen leaves. The house was somber, quiet, hidden behind two overgrown fir trees.

Her room was down a threadbare, carpeted hallway on the third floor. The other tenants crept in and out soundlessly and she was able to sleep without a problem. The room consisted of: a metal bed painted dark-green, an ancient maroon rug with a hole in it, a dresser made of ponderous wood with the patina of age and one scratched lamp with a painted scene on the base that said *Adirondack Mountains*. There was a single chair and a large closet that smelled of disinfectant. The bathroom was down the hall.

In addition to finding the room, she had another wonderful stroke of luck. At the Goodwill Store, she found a brown, genuine leather coat with a zip-in lining for eight dollars. It fit perfectly. She was beginning to get some of her old energy back, and didn't feel like sitting in her bleak room after her shift ended at the Red Dragon.

The winter carnival was being held in the central downtown area, and it was only a few blocks away. She put on her leather coat and walked through the newly-shoveled sidewalks. Although it was dark, waves of people carried her along and made her feel safe. Everyone was smiling in anticipation of the festivities. The carnival was the city's main event for the winter, with a multitude of offerings to lure everyone downtown. The street trees were lit with thousands of tiny Christmas tree bulbs, and the main stores were decorated with wreaths and additional lights. In front of city hall, excited children crowded the face-painting booths, and couples strolled the streets eating hot dogs and Souvlaki sandwiches. Dance troops performed near a children's theater. The Chamber of Commerce had built a ski-run in a parking lot, and amateur skiers floundered down the slope.

Grace took a seat on a bench near the ice-skating rink and watched the skaters while she hugged her coat tightly in the crisp air.

She began to plan. If I work double shifts at the restaurant, I'll have enough in three months to get Denny back. There's a day care facility not too far from my room called Small Gifts where he can stay while I work. The place is a big, brick building with slides and swings outside, now covered with snow, but in the warm weather, he can play outside with other children. It will be good for him to socialize, and our life will be close to normal. We can stay in my room, and I'll take him to parks and playgrounds on my day off. Then, I'll put in an application for an apartment in one of the low-income housing projects. We could live there for a few years until he starts school. By then, I'll have a better job, and we can get a place in a more suitable section of the city. This week, I'll stop over at the Municipal Housing Authority and put in an application. It takes years to get a place, but I'll be on their list.

I'll take real good care of Denny and make it up to him for the separation. I hope my parents are being kind to him, after all, he is their only grandchild, but what will I tell him about his father when he gets old enough to ask? Maybe I could say he suffered a heart attack. I can't tell him his father was murdered. In a few years, no one will remember anything about Dennis Milvern. I can hardly remember him now myself.

But as she planned and consoled herself, the camera from Channel

8 prowled through the crowd as stealthily as a pickpocket, its invasive eye recording the spectators for the eleven o'clock newscast. For one brief prying second, it captured Grace's profile, silhouetted against the ice rink, where she sat, unaware of the interloper.

On Monday morning, Katherine Denicia woke up in her friend's crowded apartment at the Palmer Heights Projects. She felt an immediate sense of dismay, as she gazed around the unfamiliar clutter of boxes and suitcases in the small bedroom. Dresses and skirts hung on hangers on the back of the door. The few intact dolls from her collection were piled in a corner. It was all so different from her exquisite apartment and so disorienting, but she was glad to be anywhere: any place that the ugly man who had beaten her couldn't find her. Lakeisha slept quietly in the adjacent twin bed, oblivious of the disorder.

She got up and dressed hastily, and spent a lot of time in the bathroom on her makeup. Her face was gradually returning to normal, but it was still discolored and sensitive. Breakfast in the galley kitchen was toast and honey with black coffee.

The Palmer Heights Projects consisted of a dense cluster of yellow brick buildings on the edge of the business section. They were ninety-five percent black, and there was a rapid turnover because of the violent nature of life there. Shootings were frequent, and several times a week the police responded to calls concerning domestic arguments, stabbings, robbery.

Katherine woke Lakeisha up before she left, so that she could re-lock the deadbolt on the front door.

She had a five-block walk to the rapid transit station through decaying streets of closely-packed houses all very much alike—two stories and an attic, a ramshackle front porch. They were all painted dull colors except for a few that were partially destroyed by fire or crumbling with neglect due to absentee landlords. The morning was cold, barely illuminated by the pinkish sky of a winter dawn. Snow was piled under the large, bare trees that overhung the street. She strode along a slight incline up to Main Street. She didn't enter the rapid transit station but stood outside near an ugly, modern sculpture, to wait for the train.

After five minutes in the biting chill, she boarded the train for downtown.

Seven-forty-five was a very bad time to ride the train, but she had an early class. The car was full of students on their way to Anston

Burroughs High. There were radios turned up to shrieking volume, and kids screamed at their friends across the aisles. One boy was urinating in the stairwell by the back door.

Katherine dealt with all the disorder by mentally reciting the phrases she had learned in her Spanish class. *Este restaurante es excelente......Esta comiendo el pollo......es muy sobrosa.* Outside the train window, daylight vanished as the car descended into an underground section near the theater district and raced through the brightly lit tunnel. Half a mile later, it emerged near the Downtown Mall. Katherine fought her way through the mass of teenagers and got off. She hurried through the three blocks leading to the campus. Rushing up the stone steps, she entered the lobby and turned down the stairway to the basement where the student lockers were situated. The basement was brightly lit, but with gray lockers lining both sides of the narrow corridor, and no windows, it seemed gloomy, threatening. The technical classes were held down here, and in the evening, academic classes also. The floors were brown tile and the walls an off-shade of beige. On the floor of her locker, under a sweater that had fallen off a hook, was the South American doll that Dennis Milvern had given to her many months ago. At that time, she was taking a class or two and she wanted to show it to a friend of hers in the Cultural Anthropology class. Marlene had lived in Mexico for several years.

"It's supposed to be from Chili," she told Marlene. "A friend of mine bought it at that place on Lilac Street, the South American store."

"It's kind of amusing," Marlene commented.

The doll was clumsily made and garish. It wore a pink and white striped dress that ended at the tops of red, high-heeled shoes. A yellow bib under a string of blue beads completed the costume. The brown face was solemn under a halo of black, yarn curls.

"It does look like it came from Chili. Women down there make these dolls and sell them through places like that store. They support entire families with the meager profits that the owner sends back to them. That's how poor they are down in South America." She shook the doll. "I wonder what the inside is made of."

"This one never seemed to fit in with the others I've collected. It always looked crude."

"Well, it does have a sort of simple charm, and you can be happy knowing that the money went to a good cause."

Katherine had returned the doll to the locker and forgotten about it.

Now, she was taking a Spanish course, and she was sure that the instructor didn't like her. She worked hard on the assignments, but she just didn't feel confident. Maybe she would show him the doll—ask about the culture of the people who made these things. Then, he might be convinced that she was a serious student. Not today, though. There was a quiz. Opening her Spanish book, she scanned the chapter. She had to get at least a B. After the test, she had an Anatomy and Physiology class, and the students were required to know the names of hundreds of bones. She knew most of them, all right, but the spelling had her baffled. She had never been a good speller, and they must be correct or the professor would mark them wrong. It was so different and so hard—the whole college thing. One afternoon, feeling totally defeated, she had gone into the darkened auditorium, where a dance class was rehearsing down on the stage, and sat in a back row and cried and cried. She was so discouraged. She had to make it! When things seemed impossible, she thought about Dennis Milvern.

"You bastard!" she muttered. "I can do this myself. I'll never need men like you again."

She used to kid herself about her dates and the subsequent financial arrangements. Sure, it had been a soft life with a lot of material advantages, but no matter—she was still a whore. Well, she'd never be one again, no matter what it took.

Chapter Nine

Martin staked out Frank Pearson. He followed him from his office to the athletic club where the man swam daily, to his apartment. He slouched half a block behind him as Pearson traveled to expensive restaurants. In the evening, he stood behind the heavy-set man in an elevator as they rode up to the twelfth floor of the Mutual Bank Building to Chez Philipe's, so close that he could smell Frank's cologne. Paco Rabanne, he guessed. Martin hated pricey aftershaves and colognes. He stared at the slicked-back hair, feeling revulsion for the person standing near the elevator door, his brief case dangling from his hand. The routine was the same, day after day. Martin was beginning to feel deflated and incredibly bored, because tailing was such tedious work. He couldn't even devote as much time to the job as he wanted to. There were other homicides piling up. The city seemed to have gone berserk—killings dominated the news every night. He was under pressure all the time, and he felt as though he was getting nowhere.

Commissioner Battaglia appeared frequently on TV repeating his message over and over: "We need more police officers, more equipment." The man was aging rapidly. Heavy circles had appeared under his eyes, and there were rumors that his health was bad. Like Martin, he swam in a sea of destruction.

Grace was eating a hamburger and potato salad at the Arms of Love when she noticed the little cook, Herman somebody or other, sidle over and tape a sign to the wall of the dining room. The notice said: SIGN UP HERE FOR BIRTHDAY DINNERS in magic marker. Then, the cook moved crablike back into the kitchen, his long white apron dragging on the floor. The flowered shower cap that he always wore listing over one eye.

The director, Jo-Jo Martinelli, was over near the front door watching out for trouble.

"Oh, no!" he exclaimed, loudly, limping over to rip the sign off the wall and tearing it to shreds. Then, he came over to sit at Grace's table.

"Herman is a problem," he complained. "He comes up with these unworkable ideas to make the place classier. It's driving me crazy!"

"He seems to care about the clients."

"Oh, he cares all right. He just wishes he were chef in a four-star restaurant instead of a soup kitchen. I don't think I've met you. I'm

Jo-Jo Martinelli, the director of this establishment!"

"Grace Milvern."

"I like to get to know my clients," he wheezed. "Did you just start coming here?"

"Yes. The food is very good. Your cook is doing something right."

"If he only didn't have these delusions of grandeur. I'll give you an example. Last fall, he decided that he wanted a harvest dinner. I said 'forget it.' He went behind my back and somehow got Walter Meiser, who helps out with deliveries, to drive out to the country and bring back a bunch of cornstalks and pumpkins for decorations, which he placed all over the dining room. The clients were going through the serving line for lunch when a large rat dashed out of the cornstalks! You should have heard the screams, the children sobbing. A woman fainted! My assistant, Gloria Morningstar's, cousin Floyd ran out the front door and got a shovel. The other Indians chased the rat around the tables until they had it cornered. People were standing on chairs, throwing dishes at the rat. Floyd beat it to a pulp with the shovel! Then, he dumped it out in the gutter. More shouts, more shrieks as people ran out the door. Some of them never came back. What if the Board of Health had gotten wind of the scene? We would have been shut down for sure! Thank you, Herman, for your big ideas. You see what I have to put up with?" Jo-Jo had a prolonged coughing fit.

"Now, he wants birthday dinners, with candles, no doubt. This place will go up like a torch!"

"At least he's ambitious."

"He's insane. Now, I must go patrol the kitchen. God knows what Herman is up to. Nice to meet you. We'll talk again." Jo-Jo heaved himself out of the chair and shuffled toward the kitchen, his carpet slippers making scuffing noises on the floor.

Inside of the room, he could be heard yelling at the diminutive cook. "No more of your idiotic ideas about turning this place into a four-star eatery. This is a soup kitchen!"

"But we need variety. A special dinner once a month. Is that too much to ask?"

"Yes, it is. We're lucky to serve food every evening, not that the menu is very expansive tonight."

"We're low on supplies. Even the County Food Bank is in trouble. We must have more provisions," the cook complained.

"Good luck! Try calling the mayor. Maybe he'll go out and catch some fish in the harbor. Oh, I forgot. The fish don't vote."

"You're killing my creativity."

"Then go and get a job at Chez Philipe, or Hyacinth's. I'm sure that they will appreciate your talents."

"You have no heart," the cook replied, sadly.

"I hear that at least once a week. Now start getting ready for the next meal."

Grace's finished her lunch. She was on the side of Herman. A cake would be nice: with pink frosting and maybe one symbolic candle. Her shift at the Red Dragon was due to start in half an hour and she couldn't be late. She was saving a lot of money eating at the Arms and even putting on a little weight. Her plans were working. Gathering up her purse and gloves, she trudged out into the snowy street.

Martin awoke covered with perspiration. He had experienced another flashback. They didn't come as often as they used to, but the nightmares were still intense, terrifying. In them, he was violently attacking another man, pummeling him. The man's face was covered with blood. In his dreams, Martin was re-living an incident from the past. He had never told Leo about it, although his partner probably was aware of what had occurred. There were few secrets in the force. The main reason he had quit vice and switched to homicide was that he had almost killed a man. The man was a pedophile, and Martin had been tracking him for months, hoping to catch him approaching children, or at least find some evidence of the guy's awful crimes. The head of a corporation, the man held a respectable position in the community, was on many philanthropic boards. No one would suspect him of criminal activities. Even his family thought that his trips overseas were connected to business interests, instead of being for the purpose of buying children for sexual adventures. Martin had assembled a lengthy dossier on the man, but he had no evidence that would stand up in court.

Then, one afternoon, when he was on his way to court, he saw the man turning into the doorway of a downtown hotel. He was pulling a young boy by the hand. The child seemed uncertain, confused. Martin hurried after them, and entered the lobby just in time to see the two entering one of the elevators. The door closed before he could get to it, but he noted the floor number on the indicator. Six. When the elevator returned to first, after a lengthy stop on four, during which he wondered if he should take the stairs, he got in and pushed the button for six. There was no one else in the elevator, so it went up immediately to the indicated floor. The carpeted hallway was very quiet, and Martin had no idea which direction to take to find the man and his prey.

The hotel was third-rate, not too heavily occupied, a perfect place for an anonymous tryst. The detective paced the corridors, listening for any strange sounds, but the halls were silent. He had covered the entire floor, and had no idea about what to do next. He decided to try another lap and set out, stopping at each door to put his ear against it and listen. When he approached 603, he didn't have to eavesdrop. There were sounds of desperate crying coming from inside of the room. He slammed his shoulder into the door, over and over, but it wouldn't budge. A chambermaid came down the hall, pushing a cart overflowing with crumpled sheets. He held up his badge and put a finger to his lips. Her eyes grew wide with fright. "The key," he whispered. She dug a batch of key cards out of her pocket and handed him one. He motioned her down the hall, and the woman scooted away, as the detective burst into the room.

The scene on the bed was terrible. The man was naked and the child, who was shrieking hysterically, was nude and bloody from the waist down. Martin grabbed the man and started hitting him, over and over. A tooth flew out of his mouth as he was punched. The guy was screaming, but Martin wouldn't stop. He battered him with his gun, bruising his eye and breaking his nose. The man's head was starting to look like a mass of jelly. Abruptly, the detective realized that if he kept on, he would kill him, and that was what he wanted to do.

"I can't do this," he moaned. Shuddering, he left the bed and drew long, rasping breaths. It took him a few minutes to become somewhat calmer. Then, he dialed his partner, Luke Dworak, on his cell.

"I'm in trouble! Get over to the Ridgemont Hotel near the courthouse and come up to room 603."

"I'll be there in fifteen minutes, maybe less."

When Dworak arrived, the scene hadn't changed much. Martin was standing, obviously shaken, near the window. The child was still on the bed crying, and the perpetrator was unconscious.

"What the hell happened?" he demanded.

Martin turned to face him, tears running down his face. "I snapped," he confessed, "and I almost killed the bastard. I was hitting him over and over like an animal, totally out of control. All I wanted to do was hurt him so bad."

"OK. We have to straighten this out or you'll be arrested for assault and much more. I recognize this guy. He's got connections all over the city. Look, I'm not blaming you. A lot of cops have done the same thing, but I don't want you to go to jail. Let me think for a minute."

"We have to do something about the child. He's injured."

"I'll call an ambulance and have him taken to the hospital. We won't have much time to figure out what to do about bozo here. Get some cold water and wake him up. I'm afraid that we will have to report this to Battaglia and explain what happened. You can say that he was in the act of abusing the boy, and you had to get rough with him to make him stop. Be upfront. You broke a lot of rules: assault, illegal entry, but the child's welfare was all you were concerned with. This guy isn't going to press charges. He might go to the pen, or not, depending on how many palms he can grease."

Martin was numb. He couldn't think.

"Battaglia isn't going to want publicity about a rogue cop. He's got enough trouble with the mayor.

The hospital will report the incident when the kid arrives, and the wheels will start to turn. All we can do is cross our fingers and hope the news doesn't get on this. Come on—this guys starting to wake up. Arrest him, and I'll call the wagon. Don't think you're the first. I've seen this happen before. It makes you understand why cops build up so much pressure that they pump fifteen bullets into some suspect."

During the next few days, Martin met with Battaglia, who suspended him for six months and ordered him to undergo mandatory counseling. He needed it. Emotionally, he was wrecked.

He moved out of his apartment and rented a rusty, dilapidated trailer on the outskirts of a small village near the beach. It was beyond minimal. There was one room with a kitchen set-up against a wall and a bath. The tub took an hour to fill and the water was the color of rust. He bought a few pots and pans, dishes, glasses, utensils and a bunch of frozen foods for the ice-crusted refrigerator. He didn't try cleaning the place, because he didn't care.

All day, when he wasn't in the city seeing the department's counselor, he walked on the beach, mile after mile. After renting a small sailboat, he went out on the lake and sailed way up toward the far end. He wanted to avoid all human contact, as much as it was possible, but he couldn't escape the nightmares that tormented him each night.

Luke came out to see him a few times to keep Martin posted on progress.

"Everybody in the city owes this guy favors, and he's calling them all in, but it will be tough for him to compromise the hospital's report. The kid's family is going to sue the predator, the city, the hotel: but no, not you. Don't worry. How are the sessions coning with the shrink? You're seeing Dr. Head. Right? Of course everybody calls him shrunken head. Get it?"

Martin was seeing the counselor three times a week. The appointments were weird. Doctor Oliver Head was a short, round man who wore green suits with vests and ankle boots. They sat on straight-backed chairs in the Doctor's office with Martin facing the man, and Head turned toward the window, so that Martin was speaking to his back.

"Some patients are influenced by the counselor's facial expressions, even their body English. I find that this way they are more open, and we will get to the root of the problem faster," he explained.

"I don't have a problem."

"Yes, you do. Nobody beats a man almost to death unless he has a problem. We will peel the layers of your mind away like an onion until everything is exposed."

But as the weeks went by, and Martin talked about all sorts of things, the pressures of the job, his failed marriage, it seemed as though they were getting nowhere. He jotted down notes when he was at the trailer, things for them to discuss at the office. Then, after two months of staring at the back of Doctor Head's assortment of green suits, Martin had a different nightmare. In this dream, his father was speaking. "We won't say anything about this. Charlie is too young to remember anything."

At his appointment the next day, he recounted the dream to Doctor Head's back.

"Who is Charlie?" the counselor asked'

"My older brother."

"How much older?"

"Just eighteen months."

"Close your eyes, take deep breaths and try to remember what caused your father's comments."

Martin did as he was told, and after a few minutes, he had a picture of Charlie crying in the bathroom and his mother washing the child's bottom. Then, his father entered the room. His knuckles were skinned and bloody, and his shirt was torn. "Gustav will never touch another child!" he stated.

Martin started to weep. "I remember," he said.

"Tell me about it," Head urged.

"Charlie came home crying and in pain. He had been sexually assaulted by the man who lived down the street, Mr. Gustav. My parents didn't report it because they didn't want Charlie to testify. They felt that being interrogated at the police station would upset him for life. They thought he would forget the incident because he was so young. My father beat Gustav severely, put him in the hospital."

"How old was Charlie?"

Martin wiped his eyes. "Probably four or five, but he never forgot."

"What happened to him?"

"He became a withdrawn loner of a child, repulsing even me, and I loved him. He got into drugs when he was a teenager. When he was twenty-one, he bought a gun at a local gun shop and took it down to the creek near our house. He sat down on the bank and placed it against his head. After he shot himself, his body fell into the water. He was discovered by a man out walking his dog later that afternoon. I like to think that the last sounds that he heard were that of the water lapping against the rocks, the birds chattering softly in the trees: that he was at peace." The detective broke down in sobs.

Doctor Head turned his chair around so that he was facing Martin.

"Now, you understand what happened in that hotel room?"

"Yes. I was subconsciously remembering what my brother went through. I was beating up Gustav."

"The onion has been peeled, and we can start healing. I will want to see you for a few more times. How much more leave do you have? "

"A little over two months."

"That sounds about right. By then, you will be able to go back to work."

The detective continued to see Doctor Head, and they discussed the problem in greater depth, but the counselor never turned his chair to face the window again.

When Martin was interviewed by Battaglia, at the end of his leave, he felt ready to resume the job.

"I'm transferring you to homicide," The commissioner informed him. "Doctor Head recommends that you not work vice. Do you still want to stay on the force? It's your call."

"Absolutely. I'm still a police officer."

"Doctor Head thinks that you are a good one. I don't know anything about your counseling sessions, that's privileged information. I can only take his recommendations. You'll be stationed at Precinct Eleven, and your new partner will be Leo Aronica. His partner was shot last week. An unfortunate fatality."

"What happened to Luke Dworak?"

"He retired after the incident at the hotel. You missed his farewell party."

Martin immediately found homicide to be interesting and challenging, and although it took him a while to get used to Leo, his chubby, effusive partner, they worked well together despite being opposites in temperament.

Chapter Ten

Ever since his conversation with Jennifer, Frank Pearson felt as though he was walking on eggs. He was afraid that she just might be bold enough to go to the police, not that they would believe her stupid story. His reputation was so solid, the law firm so well-known, that they would laugh at her fantasies, but they would be aware of him, and he didn't want that. He'd better not make any false moves. Besides, he still had no idea where Grace Milvern was.

Soon, he thought, I have to come up with a plan of action. She's in the city, therefore she can be found, but I have to figure out how to track her down.

He was besieged. There were problems with the law firm. They had engineered the sale of a prime block of real estate on Madison Street to an out-of-town company who had landed a huge federal contract for an office building on the site. Now, there was an uproar over the fact that the company was not local, and the news had started to hint of pay-offs and complicity. The firm was innocent. They had simply handled the sale, but it was making for tense moments. The worst of it was that he couldn't really get interested. He didn't care. Some spark had to be forthcoming to ignite his enthusiasm, and it had to relate to Grace Milvern.

He gazed out of the huge windows of his living room at the panoramic scene of the harbor at night. Snow was falling as though a fine lace curtain had been pulled against the sky. Tiny points of light from distant stars pricked through it. He turned and idly flipped the switch of the television set. The annual winter carnival was in full swing, attended by thousands of spectators that were attracted to it each year for the fun. He wasn't interested. All that Snow Queen crap and children's rides did not turn him on. He was about to change channels when, for one brief moment, the camera caught Grace Milvern's face silhouetted against the backdrop of the ice skating rink.

He had been sunk deep in his chair while he watched the eleven o'clock news, drinking one of the many whiskeys that he consumed each day to keep himself in a permanent fog, when her face had appeared like a stab of light on the screen.

Frank nearly fell onto the floor. "You bitch! Oh, I am going to get you, bitch!" This was the catalyst that he needed to whip himself into action! He leaped out of the chair and began to pace up and down.

"Now I can find you!" he shouted. "You'll never be safe from me!

You will regret the night you went into that liquor store!" He grabbed his coat and flew out of the apartment, heading for the winter carnival.

But after he battled his way through traffic, found an over-priced parking spot in a lot blocks away from the festivities, and searched the streets, there was no Milvern woman to be found among the groups of revelers thronging the carnival.

Frank refused to be deterred. He drove back to his high-rise and parked in the under-ground garage.

Entering his apartment, he flung his coat on the couch. After pouring a whiskey and water, he paced up and down the room. Now, where should he look for her? She had been a waitress at Russo's, so she would probably be in the same line of work. The camera had spotted her a a downtown event, so she must work downtown and even live there. Her job couldn't be a place that was too high-class, because Russo's was not much more than a neighborhood bar. How could he track her down?

He stopped pacing and gazed out the window. The snow had stopped. Ice had piled up in the river where it diverged from the lake, and moonlight glinted on patches of frozen, black water beyond the harbor. None of this registered in his mind. He was visualizing Grace with a bullet blasting part of her face off. That would be the end of her. She would be unrecognizable and unidentifiable. Dear Jennifer's meddling would have gotten her nowhere.

He reached under the kitchen counter, grabbed the phone book and flipped to the restaurant listings. Jesus! There were pages and pages of them! This would be an impossible job. He could put Discrete Detections on the job. They were good. Yes, that's what he would do. Between them, she was going to be found—and this time there would be no escape! He'd call the detective service first thing in the morning.

"You bitch! Oh, I am going to get you, cunt!" They would have to canvas all the medium-to-low-class restaurants in the city. None of the real sleezy joints, though, and no topless dives. She didn't look tough enough to work in those. And no fast food either. That was for kids.

Now, where would he look? The news camera had spotted her downtown, so she had to be in that area. Russo's had been a neighborhood bar, so the new place couldn't be too high class.

How would he track her down?

He had to find a picture of her. "She may be using a fake name wherever she working," he muttered, "so I'll need a photo to show around, but where can I get one? Of course, the paper!" There had been a picture published in the Port City News of her leaving the funeral home at the time of Milvern's funeral. It would be in their archives." I'll give a copy to Discrete Detections, and we can show it around to restaurant managers. But why should they tell us anything? Especially if they recognize her as the wife of the murdered man in the fishing tent."

"Offer them a reward. I'll pose as an insurance agent. After all, it worked before. A reward for information as to her whereabouts." Frank went to the drinks bar and poured himself another whiskey. He didn't feel drunk—only excited. Sipping it, he continued to plot.

"How much money should I offer? Fifty dollars? Not enough. Two hundred? Too much—sounds fishy. One hundred would be enough to tempt them, but not enough to make them think that something was up. I can't be recognized. That would be fatal, so I need a disguise." He examined his face in the gold-framed antique hall mirror.

"I'll just change the hair color with a hair piece," he ruminated. "Mousey brown would work. I'll wear a hat over it and glasses: very emphatic glasses—the kind that would be remembered." He would be described, if it ever came to that, as an indeterminate-looking man wearing flashy glasses. The glasses that would be long gone, pitched into the Port City River! Floating downstream in the frigid water with the beer cans, the abandoned guns and the dead fish! "I can't purchase the startling glasses at an opticians. Good Lord, no! I'll get them at the Goodwill or the Salvation Army! Maybe they will have the hairpiece too."

"You're dead, baby!!" he intoned. "Dead-dead-dead!"

He settled back in his chair to gloat. It had been so easy to get the address of the woman's parents. Any idiot would have known how to do it. He went to the city's records office and asked to see the marriage license for Dennis Milvern. His secretary could have done it in a flash on her computer, but he didn't want the firm involved in any way. The girls who worked in records were familiar. They were glad to see him, trade a few pleasantries before they retrieved the information. As he always did, he brought them donuts. Grace Buell of Cranston married to Dennis Milvern, same city. Then it had been a snap to get the phone listing and street number for the Buells. He was smart, all right.

"She doesn't stand a chance!"

Martin still had the news turned on. He had picked up a book that he started to read the week before. It was about organic gardening, but was written so dryly that his interest kept faltering. Even the illustrations were boring. He decided to have one more beer and then go to bed. Pausing in the kitchen doorway, he glanced at the television set. John Bradford was droning on about the winter carnival.

"The Snow Queen Parade has just started, and many families have gathered to watch the high spot of this alcohol-free celebration." The camera cut to the smiling, newly crowned queen, a sophomore at the university, blowing kisses and waving her wand to the crowd from a sled drawn by two horses. Her golden hair was topped with a jeweled tiara and she was wrapped in furs: fake, he hoped. The camera left her image and crept stealthily as a cat through the crowd, illuminating several small boys on skis too large for them, tumbling through the snow on a man-made ski run in a parking lot. It veered again to the Snow Queen, waving ecstatically to clusters of people.

Nice idea, Martin thought. Time the city promoted more family events, as he watched the skaters gliding over the ice in the rink. Then, he recoiled in horror as the camera focused on the face of Grace Milvern, her profile pale against the backdrop of swirling skaters, before it moved on to some clowns doing a comedy routine.

She was still in the city.

"Oh, Christ! How am I going to find her?"

He felt so powerless, because she could have gone anywhere after she left the carnival. Wearily, he pulled on his coat and headed back to the station. He had to get some men out looking for her, but where would they look? Was she still a waitress? He didn't want to think about the possibility that she might be a salesgirl or work in a nursing home.

At the precinct, he plugged in the coffee maker and started to draw up a plan of action.

Outside of his filthy office window, snowflakes drifted into the deserted street. Snow flakes, he thought, I have as much chance of locating her as I do of finding two identical snowflakes. Why couldn't she have stayed in the hotel?

"I should cut out coffee completely," he stated, as he poured a cup, his sixth today, from the automatic coffee maker on the shelf in the office. When he first started working homicide, he had gradually gotten up to six or eight cups a day because of the tension, the pressure, the excitement. On the phone or writing reports on the computer, he kept drinking cup after cup. Always on a caffeine high. Then, he injured his knee while grappling with an ex-con during a botched murder attempt. The man was so doped up that he could hardly see straight, and he had gone over in a heap when Martin tackled him.

They were in a cottage on Drake Street. The police had been tipped off by the neighbors that there was something going on. The man wanted to shoot his brother-in-law and shouts and threats disturbed the night air. It was an explosive situation. Gun shots had been fired and people cowered in their homes behind locked doors.

The guy was shooting wildly when Martin tackled him and in doing so, he twisted his knee. After limping painfully around for a week, he went to see Leo's chiropractor, Dr. Muller. The result was three months of treatments: ultrasound, adjustments, and heat therapy, before the knee was fully functional. On the third visit, Dr. Muller advised Martin to make some changes in his diet. At that time, he was eating a lot of steak and potatoes, cheeseburgers, roast beef.

"You have to limit your intake of caffeine, dairy and meat. That stuff is poisoning your system."

So, now he was down to fewer cups a day. Black, although he couldn't give it up completely, and when he was nervous, the count rose dramatically. He had become a vegetarian, and cut down substantially on cheese and milk. He didn't limp anymore, and he had lost twenty pounds.

Studying the assignment roaster, he worked on the names of cops who would be available to search for Grace and tried to think about where to send them. There weren't many who could be pulled off other investigations. Homicide was enjoying a renaissance in the city.

His desk was piled with work. A woman had been found floating in the river near the water intake station with a bullet in her forehead. There was the shooting of the guard over at Port City Community late last night. This one puzzled him. Why would someone burglarize the registrar's office at the college and shoot a guard? It made no sense. He and Leo couldn't come up with any answers. Commissioner Battaglia had immediately stationed an undercover officer at the college, but there were no leads. Nothing had been taken from the registrars, but papers and computer sheets were scattered around the office. The ladder that had been used in the break-in was still standing against the wall when the police arrived. The guard seemed to be an ordinary citizen with no connections to crime. He'd think about it later. The main thing now was to find Grace Milvern. Sometimes it was better to prevent a crime than to solve one.

He was at a dead end in too many killings. Nothing had turned up on the Milvern homicide and Grace Milvern was still missing. He was still shadowing Frank Pearson as much as possible, but the man never deviated from his daily routines. Homicide was like that, he consoled himself. Things would lay around gathering dust for a long time, and then, suddenly a crack would appear in the solid wall of inertia, and the facts would rapidly fall into place. The killer would be found, the crime explained. Either that or or nothing happened, and the case would die. Half of the homicides were unsolved. There were murderers walking around all over the Port City chuckling to themselves, because they had gotten away with the big one.

He fought down the impulse to pour another cup of coffee. He had been so sure that Frank Pearson would lead him to Grace, but the elation he felt when Jennifer Pearson sat in the chair across from his desk was short lived. He could never prove that Pearson had killed Nathan Scortino, unless he could find Grace and convince her to make the identification. The team could work on it tomorrow. As If searching for her wasn't enough to occupy him, he had to work on the speech he was presenting to the Criminal Justice class of the University. His topic was famous homicides in the area. He would explain how the police dealt with them and the possible solutions. Ha! He felt like a fraud.

"Good evening. This is John Bradford and this is the evening news. Last night, the Port City recorded its fourteenth homicide. Alejandro Gomez, a security guard at the Port City Community College was shot to death during a break-in. He apparently surprised his assailants as they were looting the college Registrar's Office where they had gained entry through a ground- floor window. As of tonight, police have no leads. At the same time that the guard was killed, there was a drive-by shooting at the rear of the college. Several shots were fired through the window of a first-floor music room. This drive-by is believed to be unrelated to the killing of Mr. Gomez, but police are not sure as to why the two events occurred simultaneously."

Mr. Gomez had only worked at the college for three months. He leaves a wife and six children.

In other news tonight, a trapped deer was rescued from the ice covering the frozen ice at the City Municipal Beach........."

"He surprised us, Jack," complained Gene Lempke. "We had gotten into the room, and I had just printed out the information when this guy bursts in on us. He threw the light switch and saw us plain as day. The door wasn't even locked! He came right in!"

The two were in Jack D'Angelo's office, standing before his desk.

"Which one of you shot him? I specifically said there was to be no shooting." Jack asked, even though he knew the answer.

"George shot him. I had the printouts in my hand. It happened so suddenly. The guy should have been at the back of the building, investigating the drive-by."

"I had to do it," muttered George. "He saw us. I got a record. We'd be dead meat. The cops know me."

He shivered slightly, remembering the excitement of jimmying the window, and how the pressure mounted in the dark room, illuminated only by daggers of light from Leo's flashlight. The wonderful intoxication as they prowled through the office, Leo working the computer while he broke into file after file. Then, the climax. The guard emerging through the doorway, back-lit by the light of the hall, his finger pulling the trigger, his whole body suffused with the thrill of the moment.

Jack swiveled his chair around so he wouldn't have to look at these punks. He stared out the window at the ice-filled harbor. In the distance, a lighthouse blinked off and on, off and on, a halo of red light.

None of this was what he needed. He wanted things to be clean, but these two idiots were unable to do a simple job. Instead of employing a squadron of lawyers to keep him out of trouble, he should have hired reliable help. He hated making mistakes, and this was an important error.

"You did get the information?" he asked, wearily.

"Right here," Gene responded. "She lives at 51D Palmer Heights. That's the big housing project over on the East side."

"George, you can leave for now. I don't have to tell you not to discuss this. If you mention a word to anyone, I will send you straight back to prison where you will certainly be killed, because I have connections at all of the correctional facilities of this state."

Jack turned to the window again. He had to think. Should he have Gene stake out Palmer Heights? No, the idea of the Jordan woman keeping product in her apartment had backfired. Another line of direction was needed. He had the address for use in the future, and that was enough. First, though, the woman had to be zeroed in on. She might not have the product, but she could know something.

"Gene, no one saw you or can connect you to the slaying of the campus guard. If anyone even infers that you were involved, I will provide you with an air-tight alibi. Now, what I want you to do is shadow the Jordan woman when she is at the college."

"No, Jack! I'm not going back there! It's too dangerous!" Gene sputtered.

"Nonsense. I want you to follow her around and see if you can pick up any information."

"I'm not going back to that place!" Gene protested.

"See if you can find any clues that will lead us to the whereabouts of the merchandise. You can hang around the student union. Listen to conversations that she's involved in. Be very cautious, though. One George-type experience is all I can take. Just report anything back to me."

"But I said....."

"And dress like a student. Wear jeans. Carry books. Here!" He crossed the room to the massive bookshelves and took down several large volumes.

"Tell anyone that you are studying psychology. All students have to take psychology."

"Please, Jack. Get Mike Stokes to do it. He's younger and would fit in with the other students, I'm forty, for God's sake. No one will believe that I'm going to college."

"You will find that there are many students much older than you. Do it or I will send an anonymous tip to the police. Within the hour, they'll toss you in the slammer and grill you until you confess to the break-in."

Gene picked up the books dejectedly.

"Remember. Report back in a few days."

Martin and Leo were having lunch at a wonderful restaurant in the Friends Co-Op on Sloane Street. It did have a small list of meat selections. so Leo was satisfied with his ham sandwich and a side of potato salad. Martin was enjoying asparagus ravioli with tomato sauce.

"How is Tina getting along?" he asked his partner.

"She's out of her cast and raising hell!" Leo replied, glumly. "Once again, she's staying out late, defying her mother and me. One good thing: that boy dropped her when she had the cast put on. He's got another girl, and Tina is miserable and furious. And of course, it's all our fault. Her grades are in the pits, and she's been cutting classes. Maria had to go to the school several times! What else can we do? We wanted her to have counseling, but she won't go. She'll get in serious trouble, you wait and see."

"How about your son, Rocco?"

"He was accepted into the honor society at St. Anthony's. If only all my kids were like him! He's a wonderful student, never gives us any trouble."

"Tina may straighten out. Don't give her too much aggravation."

"Easy for you to say. You aren't even married!" Leo knitted his copious black eyebrows.

"And I am eternally glad that I'm not. As they say: been there, done that."

"Anything new on the Jordan beating?"

"No, I think it might have been one of her disgruntled clients, in which case, we'll never learn anything."

"Must have been a real angry one. That apartment was demolished! Are we having dessert?"

"They do a good walnut cake."

"OK, then we must get going."

Chapter Eleven

Gene Lempke finished his hamburger while seated at a table in the crowded, noisy student lounge area. The burger had been dry. Probably made hours in advance and kept warm. He was no gourmet, but he did like to have a substantial lunch, and this assignment at Port City was causing him some distress, especially as he couldn't eat in the dining room run by the Culinary Arts students. He had to stick close to the Jordan woman. Also, he had recently discovered a great little eating place a block from the campus where they made a roast beef sandwich with gravy and a side order of the best Cole Slaw he had ever tasted. Tangy, and not heavy on the mayonnaise: sour cream added, he thought. He couldn't go there until his quarry, Katherine Jordan, was on the rapid transit heading for Palmer Heights. He watched some students playing cards at a near-by table. Christ! He thought that students put in a lot of time studying. This group had been in the lounge for three hours, and he knew that they were betting on their games. When did they go to class? Some of the students were so messy. Fastidiously, he picked up his paper plate and napkin and took it over to a receptacle after wiping the crumbs from the table. The walls of the lounge were plastered with posters advertising some big rally or march to be held in front of city hall next week. Something about tuition hikes, it looked like. He hoped the Jordan woman wasn't planning on attending, because he would have to follow her. He decided that he hated students.

He took out one of the psychology books that Jack had given him out of his back pack and pretended to study. Cognitive Psychology. It made absolutely no sense to him. No one seemed to have any questions about his student status. Jack had been right. There were a lot of older students here and he blended in. There had been one bad moment when a security guard stopped two guys who were harassing another student and demanded to see their student ID's. He was afraid that they might ask him also, and he didn't have one, but they were too busy throwing the two non-students off campus.

Katherine Jordan, seated at a table across the lounge from Gene, finished her salad, got up, and picked her way past the crowded tables to the basement stairs. Spanish class was next, and it had continued to be a problem. Professor Sanchez definitely didn't like her. During the last class, her pen had run out of ink, and she whispered to the boy sitting next to her, asking if she could borrow a pen from him. Sanchez interrupted his lecture to ask if she could please try to confine her socializing to after class hours. She had been embarrassed, and it was unfair. She had whispered quietly. Some of the other students were almost raucous, but he never got on their case. Standing in front of her locker, she wondered: should she show him that South American doll that Dennis had given her? It might be a good ploy to convince him that she was interested in Spanish culture. She decided that it was worth a try, and she was ready to try anything. She had to get at least a B in the course or her average wouldn't be high enough to be accepted into the nursing program. She picked the doll up, along with her books and headed for the elevator.

Gene had been lingering in front of a locker down the hall from Katherine. When she headed for the elevator, he followed her. He caught up with her in time to push the up button before the door closed. Positioning himself back against the rear wall, he watched the numbers as the car rose. Katherine didn't notice him. Four students got on at the second floor that created more of a boundary between him and the woman. Katherine exited at three, and Leo waited until the doors had started to close before elbowing his way to the front of the car.

"Whoops, sorry. My floor," he apologized as he hit the button to open the door.

The Spanish professor stood at the door of the classroom, waiting for students to appear. Leo paused and pretended to study a bulletin board advertising Math Anxiety Workshops, as Katherine showed the doll to the professor. He could overhear their conversation.

"Well, it's not a bad example of the sort of thing made by native Chilean women. It is rather large, though, for this type of doll. And it's much heavier than other dolls of this type."

Gene pricked up his ears. He edged a little closer.

"Where did you buy it?" the professor asked.

"A friend of mine knew that I was interested in the culture of South America," she improvised. "He gave it to me as a birthday present. Could you tell me something about the conditions that these women live under? The ones who make the dolls. I want to know more about their lives."

"Holy shit!" Gene muttered. "That damn doll she's got! That has to be where Dennis stashed the merchandise! I've found it!" He hurriedly left the third floor, took the stairs in large strides, ran to his car in the student parking lot and headed for Jack's office as fast as he could travel.

Jack had just come back from playing squash at his club when Gene brought him the good news.

"The product is hidden in a stupid doll that she's keeping in her locker at the college!" he chortled. "It's gotta be in there."

"Well done, Gene. My estimate of you has gone up. You can suspend your surveillance of the Jordan woman."

"I don't have to go back to the college?"

"No. I think we will have George retrieve the doll. You've done your part and done it well."

Gene sighed with relief. Maybe he'd stop on his way home at the little restaurant with the marvelous cole slaw.

Although he was happy with Gene's news about the product, Jack D'Angelo had become bored with the whole Milvern problem. There were so many other interesting deals to hold his attention. A private developer was negotiating the purchase of several blocks of his inner-city housing holdings for the eventuality of demolishing the area and constructing a large plaza with a supermarket, bank, fast-food stores, a pharmacy and a commodious parking lot.

Tapping an untouched market was how the developer described the project. Of course, the bleeding hearts were already sounding the drum roll. "Where will the residents go? They can't afford any housing except what they have. It may be shabby, but it's a neighborhood. This can't be allowed to happen."

Well, it could and it would, and he was going to make a tremendous profit on his miserable clutch of welfare shanties.

He also owned a large, brick rooming house that the prison system deemed suitable for sheltering semi-released prisoners in a halfway house situation. It was stuffed with citizens of the ghetto. He would clear a mint on that one. The place was in a wrecked section of downtown surrounded by boarded-up buildings and storefronts that sold canvass, plexiglass and army-navy equipment behind heavily iron-grilled doors. He was also contemplating the purchase of a nursing home. After all, people were living forever. Even though they scarcely resembled humans at the end. There was federal money available for that deal. Lots of it.

Yes, there were plenty of exciting things, opportunities in the wind these days, and he was intrigued by them, but he still had the Milvern problem on his hands. It must be solved soon! He couldn't afford to be viewed as weak. He recalled his lessons from prison. Always be on top and punish any infraction against your authority. And now, thanks to Gene, he knew where the product was hidden. The next day, he summoned George to the office.

He deeply regretted not developing a better cadre of henchmen, he thought as he studied George. The man resembled a large, gray lump of suet, in his denim western-style suit, with his pasty skin and his huge head. Well, he had to work with what he had. Too late for a change in the ranks, but Arnie Levenson had mentioned a man who had just moved to the Port City and was looking for work. Perhaps he would interview him after this Milvern business was completed. Now, he must persuade George to retrieve the merchandise and at once! The doll had to be recovered, and if George had to kill the Jordan woman, that was unfortunate. He probably would anyway. It would make the whole adventure worthwhile in his demented brain. Oh, yes, he would do it. That was the only virtue of employing a psychotic killer to do jobs. He'd squash that Jordan woman like a roach and come panting back to the office with the doll under his arm.

Jack had always suspected that Milvern had given the package to the Jordan woman. It was the sort of stupid romantic gesture that the jerk loved.

He summoned George, that psychotic hit man, to the office.

"I have to go back to the college?" George's face moved restlessly under his stetson hat. His tiny, cold eyes registered alarm. "After I wasted that guard?"

"Yes, George," Jack soothed him. "We must finish the job now that Gene has discovered where the product is."

"I don't want to go back there."

"You have to, but the plan will be air-tight and quite simple. The woman whose apartment you trashed has a doll in her locker in the basement of the school. The doll contains the merchandize we have been searching for. Follow her to the locker and take it. Couldn't be easier."

"What if she don't go along with the idea? Can I use force?" Dolls and schools. The things he hated the most, but if he could strike back at them, hurt someone—it would be all right.

Jack knew only too well what George meant by force. The gun would appear, and there would be a bloody body on the floor.

"Whatever needs to be done," he murmured.

"What do I put the damned doll in? I'd look stupid carrying a doll out of there."

Jack went to the closet and took out a gym bag. It was bright blue and had a silhouette of a runner on the side.

"Put it in this. If anyone stops you, say you're on the track team."

"When do you want it done?'

"She has an evening class tomorrow night. Gene gave me her schedule. Wait near the front entrance until she arrives and follow her into the school, but don't let her see you. She has to go to her locker to get her books, and you can take the doll from her there."

George clumped out of the office carrying the gym bag.

"I'll have to eliminate him after he brings the product back. Maybe I'll get Gene to do the job. He's in so deep that he can't refuse. George may be dumb, but he's vicious and will do anything, including turning on me, to stay out of prison. I guess that this will have to be George's last stand."

Jack and Raven were seated on spindly gilt chairs at a boutique called Lovely Body in the business district. Raven was wearing tight black slacks and a purple lace blouse. Her fur was draped behind the chair. Around them was a huge showroom where racks of lurid and colorful clothes crowded the walls. Tables were piled with crotchless panties, garter belts, embroidered stockings. Mirrors of all sizes were everywhere, and plaster busts of female heads with flowing hair covered the walls. Music from stage productions and Judy Garland show tunes throbbed incessantly. The floor was carpeted in a dense aqua shag, and the windows hung with heavy plum-colored satin drapes that admitted no light. Intrusive floral perfume had been squirted liberally over the area.

They were there because Raven was going to audition for a role in the upcoming revival of Gypsy, the musical about Gypsy Rose Lee, the famous stripper. Raven wanted to audition wearing a stripper's outfit, an idea that Jack assumed most of the girls trying out for the starring role had also thought of. Raven's ideas concerning acting were usually unimaginative, which was one of the reasons she was a fourth-rate thespian. He had accompanied her because this theater thing was a side of the city that he had been totally unaware of, and he thought he was familiar with everything. The philharmonic was well-known territory, and he patronized the art museums. He had dined at every decent restaurant in town and had placed bets at the racetrack and the casino. This, unknown to him, facet of the lower side of the theatrical world, was new and, for the moment, interesting. Besides, she was gorgeous, and it took his mind off his business problems, which were many.

As they watched, a tall man with shoulder-length blond hair and discrete makeup, wearing a white jump suit unzipped to the waist, held a transparent bra up against his hairy chest. The bra was decorated with feathers where the nipples would be.

"This is our Indian number. Very popular. It comes with a variety of feathers to match different scenarios." Lovely Body catered primarily to the stripper trade, female impersonators and drag queens.

The salesman held a sheer bikini against his pelvis. "These panties complete the costume." Like the bra they were transparent and also decorated with detachable feathers.

"I would like to see more of a selection," Raven commented. "Do you have anything with roses?"

The salesman sighed. Because of the upcoming audition for the Gypsy Rose Lee role, every would-be star who had come in searching for costumes wanted roses. He disappeared behind a door and emerged with a new outfit. This transparent set of bra and panties was similar to the Indian-themed ensemble only instead of feathers, there were rosebuds in strategic places. He held the bra against his torso, coyly.

"It's very artistic," he purred.

"What do you think, Jack?" Raven whispered.

"I think that every actress auditioning for the role will choose roses. Pick the Indian costume."

"I would like to see a robe, also. Something not too flashy, but interesting, and a garter belt and open work-stockings," she addressed the salesman.

"Gypsy wore garters," she whispered to Jack.

"Hurray for Gypsy," he commented.

"I thought that I would enter wearing a robe and then slowly remove it a little at a time, like a mini- strip tease. Get into the spirit of the role immediately."

"How very novel. I'm sure no one else will think of that." She missed his sarcasm.

The evening before, they had dined again on over-priced, uninspired food at Cinimatricity so that she could be seen again and appreciated. Instead of the violinist, there were drag queens modeling lavish evening gowns while acting out short skits. He found the spectacle of six-foot-four-inch men in towering high-heels wearing lace and velvet and padded bras hysterically funny, and he had to hold a handkerchief in front of his face to conceal his guffaws. They wore marvelous wigs though, he had to admit, and their makeup was expert.

Jack loved makeup on a woman, but he hated to see five-o-clock shadow poking through cream foundation. These guys were good, but he found their bitchy attitude irritating. They had gone back to Raven's apartment for a few hours, and he had the cuts and scratches to prove it. He sensed that she would like to have him create some havoc of his own, but he wasn't like that. No way would he ever be rough with a woman, and he didn't understand men who were into that scene. His thumb was sporting a bandage today, thanks to Raven's inventiveness. She had been leaning seductively over him as he reclined on her bed, pretending to be a tiger. Flexing her fingers as though they were claws, she swiped at his chest, growling, her luscious breasts swinging near his stomach. Then, all of a sudden, she swooped down and bit his thumb, hard.

"Ouch!" he yelled as she laughed with delight.

"Kitty bad?" she asked.

"Kitty better stop the attacks," he admonished her. "Jack doesn't like games!"

The rest of the afternoon proceeded without further incident, and he was pleased to note that he had left a streak of blood on her expensive sheets. Served her right.

Raven bought the Indian costume, the robe, the garter belt and stockings at an incredible price. For a minute, he debated buying the clothes for her, but decided against it. This relationship must be kept casual. He didn't want her to get the idea that there was anything serious to it.

He dropped her off at her place and went to his office, where the problem of expanding the members of his staff confronted him. Losing Dennis Milvern had left a hole, and George was always an unpredictable problem. That left Mike Stokes, and he was only good for reconnaissance work and a little breaking and entering. He did not want to hire another psycho-sadist like George. Arnie Levenson had told him that a man called Lizard Jacobi was looking for work. He was from out of town and wanted to get established in the Port City. Perhaps he would interview the man. Gene Lempke was back on assignment for Arnie Levenson, and he hadn't been too impressed with Gene, anyway. Except for discovering where the product was, he hadn't accomplished much. He preferred a cadre of four men, one experienced in debt collection, one familiar with the drug world and one for minor tasks. A really accomplished hit-man was another necessity. He wondered what this Lizard guy's specialty was. He assumed that Lizard was not his real name.

After picking up the ridiculous glasses at the Goodwill and purchasing a cheap wig at a Francie's Hair Boutique in the Downtown Mall, Frank set out on his quest to find Grace Milvern. He was armed with a list of restaurants in the downtown area. To make sure that no suspicion was attached to him, he followed his usual routine, arriving at the law firm's offices at nine. All morning he conferred with either clients or his partners. At noon, he left for his daily swim at the Athletic Club, leaving word with his secretary that he would be at the County Court Building during the afternoon. After he had duly backstroked the length of the club pool for half an hour, he lunched with a fellow lawyer in the club restaurant on steak and a Cobb salad. Then, he walked two blocks to the Court Building. He planned to proceed this way until he found the Milvern woman.

Carrying the briefcase that contained his disguise, he entered the building by the front door, supposedly to attend a trial. There was a long, involved case that the firm had represented in a land acquisition a long time ago. The firm was in no way implicated, but it was logical hat Frank would be watching the proceedings. He would catch the results on the news each night, so that he could respond to his partner's questions if anything interesting came up.

Frank got into a crowded elevator. He waited patiently as it descended to the basement, and then elbowed his way out. The men's room on that floor was deplorable. Obscenities written in ball point pen covered the white tile walls, and it looked and smelled as though someone had recently thrown up in the sink. Some strange curdled pink mess floated there. Apparently the maintenance staff never cleaned the place. A year ago, a man had been fatally shot in this room. It suited his purpose perfectly because no one would be in there, and it was the last place anyone would expect to find him.

He entered a stall and opened the briefcase. The rank odor of the room made him gag. Carefully, he positioned the wig over his own hair and donned the long beige coat that covered his well-tailored suit. Now, when he left by the basement stairway, he was not liable to be recognized. The glasses would be left off until he approached the restaurants. Taking a large paper bag out of the coat pocket, he placed the briefcase inside. The last vestige of his lawyer persona was gone. He looked ordinary.

Martin had been following Frank Pearson every day. Although he had men checking restaurants, he was sure that Frank would lead him to

Grace before the police found her. He was a ways behind the heavy-set man with the slicked-back hair in an elevator as they rode up, as usual, to Chez Philipe, the extremely expensive place patronized by bankers, upper-grade judges and politicians. Martin always took a table in a far corner so he could observe his quarry from a distance, yet remain invisible. He ordered something vegetarian, wincing at the prices listed on the menu. After lunch, he walked several yards behind the man when the lawyer entered the County Court Building.

When Martin tried to get on the elevator on first floor, there was no room for him. A large black woman carrying a baby had pushed in before him and occupied the remaining space. The courtroom was on the second floor and Martin assumed that it would be Frank's destination. He watched the floor numbers light up as the elevator descended to the basement. Whistling, he waited for it to arrive back on first, but when the doors opened, he was once again facing the large woman whose baby was now squalling loudly.

"We full, mister," she informed him.

He shrugged his shoulders as the doors closed and took the stairwell to the second floor. Lawyers, clients, masses of people were milling about in the corridor in front of the courtroom, but he didn't see Frank Pearson. Puzzled, he scanned the hall and then entered the courtroom.

He recognized the guard at the door immediately. It was Darryl Pleasance, an amiable black man who had worked at the court for years.

"What are you doing here, Martin? Shouldn't you be out fighting crime?"

"Crime can wait. I'm looking for Frank Pearson. Know him?"

"Sure. Big-shot lawyer. Naw, he hasn't been in today."

"Funny. I saw him downstairs."

"Maybe he got detained."

"Just don't mention that I was looking for him."

"Would I do that, Marty?" The guard grinned.

Martin went back into the hall and waited around watching for Frank, but no luck. The guy had probably gone into one of the hundreds of offices in the building. Finally, he gave up and returned to the station and the mountains of paperwork waiting for him.

Chapter Twelve

Frank patiently covered the restaurants on the outskirts of the theater district. At each place, he took out Grace's photo and put on his ridiculous glasses with the over-sized mottled turquoise frames. Then, he showed the photo to the manager while giving him the insurance spiel. None of the men had seen her. He planned on canvassing ten or twelve places each afternoon, and was not at all discouraged that the first day's work had yielded nothing.

The manager at the final place, the Downtown Grill, scanned the photo, screwed up his eyes.

"I think she's the one who applied for a waitress job. We didn't have any openings—couldn't hire her."

"Did she leave an address or a phone number?"

"No.

"She didn't tell you her name."

"No. But how many of you guys want this babe? The police were here an hour ago asking about her."

Frank wasn't worried that the cops were ahead of him. He knew that these places paid under the minimum wage or had health violations. They were never going to admit hiring her to the police. They might fire her, though. He'd better step up his search. He'd call in sick tomorrow and spend the whole day tracking her. Time was of the essence.

Grace was still eating at the Arms of Love, and as she looked around, she realized that the same people dined there each day. There were the retirees, the veterans, families with small children, Gloria Morningstar's Indian relatives, and Gloria's angry daughter who pushed two children in a carriage. One was a new baby, the other a toddler. The food was good, so she surmised that Herman was still on duty in the kitchen.

The director, Jo-Jo Martinelli, decided to sit with her again today, while he kept a wary eye on Herman. The weather was fine. Lambent clouds were caught in a blue sky, and the ice had melted from the sidewalks enabling more clients to come for lunch.

"Not a bad crowd, considering that the forecaster actually predicted six inches of snow. Why can't they get it right or at least be honest? I would like a weather reporter to say: "It might snow or on the other hand, the temperature could warm up. We really don't know. We can offer you a few options and see what works out. Don't make any plans based on our predictions because we have no idea what will happen. Just cross your fingers and hope for the best."

Grace laughed. "Or people could open a window and stick their heads out."

"That would work. Are you employed in the downtown area?" he rasped. Jo-Jo looked weary. His color was bad and his hands shook. Grace figured that his was an exhausting job with little thanks.

"I'm a waitress at the Red Dragon, but I really need to eat here. The pay isn't much."

"Don't apologize. See that man over there? He's an adjunct professor at the university. They don't provide a large salary for part-time faculty. Anyway, we're not here to judge."

Just then, an argument broke out between two men sitting together at a table. Soon, there was shouting and chairs were overturned. Jo-Jo left the table and rapidly approached the pair. Gloria Morningstar's relative, Clyde, went to stand with him.

"Keep your problems to yourself or you won't be allowed to eat here. Now, put the chairs back and be quiet!" the director admonished them.

Both men were wild-eyed, ready to throw punches.

"You don't want me to call the police!"

At that threat, they both righted the chairs and sat down, reluctantly.

Jo-Jo returned to Grace's table.

"Both of those guys are former mental patients," he explained. "When they closed the psychiatric facilities, a lot of the patients had nowhere to go. Some of them come here, but they really need treatment, supervision, and medication. The governor decided to save money and put it elsewhere, like into big administrative raises," he sneered. "This place is where the money should go, but no one gives a damn!" He slammed his fist on the table, beginning to get worked up, and his breathing was labored. Gloria Morningstar appeared from the kitchen holding a glass of water and a pill. Silently, she handed them to him, and he gulped the medicine down.

"He's not supposed to get upset," she explained. "Come on, Jo-Jo. Herman wants to consult with you about tomorrow's menu."

Jo-Jo heaved himself up and walked unsteadily through the kitchen door, leaning on Gloria's arm.

Grace finished her lunch and left. She would be back tomorrow.

Katherine shivered in the chilly night air. Even her heavy suede coat didn't seem to cut the wind, and the three blocks from the rapid transit to the school were unbearably long. She passed knots of people huddled in the doorways of restaurants and office buildings, waiting for buses. The night course was a pain. She liked Anatomy and Physiology, and it was required for the nursing students, but being downtown on a weeknight was no fun. After class ended at nine-thirty, the guard from the school escort service would walk her to the rapid transit station for the trip home. That journey always scared her more than the ride in, because so many strange people were on the train. Now, she clutched her purse in front of her and didn't look to either side until she arrived at the imposing Gothic building with the carved stone eagle over the front entrance and hurried up the steps.

Inside the lobby, she turned to the elevator to go to the basement. She felt guilty taking it for only one flight, but there was no time to walk down the stairs. She had to get her textbook from her locker or the professor wouldn't let her into the class. He was very strict.

She hated the basement. Last week, a man was discovered in the women's lavatory. He was in a stall, poised on the toilet, peering over the top of the cubicle. The girl who entered the restroom looked up and encountered his eyes, spying on her. She screamed and screamed, and he bolted out the door. Security searched the building, but he hadn't been caught.

Impatiently, she waited for the elevator to disgorge a group of students and then got on with some other people.

The car descended slowly toward the basement and then stopped halfway down.

"We're not moving," one of the students complained.

Katherine angrily jabbed the button for basement again and again. Nothing happened.

"Push the emergency button," a boy suggested.

She did and a loud ringing sound responded, but the car was not moving.

"I'll never get into class if I'm late." She was near tears.

"What are you taking?" a girl near the closed door asked.

"Anatomy and Physiology."

"Professor Rashoon?"

"Yeah."

"Oh God. I had him last semester for Biology and I was lucky to get a C. His final exam was so hard that half the class flunked it."

"Great." muttered Katherine.

The elevator was still going nowhere, and she kept on pushing the emergency button. Thank heaven the car wasn't crowded. She didn't think she could bear it if she were stuffed in with ten or twelve other bodies.

"Why doesn't this thing move?"

George had slipped quietly into the school, taking care not to call attention to himself when he entered the lobby. Tailing the Jordan woman had been easy until she entered the school. There had been a cluster of students talking on the front steps, and he momentarily lost sight of her as he jostled his way through clouds of cigarette smoke. Once inside the building, she was nowhere to be seen. He felt that Jack hadn't given him enough information. The locker was in the basement. How the hell did he get down there? He walked across the lobby to an elevator near the side door.

"This thing go to the basement?" he growled at a pallid-looking young man.

"No, you have to take the one near the backdoor, or the stairs over beyond the switchboard."

George set off in search of the elevator.

The security guard on duty that night was Orrin Jones, a fat, arthritic black man who could not walk very fast. He had been standing near the front door when George entered the building, and he didn't like what he saw. The man looked awfully bizarre for a student with his huge pumpkin-shaped head and hulking body. The guards were under strict orders to stop any suspicious characters, and there was an undercover cop posted in the building since the killing in the registrar's office.

He didn't want to stop this one. The guy looked dangerous.

"It's your job, Orrin. Get those legs moving."

"Mister," he called, as he lumbered after the strange figure. Maybe he was one of those homeless people who had been sneaking into the building to sleep on cold nights.

George stopped. Trouble! He knew that he shouldn't have returned to the school. Damn Jack! He eyed the security guard.

Orrin rolled his head apprehensively as he approached the stranger.

"You a student, mister? I got to see your identification card."

"I just stopped to see a friend," George muttered.

"Have to ask you to leave then. Only students allowed."

"This will only take a minute."

"Sorry, but I tell you that you got to leave the premises."

George glanced rapidly around. Classes had started a few minutes ago, and he and the guard were now alone in the lobby. Beyond him, he could see the stairs that led to the basement where the lockers were located.

"Mister, you hear me?" Orrin barked.

That did it. George hauled off and swung at the man. The punch caught the guard in the jaw, and he collapsed in an ungainly heap on the terrazzo floor near a pillar. George ran to the stairway and clumped down the stairs.

Panting, he arrived at the basement, but he didn't know where to go. There were soft-drink machines and candy dispensers on one side, and the other was lined with lockers. Christ! How was he going to know which one belonged to the Jordan woman. If he had to walk around until she showed up, it could take hours. The guard would come to—there would be a commotion and someone would find him. What a bunch of shit! What time did Jack say that her class started? He couldn't remember. He roamed up and down the corridor, knocking aside the few students still at their lockers. There was no sign of Katherine Jordan.

Upstairs, on the first floor, Orrin was beginning to regain consciousness. From where he was lying on the floor, tall pillars holding the ceiling up swam into his vision. He shook his head like a dog. He hurt powerfully, but he guessed that he was in one piece. He wanted to go home. Get out of this crazy place, but he knew that if he did leave, there would be no job next week, and he really needed this job.

Clutching one of the pillars, he forced one knee up, and then pushed his bulk to an upright position. He was dizzy, and he hung on to the column.

No matter how painful it was, he had to get to the security office and tell the chief to call the undercover cop. He wobbled from his stance near the pillar and staggered to the wall. Holding onto it, he inched his way into the office. Inside, Jerry Stomski, security head, was at his desk reading a paper.

"What the hell happened to you?" he asked.

"I got decked by a weirdo who is now loose in the school! Call the cop!" He sank to the bench.

"What did he look like?" Jerry was on the intercom. "Sixteen oh seven. Report to the security office at once. Emergency."

"Big guy. Crazy looking. Like some kind of psycho. Carrying a gym bag." And Orrin crumpled over in a heap.

The policeman who had been working undercover was at the rear of the school checking the hall near the receiving room where the back doors led to the loading dock. His radio crackled with static.

"Suspicious-looking male assaulted a security guard on first floor. Suspect is somewhere in the building. Looks dangerous. Ten four."

The cop responded. "Will check first floor and then proceed to second. Suggest that security start searching on fifth and work down. I need a description of suspect."

Back in the office, Jerry Stomski swore. "Damn! We're short-handed tonight. I've only got Orrin and he's not in good shape! What the hell!"

"Orrin!" he shouted at the inert figure on the bench, "get up to fifth floor and look for the guy who slugged you! Work your way down through four and three. The cop in checking on the first and second floors."

"I can't do it, Jerry. How do I know that he isn't armed. I'm not! I could get shot!"

"He doesn't know that! Put your hand in your pocket as if you had a gun. He'll think you're armed."

"I don't like it," Orrin insisted as he started toward the front elevator to get to fifth. "Man's already assaulted me."

The cop found nothing suspicious on the first floor. The administrative offices were closed, and there were no classrooms there. He took the stairs to second floor, his hand on the gun that was concealed under his jacket. The student offices and the atrium where the lounge and lunchroom were located were on second. His eyes swept the open area. Clusters of evening students were eating and studying at the round tables. No sign of anything suspicious. Where could the guy be? The building was so vast, so complicated.

He walked down a hall and paused at a room whose door was open. It was the Campus Ministry. Several students were seated on a couch sipping coffee. In the office area beyond the, a woman wearing slacks and a sweater with a large cross hanging on a chain, was seated at a desk. He assumed that she was the director.

He approached her.

"Could I speak to you quietly for a minute, Ma'am? I don't want to alarm the students."

The woman got up and shut the office door.

"I'm an undercover policeman."

"Sister Rose." She held out her hand.

"I've been stationed in the building since the killing last month."

"I'm glad that you are here. We were afraid that no one cared about what happened on campus."

"Security has just informed me that there is a suspicious-looking person in the building tonight. He assaulted a guard on first floor."

"I haven't seen anything strange, and I've been in and out of the Ministry all evening."

The policeman looked perplexed. "I've checked out the lower floor and the security person is working his way from fifth on down. Look, you know the layout better than I do. What would you suggest would be the best place to look?"

"You don't have any idea of what he's after?"

"He told the guard that he was looking for a student."

She spread her hands out. "He could be anywhere. In the stairwells, the bookstore, the basement."

"The basement!" The cop's eyes lit up. "That's the most secluded place in the building. Lots of funny nooks and crannies. If he's looking to abduct someone, he could do it there and not be observed!"

Her eyes widened. "I hope he hasn't got one of our students."

"I hope not. Thank you sister. I hadn't thought of the basement."

"There are some classrooms down there and all of the lockers."

But the cop was already rushing out of the office, checking his gun as he turned into the stairwell.

Inside of the elevator, Katherine was feeling really trapped. The other students had stopped joking and were looking nervously around. She fought down the panic that came from being confined in a closed space. "Someone will get us out soon", she rationalized. A boy near the door had started yelling, "We're stuck, get us out of here!"

Frustrated, she pushed the alarm button for the hundredth time.

Then, with a violent lurch, the elevator started up and began to descend. It reached the bottom and landed with a thump. The students inside the car cheered as the doors parted slowly. Kathrine picked up her purse and books from the floor and followed the others out into the hall. She started toward her locker just as George rounded the corner.

She was going to be terribly late, if Professor Rashoon even let her in, and it would affect her grade. What could she tell him? Would he believe her about the elevator?

She looked up, and her eyes met those of a man coming down the corridor toward her. She stared at the huge grayish man in a bulky overcoat carrying a gym bag, and a shock of recognition flooded her. This was the person who had broken into her apartment and beaten her so severely. What was he doing here?

She turned and ran back to the elevator, arriving just as the steel doors clanged shut. Hysteria rose in her as the man walked steadily down the hall. Screaming, she banged on the heavy metal elevator doors. Then, she began to run the other way. She stumbled past the closed and darkened audio visual room. Classes had started. There were no students in the hall. She ran past the International Center. The man tramped after her. "Stop Bitch!" he called.

She had just reached the door to the drafting class, striking it with her fist to get the attention of the students working silently at the high tables, when the man caught up with her. He grabbed her by the shoulders, spun her around and slammed her into the wall.

"What do you want? Don't hurt me!" she gasped.

"Where's your locker?" he growled.

"On the other side, near the pop machines." He shoved her in that direction.

"What do you want?" she quavered.

"Shut up!" He wrenched her arm behind her back. "And don't talk!"

The pain in her arm was terrible, and she stumbled as he dragged her down the hall.

"Which one is it?" he demanded.

"Over there. Please let me go," she begged.

George hustled her toward the locker she had indicated. "Open it!" he commanded.

Just then a student wandered down the hall, looking lost.

"Act normal," George hissed, tightening his grip on her arm. "Feel that gun? I'll waste you if you don't behave!"

The student drifted over to them. "Do you know where the Spanish 101 class is?" she asked. "It was moved from 342 to the basement, but I'm not sure where."

George poked Katherine.

"I don't know," she stammered.

"Which direction do I go to get to B-12? It might be over there."
"Around the corner," Katherine responded, her eyes pleading, trying to signal her distress.

But the girl was absorbed in her own search for the Spanish class and noticed nothing. Biting the tip of a pencil, she walked around the corner.

"The locker!" George reminded Katherine. He wrenched her arm fiercely. She stifled a scream. With her free hand, she fumbled with the combination of the lock.

"I can't do it!" she gasped. "You've got to let go of my arm!"

For an answer, he smashed her forehead against the locker. A line of blood opened up over her eyebrow.

"Turn the damn dial!"

Her hands were shaking so hard that she could barely hold the dial, and her brain refused to remember the combination, but after several false starts, the locker clicked open.

George let go of her arm and reached eagerly inside. Katherine buckled against the wall, holding her injured arm. He was going to kill her, she knew it. Her vision was distorted, and everything was beginning to turn red.

He bent over and lifted the gaudy doll up from the floor, tucking it against his side near the gym bag. Then, he raised the gun and pointed it at her head.

"Say goodbye! Bitch!" he sneered.

The undercover cop had dashed down the stairs, taking them two at a time. When he came to the basement, he remembered that it was designed as a square, and if he kept going, he could cover the whole area. He sprinted past closed offices and rooms where instructors could be seen through the door windows, gesturing at their students. Turning a corner, he passed the elevator and the men's lavatory. Down at the far end of the hall, he spotted a strange-looking man holding a gun pointed at a black woman who had slid down the side of the wall onto the floor.

"Stop!" he yelled, holding his gun in front of him with both hands.

The man in the gray overcoat turned his attention from the woman on the floor to the intruder, but he was so burdened with the cumbersome doll and the gym bag that the shot that he fired went over the cop's head. The policeman fired instantly. The bullet went through the brightly colored cotton skirt of the doll, shattering its body before burying itself in George's chest. George sank to the floor, clumsily, the gym bag falling next to him. The violated doll lurched onto the linoleum floor, fine white powder spilling out of its side, sifting around George's head in a soft cloud.

The cop ran over and yanked the gun out of the fallen man's inert hand. The weird guy lay in a heap, bleeding profusely. The woman was still crumpled up against the row of lockers, wide eyed.

"Oh my God," she kept repeating, over and over.

Alerted by the sound of gunshots, classroom doors opened and students and faculty poured into the hall.

"Call security!" the cop commanded. "And keep back! I'm a police officer. Don't approach the crime scene!"

"Get back in the room," the drafting instructor ordered his students. "Everybody back inside."

They were slow to return, staring at the man bleeding on the floor and the shaking girl.

"It's all right, miss," the cop told Katherine. "He won't hurt anyone again."

But she just stared at the blood seeping through the pile of white powder staining the floor. Some of the powder had dusted George's face, making it look like snow on a pumpkin, and it was obvious that he was dead.

Chapter Thirteen

The two detectives were working on the piles of paperwork covering their desks. Case after case had to be documented, and it took hours. They were always behind.

"What was the address of the guy who killed his girlfriend's kid, Leo? Last October—The baby wouldn't stop crying, and the man hit him hard enough to fracture the child's skull. They were going to get married the following week, but homicide got in the way!"

"Fifty-two Skillen Street. Speaking of marriage, Marty-- why don't you and Ellie get married? She's the best girl you've dated and you two like each other."

"We have no desire to complicate things, and although we are fond of each other, that's as far as it goes. Besides, why ruin a nice relationship with marriage? Yours is the only one that I know of that's worked out. All the rest of the precinct is divorced or running around. Look at Polarski. He's on his fourth trip to paradise."

"Police work takes a toll on relationships."

"All the more reason for me to stay single."

"Maria liked your girlfriend, but she didn't understand why her parents gave her a boy's name. It used to be that you had to be named after a saint."

"Ah, those were the days! Instead of Elliot, she could have been christened Nympha."

Leo chose to ignore the sarcasm.

Martin and Ellie and Leo and Maria had double dated a few weeks ago against Martin's better judgment. Two committed vegetarians and two determined carnivores. The evening at Pasquale's Italian Garden was uninspiring, food-wise, but Ellie had been amused. She was much more tolerant then he was.

"Try a bite of this meatball," Maria insisted, shoving a tomato-drenched, loaded fork at Ellie. "It may change your mind."

"She's a vegetarian. She doesn't eat meat," Martin warned Leo's wife.

"It's all right, Martin," Elly soothed things. "It looks delicious, but you had better eat it, Maria, not me. I wouldn't appreciate it."

Martin hated people who were always trying to make you share food. If you ordered it, eat it, and stop passing it around. Try some of this, try some of that. No way! His pasta paella was depressing, and Ellie winked at him as she worked bravely on her fettuccine with spinach. Restaurants should be barred from attempting dishes beyond their expertise. The accompanying salad was basically exhausted lettuce and cucumber with some tasteless dressing. Why did Leo think this place was so great?

But one amazing thing had happened at the restaurant. There had been a trio: accordion, drums, clarinet playing dinner music, and Leo had gotten up and approached the group while they were waiting for coffee to arrive. After some intense conversation, the trio began to play, and Leo came back to the table and led Maria out onto the tiny dance floor.

Standing a ways apart, facing each other, they began a frenzied, rhythmic dance; snapping their fingers, circling each other. The dance involved teasing, enticing behavior while the accordion pumped out the accompanying music. Leo's rolls of fat bounced up and down as he snarled, stamped his feet, and Maria was seductive, inviting, raising her skirt flirtatiously as they ogled each other. When the dance was over, the restaurant patrons all stood and clapped, and Leo and Maria bowed and waved.

"Leo!" Martin exclaimed, when they returned to the table. "This is a totally different side of you! I can't believe it!"

"Now you know why I married her," he said, patting his wife on the shoulder, breathing heavily. "We always dance the Tarantella at family weddings."

"What does the dance represent?" Ellie wanted to know. "I've never seen it performed before."

"It's an old Italian folk dance," Maria responded. "My mother always told me that if you danced it after being bitten by a Tarantula Spider, you would be cured of the bite. That's where the name comes from."

"Sounds a little strange." Marty commented.

"Marty! If my mother-in-law said so, it is true!"

Martin realized that Maria's outfit had been chosen with the dance in mind. She wore a black skirt and a red and white flowered blouse, high-heeled shoes.

He was sure that the dinner would have to be repeated if only so that they could see Leo and Maria dance again, but hopefully, at a better restaurant.

His pager went off at that moment while they were working. He listened to it briefly and then put it back in his pocket.

The dispatcher came on the loudspeaker to announce a possible homicide.

"Come on, Leo. They're playing our song."

The latest suspected homicide occurred in a rooming house on a dilapidated street not too far from the downtown district. The two detectives left the car cautiously, and approached a man standing near the streetlight. The house was three-stories high with a wide front porch where several decrepit rocking chairs were positioned. It looked like most of the many rooming houses in the area, with a trampled front yard and worn paint.

"Did you call it in?" Martin asked. The man was staring nervously at the house. He was dressed in work clothes and had a tool kit on the ground next to him.

"I'm the landlord. I was over here repairing an outside plug when I heard shouting and gunshots. Some of my tenants are parolees and others were released from the Psych Hospital. We've had problems. Social Services is here a lot. I'm not sure if anybody got killed, but I don't want to take chances. I called the precinct right away."

"You don't live on the premises?" Leo asked.

"God, no! These people are crazy. I just rent out the rooms."

"Stay out here. We'll check things out. Is the front door locked?"

"No. You can go in. The shots came from the third floor as near as I can figure."

Martin and Leo went quietly up the bare stairs in the dingy hall. Apparently not much maintenance was going on here. The place was dirty and dimly lit.

They knocked on each of the four doors leading off the hallway. There was no answer from three of them, but the fourth produced a loud unintelligible shouting. Martin drew his gun, stood off to the side, while Leo kicked the door open.

A wild-looking man with tangled hair, dressed only in underpants and a shirt, waved a shotgun at them.

"Put the gun down!" Martin commanded.

The man threw the gun at the detective and rushed at Leo.

"Hey!" Leo shouted, as the man grabbed him by the arm and bit him viciously!

Martin struck the assailant across the head with his gun, and the man dropped to the floor, howling in pain.

Wincing, Leo pulled his phone out of his pocket and called the precinct. "Need back-up, and a straight jacket for a violent suspect. Bring the wagon for one dead victim. A shooting." He relayed the address.

The body on the filthy bed was dressed only in a pair of shorts.

The carnage from the shotgun blast was extensive. His chest was blown away, and there was a large blood-spatter on the back wall. The mattress was soaked in gore.

Martin kept his gun trained on the creature who shouted expletives at them. "Fuckers! Clyde stole my money!" he yelled. "I got a right to get it back!"

"Don't move or you're dead and shut up!" Martin admonished him. The suspect quieted down. There was no conversation until the team arrived, jacketed the man and loaded the dead one into the wagon. Both of them were headed for County Medical that had a functioning psychiatric ward. The scene was taped off for later scrutiny and the door sealed.

The landlord was standing on the porch when they emerged from the house.

"This is bad," he said. "I've had trouble, but never a shooting on the premises."

The two detectives took his name and address and told him to be available for a further interview.

"Who's going to pay for the clean-up?" he complained. "I got to rent this room."

"Maybe you should be a little more selective about who your renters are. Don't rent to someone who will shoot up the place."

"Marty!" Leo shouted." You got to take me to Flowers right away! That guy bit me! I need a tetanus shot and the wound disinfected! It hurts like hell."

"How could he bite you through your jacket?"

"He bit me down below on my wrist!" Leo held up his arm where blood trailed from a nasty laceration.

"Hey, he did get you! We're on our way."

The emergency room at Flowers was packed. All the chairs were taken and injured people stood leaning against the walls, some moaning, a few sobbing. Although the admittance nurse was doing triage on patients, the detectives were admitted at once. "It makes everybody nervous to have you wait out there. Some of our clients are afraid of being arrested."

Leo was taken to a curtained enclosure where an intern came in, washed out the bite on his wrist, gave him a shot, and bandaged the wound.

"Busy day?" Martin queried.

"The worst this week and we aren't even close to the weekend!!"

"The homicide business is picking up also."

"Well, if yours does, ours is bound to follow. Is there a full moon or something? I feel like howling."

"I wish I knew. Come on, Leo. The blue line awaits."

"I got to stop home and change into my other jacket. This sleeve is covered with blood."

Martin examined it, critically. "You're right."

"I lose more uniforms on this job. This is the second one this winter!"

"Switch to Traffic Patrol."

"Yeah, sure. Then, I can get run down."

Martin had not been shadowing Frank Pearson lately. There were too many other cases to work on, and he and Leo were busy. Homicide was rampant in the Port City. Martin and Leo were driving on the West side not too far from Leo's house the following day when they noticed a girl walking along, talking on a cell phone. She was dressed in full Goth attire with black clothes, black makeup and black fingernail polish.

"Stop the car, Marty! That's my kid, Tina!"

Leo jumped out of the car and ran up and grabbed the girl by the arm.

"What are you doing?" he demanded.

"Let go of me," she cried, defiantly. "I'm not one of your stupid criminals."

"You're skipping school. There's a truant officer for kids like you. Do you want me to call him, or do you want to go back to the school with Marty and me? The principal will call your mother, or he can talk to me. Make up your mind!"

"Why don't you just let me alone?" she whined. Leo took out his phone. "O.K. I'll call the officer, and he can pick you up."

She wrenched her arm out of his grasp and walked over to the squad car. Martin shoved the passenger door open, and Tina got in.

"Why do you do it?" Leo questioned her. "Why are you dressed like this? You didn't leave the house in these clothes this morning."

Tina stared ahead, refusing to answer.

When they reached the school, Leo yanked his daughter out of the car and marched her up to the front door. Martin called the precinct and told the dispatcher that he and his partner would be on a personal errand for a short time. He believed in keeping things on the up and up.

Fifteen minutes later, Leo appeared.

"Well, she's got detention and has to see the school counselor twice a week. Not that it will do any good. She was just as defiant with him as she was with me. I don't know what to do."

"I wish I could help."

"Marty, nobody can help. It's our problem, but I don't know what the Hell to do about it."

"Are her friends into this Goth business also?"

"Do you think we know her friends? She stopped bringing them around after that fractured ankle episode. She doesn't want to have anything to do with us. Maria is pretty distraught." Leo knitted his bushy eyebrows.

"Let's hope it's just a phase."

Frank doggedly continued his rounds of the restaurants. He canvassed a small, dark eatery near the music hall whose front window was completely suffocated by closely-packed snake plants. They used to be called mother-in-law's tongue. He disliked them. They were ugly. Grace had never been seen in that place. Next, he tried a place that specialized in Greek cooking, but the owner didn't recognize Grace's picture.

Now, he was in a third-rate Chinese dump talking to the owner. He watched the man carefully as the photo of Grace was examined. He never trusted the Chinese—crooked as lightening. This one looked like a Tong member.

"Why you want lady?" the man asked.

"I'm representing the insurance firm of her late husband. She was left money after he passed away from a heart attack, but we have been unable to locate her. We know that she sometimes works as a waitress, and we thought that by checking the local restaurants we might turn up some information about her whereabouts." He pushed the over-sized turquoise-rimmed glasses back up onto the bridge of his nose.

"What if I know her?"

"Our company is willing to pay a reward for information concerning her, but it must be concrete facts. We wish to contact her. Do you recognize the woman?"

"How much reward?"

"One hundred dollars."

The man stared at the photo, his mind working.

"She works for me. Come back at four o'clock."

"Is Grace one of your waitresses?"

"Sally in the picture."

"Four o'clock, you say. It's three-thirty now. I'll just wait and give her the good news." He took two fifty-dollar bills out of his wallet and handed it to the man. The money disappeared like magic.

Frank went over to a booth near the fly-spotted front window, ordered a pot of tea and an egg roll from the waiter and settled down to wait for Grace. Then, he called the owner over to his table.

"Don't say anything to the woman. I want to surprise her."

The gun was in his pocket, along with a set of handcuffs. He wasn't planning on killing her anywhere in the vicinity of the Red Dragon. He'd grab her before she came in the door and hustle her into his car, take her to the waterfront. She could join the remains of the victims the old Mafia Black Hand used to rub out years ago: all those bodies that were reputed to be dumped in the river. Santa Lucia Place had been a festering mob slum before it was demolished and the Stanley Towers constructed in its place. Formerly, there had been dives with sliding hatches in the floors. The victims would be iced and slid right into the water. He pictured the river bottom covered with stacks of calcified skeletons, boats gliding within a few feet of the bones. Soon Grace Milvern would be one of them.

He waited calmly. The tea was good, but the egg roll was greasy.

Grace was watching her reflection in the store windows as she walked down the street to the Chinese restaurant. The coat looked terrific. She wondered if she should call her parents in Cranston. She had no desire to talk to them, listen to them whine about what a chore Denny was, but if she didn't, if they didn't hear from her soon, they might do something drastic. She could easily imagine them putting the child in a foster home. She had to reassure them that she was saving, and it wouldn't be too long before she was able to take him back. God knows she wanted Denny with her, but she had to have more money.

She was almost at the door of the Red Dragon when a man came out of the place, walked up to her and grabbed her by the arms. He wrestled her over to a car that was parked at the curb.

Grace screamed "Let me go!" but the man yanked her arm behind her with such force that she almost passed out with pain.

"Scream again and I'll break it!" he threatened.

Several people were standing near the restaurant, watching the drama, but they did nothing to interfere. They pressed back against the building as though he might harm them also.

"Please help me!" Grace implored, as her abductor thrust her into the back seat of the car. He pulled her arms in front of her as she fought him furiously, and snapped a pair of handcuffs on her wrists. She kicked at him, as he shoved her back into the rear seat, ripped a length of duct tape that was hanging from the car ceiling and plastered it over her mouth.

The man leaped into the driver's seat and drove off with Grace banging the handcuffs against the rear window, trying to attract someone's attention. Her frightened face pressed against the glass.

When Frank stopped at a traffic light, he turned around and slugged Grace brutally across the head, knocking her unconscious. She fell back in a heap, the handcuffs held awkwardly in her lap. His destination was a section of the city called the 'flats' where the river wound its way around deserted grain elevators. It wasn't totally frozen due to the chemicals and industrial waste polluting it. No one went there. Even bird watchers avoided the area.

Rush hour was approaching, and the traffic was beginning to be heavy. Frank turned the corner near the new bank complex and drove past the government office building. He was very controlled at the wheel. It wouldn't do to call attention to the vehicle by erratic driving. The streets changed from business ventures to cheap, antiquated buildings, including boarding houses and bars. This was an old section of the city that some found quaint, known mainly for producing politicians.

Snow was falling on the slushy streets, and he handled the car with care, as Grace lay supine on the back seat. His mind went over the steps necessary to getting rid of her. He had cased the area earlier in the week, parking on an abandoned access road. It was an area where only the gulls went, perching on rusting oil drums, slumped mattresses, bags of frozen garbage that sat rotting in the filthy snow. He made his way down the bank of the oily scum-green water, where the ice was thin, protected by the industrial structures. There would be no problem. The place was deserted. He had a cement block in the trunk of the car, just like the old-time Mafia. After he shot her, he would tie it to her legs and heave her into the toxic foam, watch the water close over her head. If, by some miracle, she surfaced in the spring, so what? There was no reason to connect him with her disappearance. The police would link the killing to that of her husband. He'd be in the clear.

He drove down Cleveland Street. One more block, then over the bridge, drive past the cereal plant and then turn down the rutted street that led to the access road. He could see the swarms of birds that always circled the plant, lifting off the roof and then re-settling themselves in the chill air.

Just ahead of his car was a rusted red pickup truck with a bumper sticker that proclaimed *I'm the NRA and I Vote*. The truck braked unexpectedly.

Frank fumed. What the hell was this? The truck didn't move. Then, he watched with alarm as beyond the truck, guard rails clanged shut across the entrance to the bridge. Stoplights came on and flashed. Traffic sat motionless as the bridge started to slowly rise.

"No! No!" he sputtered. "They can't lift the bridge now. It's not allowed to be raised between the hours of four and seven! There's a sign posted right on it, for God's sake!" The structure continued to rise.

But plunging determinedly through the brackish water and floating ice came the icebreaker. The William J. Staunton, famous locally for rescuing stranded boats that were trapped in the river. It's horn bellowed twice as it approached the rising span.

"Fifteen or twenty minutes! It will take that long for the damn thing to clear the bridge!" he shrieked.

He turned to check on Grace. She was still out cold. His fingers itched to shoot her now and get it over with. He had waited so long for this moment, but he couldn't do it. He didn't have the silencer with him, and the report of the gun would make a significant noise. If he shot her in the car, there would be blood all over. No, he must get her to the flats.

The top of the icebreaker was visible from the road as it moved slowly through the water. A deck hand waved to the idling cars, who honked their horns in response.

Frank was going crazy. He was covered with perspiration.

"I've got to get out of here," he muttered. The woman was going to come around any minute and start yelling and attracting attention. It wasn't dark yet, and he could see the faces of the people in the car behind his. They would know something was fishy when she started banging those handcuffs around.

If he struck her again to shut her up, they would see that too. He had to move. There must be another way to get to the flats. If he drove back down Cleveland and cut over to the Shoreline Bridge, he could get on the Lake Shore Road and find the access road from there. It was a long way around, but the alternative was staying in this unmoving line until Grace came to.

Why the Hell hadn't he brought a rope to secure her? He

thought that the tape and cuffs would be enough. There should have been chloroform to knock her out. He thought that he had planned everything out so well. Grace moaned slightly from the back seat.

That did it. He swung the car around, barely missing the bumper of the pickup and turned out into the other lane of the street. After racing down the wrong way on Cleveland, he careened around the corner of Chicago, still driving in the opposite lane. Frank was so worked up that he didn't notice that the light at the intersection was red when his car hurtled through. A large tractor-trailer was slowly turning the corner, easing into the line of traffic waiting at the bridge.

The driver of the truck threw on the brakes as he saw the speeding car, wildly out of control, skid through the intersection. He was unable to stop as he rode the brakes and yelled. The truck collided with the driver's side of the car and slammed it into a light post where it came to a halt, bent at a crazy angle. No sound emerged from inside of the wreckage.

Chapter Fourteen

Martin sat sipping coffee at his desk in the precinct house. He was thinking about the man that the undercover cop had shot in the basement of Port City Community College. George Shaunessy, a small-time local hood. He had a long arrest record, had done time more than once. Martin sensed a vast web spreading out over the city. Somewhere in the center was the person or persons who controlled things, who had sent Shaunessy to get the drug-filled doll at any risk. Who were they? Maybe he would never find out. It could be any of the major drug dealers in the city. Could this be traced to Jack D'Angelo? Well, from here on in it was the Narcotics Squad's concern, not his. He'd have to assume that Shaunessy killed Dennis Milvern, so that homicide was solved.

It was clear that Katherine Jordan had no knowledge of the drugs hidden in the doll, but would she be all right? She had been through hell. Could she put her life together and finish school?

"I'll check on her in a few weeks," he murmured. "She's going to need a lot of encouragement."

Outside of the building, fire trucks, rescue vehicles, ambulances raced by the station house with sirens shrieking. Martin stuck his head out the door into the reception area.

"What's all the excitement outside?" he called.

"Wicked crash down near Chicago Street," the dispatcher responded. "We just got the call. Some guy ran a light traveling at a high speed and was hit by a semi."

"Fatalities?"

"No word yet. Morganti and Berkowitz are at the scene."

"I'm on my way home. Call me if I'm needed."

The bird feeder was empty, and Martin carried a sack of seeds as he stepped through the sliding glass doors onto the roof of the garage. A large brown shape darted under the feeder.

"Oh, shit! A rat! How did it get up here?" He carefully examined his garden. The wooden box that he used to store tools bore gnaw marks.

"I'll probably have to take down the feeder to get rid of him. Just when the juncos were starting to come around," he mused. Angrily, he shook sunflower seeds into the feeder.

"I can't use poison, that's out. They say that if you see one rat, you've probably got a dozen. Maybe Ellie can tell me about some organic remedy. I'll ask her tomorrow." Wearily, he stepped back into the apartment and sank into his red recliner. There was a stack of neatly piled newspapers next to the end table. Someday, he'd get caught up on his reading.

When he turned on the TV, John Bradford's face filled the screen.

"Good evening. This is the six o'clock news. We begin with a puzzle. Police are trying to understand a strange accident that occurred late this afternoon. A prominent Port City attorney was found pinned beneath the steering wheel of his car at the scene of a two-vehicle pile-up. Frank Pearson, a well-known real estate lawyer was reported to be wearing a disguise consisting of a wig and over-sized turquoise-rimmed glasses when he was found."

Martin sat bolt upright in his chair and listened intently.

"An unidentified passenger, a woman in her early twenties, was discovered unconscious, gagged and handcuffed in the back seat of the vehicle. She and Mr. Pearson have been taken to Port City Medical Center where Mr. Pearson is listed in critical condition. Harvey Gunnite, the Action Reporter, is on the scene."

"Yes, John. We are talking now to the driver of the tractor-trailer that struck the Pearson car, Les Marone. Mr. Marone, can you tell us what happened to cause you to hit the car?" Harvey's luminous green eyes were full of concern. Behind him, the wrecked car was seen, surrounded by policemen and a towing service.

The driver was a man in his forties, balding and pudgy. Long sideburns extended over his jaw in a point. Snowflakes were caught in his bushy eyebrows.

He was obviously shaken, and close to hysteria.

"That car came barreling right through the intersection, went right through a red light! I hit the brakes—couldn't stop—this rigs big, you know. I wasn't going more than twenty miles an hour, but I ran into the car and pushed it up against the light post. I couldn't help it! He ran the light! That's what happened!"

"Thank you Mr. Marone. Now, back to you John."

"Thanks Harvey. We hope to bring you more on this strange accident as soon as we have more facts."

"In other news—the Center Plaza bank was robbed this afternoon for the second time in twenty-four hours....."

Martin had his coat on and was halfway down the stairs by this time, not bothering to turn off the set.

Grace was in incredible pain. Her wrists felt as if they had been broken, and her mouth was raw where the tape had been removed by the aide in the emergency room. He had been so careful, peeling it off slowly, but it was still excruciating. Then, he had to get a service man to come to the ER to saw through the handcuffs. The aide spoke consolingly to her as the cuffs were removed, but there were pains everywhere. Her neck felt frozen. Could it be broken? Her leg was in agony.

"You had better have x-rays on that leg and your neck. We'll take you to x-ray right away."

She gasped as she caught a glimpse of her swollen, purplish limb as the aide helped her onto a gurney, before she was wheeled down the hall.

In the hall, everything was so bright. The lights hurt her eyes, and the noise was terrible. Crying women, screaming children, moans, grunts. Nurses and doctors were dashing back and forth. It was like a vision of hell. They maneuvered around a cart carrying a man whose chest had been shattered by gunshots. There was blood everywhere, and an orderly ran along side of the cart holding a bottle of fluid that attached to the man's arm.

"I can't stand it here..." she started to say.

"We'll have you in a room as soon as we find out what's the matter with you," the aide explained. He had a nice face, square chin, gray hair.

Another technician took the x-rays after laying her carefully on a stainless-steel table and covering her torso with a lead apron. The pain was terrible. When they moved her back onto the gurney, she started to scream. She was unable to stop. Over and over, she shrieked.

"It's all right," the aide said, patting her shoulder. "You're having a reaction to the accident. You'll feel better soon."

He held her hand tightly, and everything began to fade, as the room turned into a black tunnel that enveloped her.

Jack D'Angelo sipped an Old Fashioned from the private bar in his office. Too bad about George. It was inevitable, though, and it saved him the trouble of having to arrange his execution. The lesson was there, even though the merchandise was unrecoverable. It had been tracked down, that was the important thing. No stone was left unturned. It was an object lesson—that he would go to any length to make sure that no one held out on him.

A meeting was scheduled at Hyacinth's restaurant next week, and other issues would be tackled. He needed to buy a judge. There was a large stack of housing violation notices on his desk at the office. An honest, but stupid, housing inspector was determined to get him.

"We'll see about that," he murmured. He had stopped seeing Raven Saint Clair. During the last athletic session she had given him a serious black eye. It was puffed almost shut. He had seen his physician who assured that the swelling would recede in a few days. He couldn't appear at the next business meeting looking damaged. She may have been gorgeous, but she wasn't worth the trouble. Part of her rage was due to the fact that she had been rejected for the Gypsy Rose Lee part. Now, she was due to go into some ghastly production of Cabaret, but not the Liza Minelli role. Madhouse Productions had cast her as one of the dancers. Well, she certainly was decorative, but she couldn't act worth a damn.

Lizard Jacobi was due in a few minutes for his interview. Perhaps the man would work out. He really needed more staff.

"Why do they call you Lizard?" Jack asked the nondescript man sitting in the chair across from the window. He resembled a middle-school English teacher, not someone in the trade, but then, compared to George, anyone looked unprepossessing.

"Because my heart is green," he answered, sounding like a teacher explaining an assignment. He wore gold-rimmed glasses, a sport jacket and tie. His hair was somewhat balding, and he was very clean-shaven.

It must be a joke, Jack thought, and laughed in appreciation.

"Can you tell me something about your history, your specialty?"

"Yes. I was employed in a city down in the next state by Klauder Associates. Have you heard of them?"

Jack had to confess that the name meant nothing to him.

"There was an altercation that went bad, and I was advised that it would be prudent to take up residence elsewhere and seek another employer. References will be furnished if you require them."

"Perhaps."

Lizard didn't go into any further detail about his previous confrontation, but it had been an explosive situation. He had completed a successful elimination for the Klauder Syndicate when he was surprised by several armed men from a rival gang. He only escaped by leaping through a plate glass window, speeding during a high-speed chase that traversed busy city streets, and eluding the pursuers by driving through a little-known alley. He left his car behind an abandoned building for four days while he holed up, cut and bleeding, in a nearby flophouse. The owner of the place had been the recipient of some of Lizard's favors, and he arranged for a nurse to come to his

God-forsaken room minister to his wounds.

"It's a miracle that you don't have blood poisoning," she exclaimed, viewing the festering mess on his arms and legs. She cleaned him up, bandaged him, left a supply of antibiotics and a number for him to call if an infection seemed to be setting in.

Then, the landlord brought a message to Lizard from the Klauder people, who sent his compensation and urged him to leave town. He followed their advice.

"My specialty is elimination, and I must say that I am very good at it. I also practice a little light intimidation and debt collection."

"You're an all-around sort of associate."

"I have a philosophy concerning my involvement with ecology. You might say I'm an urban eco-terrorist. I believe that all the problems that beset the planet are due to over-population. Human nature hasn't changed since the time of the Cro-Magnons, but when the population is kept below a certain point, problems are manageable. There are simply too many people in the world. My mission is to eliminate some of the more noxious specimens. This will contribute to the well-being of society." His pale blue eyes were very sincere, and he spoke with passion. "My work will also prevent wanton depleting of the earth's natural resources."

Jack had to turn and face the window. Another head case. What do I do to attract them? First George, then Raven Saint Claire and now Lizard Jacobi. Well, this one is not a thug, like George, and he is presentable and experienced. He spun the chair around.

"Are there other urban eco-terrorists? Do you have meetings?"

"Not yet in the Port City. I hope to form a chapter when there is more interest in the mission."

"All right. I think that I can use you. Your assignments will be varied. There will be an occasional elimination, but for now, I'd like to have you start on debt collection. It will help you get a feel for my organization. I have a small staff. You and Mike Stokes are it at the moment, but I hire temporary help from some of the other agents in town. You may be loaned out to other organizations if needed. I can guarantee that they are reputable people. Competent elimination specialists are rare, so I'm sure that there will be a satisfying amount of work. Remuneration, of course, will be by the assignment. My secretary will explain the schedule for compensation, and direct you to your first debt assignment."

"Thank you Mr. D'Angelo. I'm sure that this will be a fruitful endeavor for both of us."

Jack stood up. The interview was over. He shook hands with Lizard. The man's hand was dry, actually somewhat reptilian. He proceded to the secretary's outer office.

"Well, now I have staff again. Things are looking up."

"Grace, Grace. Are you awake? Can you talk to me?"

She opened her eyes. She was lying in a hospital bed and standing next to her was Detective McCallister.

"I'm sorry that I let you down," she whispered.

"Don't be. I'm just glad that you're alive. You could have been killed in that crash. What was he going to do to you?"

"Kill me. He grabbed me in front of the Red Dragon and knocked me out. The next thing that I remember was waking up in the ambulance. Where is that man? What happened to him?"

"After he snatched you, he drove to Chicago Street and crashed the car going through a red light. He's in critical condition with multiple injuries. They don't think he will make it."

"But the crash---?" Grace was beginning to feel very foggy. Martin's voice seemed to be slurred, indistinct.

"The car was struck by a tractor-trailer. It was a bad accident. You're lucky to have survived."

"If I hadn't run out on you at the hotel---but I had to find work, so I could get Denny back."

"Look, don't try to talk about it now. I'll come back tomorrow when you're stronger."

"Will you explain everything to me? Tell me about Dennis's murder and the man who abducted me."

"Everything. I'll tell you the whole story." Martin stood by the bed for a while as she drifted off to sleep. Then, he reached down and patted her arm. Yes, tomorrow he would tell her everything.

Right now, he had a strong urge to find Ellie. Mentally, he pictured her in her jeans and her green gardening clogs. He needed her calmness and her restorative nature. She worked inside of the greenhouse at Plantasma in the winter, transplanting and a bunch of other jobs that he was unfamiliar with. He would swing by and spend a few minutes with her. Get his mind off the job.

Leo had really disintegrated. His uncombed hair flopped over his face, his eyes had deep purple blotches under them, and he was unevenly shaven. He and Martin were having lunch at Pirell's Pizza House, a choice that usually pleased him, but today, he barely noticed the food.

"You look terrible! What's wrong," Martin asked his partner.

"Maria and I have finally turned a corner on the Tina business, but I can't tell you how much it's taken out of us."

"What's happened? I thought she was in counseling at the school."

"Oh, she was, she is, but she had to go off on her own. She's so headstrong, and she knows everything, of course. Everybody else is stupid!'

"What did she do?"

"Marty, you won't believe it! The dumbest thing in the world! Any idiot would see through it, but not 'Miss I Know Everything.' Her friend, Debby, had been corresponding with a man that she met on the internet, and he told Debby that he represented a modeling agency and that the business was looking for young girls to promote as models. They wanted a Goth look, because it's so popular with the teenagers these days. Idiot Debby, who is just as naive and dense as Tina, told my daughter about it. Well, Tina was all excited. A chance to be a famous model and make enough money to get her own place. She's been wearing all that black stuff and painting her fingernails lips, and eyebrows black. You've seen her. She looks awful! She got in touch with the man."

"How did she do that?"

"Debby's computer. We've denied her use of the family one except for school work, and she and Debby skipped out before the final period at school and went right over to Debby's house to contact the guy!" Leo shook his head.

"And then---?"

"He talked Tina into meeting him at a hotel downtown! Said that the interviews were being held there, and my brain-dead daughter believed him! She went merrily off to meet a total stranger in a hotel room, convinced that her rebel look was so special that he would sign her up on the spot!"

"I've got a bad feeling about this," Martin said.

"Sure you have. You worked vice before changing to homicide. You know where this is leading. No talk about photos, a scrapbook, resume, recommendations, nothing. She went up to the designated room, and, of course, he was waiting eagerly. They talked, and he informed her that she would have to spend an hour with his associate who would evaluate her presentation. The other guy stepped out of the next room and started asking her personal questions, none of which had anything to do with modeling. She began to get nervous and started backing toward the door, when the man grabbed her and tried to yank her over near the bed. Thank God for girls basketball! She is strong! She kicked him and ran out the door."

Martin was horrified. "She doesn't know how lucky she is. Most girls don't get away from these pimps."

"Yeah. They wanted to put her into prostitution. You can make a lot of money off a fifteen-year-old!"

"And she actually thought that she was going to be a model!"

"She was absolutely sure! I wonder how many girls have been trapped by these guys. Even her friend, Debby, was interested. She's not Goth enough, though, so she didn't think her chances were too good."

"It makes me sick! I used to see this stuff years ago, and I couldn't take it. So many ruined lives, both boys and girls, because they will believe anything. Usually, they are transported to another state and kept virtually imprisoned, hooked on drugs, and unable to communicate with their parents."

"What happened next is that she kept running until she got to a fast-food store and called Maria. The first man had confiscated her cell phone when she arrived, saying that they didn't want any interruptions during the interview. Of course, she fell for that. Maria was just leaving for her job at the drugstore, but Tina was screaming and sobbing, so she quick got someone to change shifts with her, and drove off. She picked the kid up and took her straight home. Once they got there, she made Tina wash all the black crap off her face and get dressed in jeans and a sweater. Then, she drove her to the family doctor and demanded that she be examined. Maria was afraid of rape, but she knew the Tina wouldn't go to the hospital for a rape kit. He gave her the works. She had not been sexually assaulted; in fact, for all her worldly attitude, she was still a virgin. Mainly, she was hysterical, so he prescribed some strong medication to calm her down."

"I hate to say it, Leo, but maybe it was all for the best. She was on the wrong track, and now she knows what the real world is like."

"But now, she won't go to school, because she says everyone will know about the fiasco and will shun her or mock her."

"Transfer her to another school."

"Maria wants to put her in a strict Catholic school, but we can't afford it with Rocco at Saint Anthony's. I don't know what to do." Leo rubbed his forehead.

"Doesn't Maria's sister, Nancy, live in Madison? That's not very far. It's on the fringe of the city. Could your daughter live with her during the rest of the school year? She'd be supervised, and she could get a fresh start away from her Goth friends."

Leo pondered this idea. "You know, Marty, that might just work. She's be close enough so that we could see her, and who knows what next year might bring. I'll suggest it to Maria. I think that Tina would go anywhere to avoid having the other kids know what happened."

"Have you spoken to the Vice Squad about this?"

"Yes, this morning, while you were over seeing Grace Milvern at the hospital, I gave them the story. They are getting hot on it. One sergeant has been posing as a teenage girl in those chat rooms, hoping to lure some of these sickos into meeting with him. They've been aware of this group for a while, but hadn't had any luck tracking them down. They want Debby's e-mails, but of course neither she or Tina will cooperate."

"It could have been worse, Leo," Martin reiterated.

"I know. I guess Maria and I have a strong marriage to be able to survive this. You never know when you are going to be tested."

"Come on, comb your hair, and let's get back to work. Do you want a doggy bag for that pizza?"

"No. I couldn't eat it. I'm too depressed."

"Cheer up. You and Maria will be dancing the Tarantella again soon."

Chapter Fifteen

Katherine Denicia was meeting with her adviser, Maxwell Emanuel, in the counseling center at the college. She had missed two weeks of classes because she was in bad shape from the incident in the basement, but he had advised her to provide a doctor's signature and to talk to each professor about why she had had not attended classes. Not all of them had been agreeable to letting her continue with the program. Her Spanish professor said that she could try and catch up, but she had to get the class notes from another student. The Nutrition instructor was an adjunct, and he didn't really care one way or another. He had classes at two other colleges to worry about. Professor Rashoon, who she had for Anatomy and Physiology, her most important class, flatly refused to allow her back.

"This course is a foundation for the nursing program. You have missed too many sessions, not to mention the labs. It would be impossible for you to pass. I advise you to withdraw for a semester and register in another program next fall. Are you interested in Culinary Arts? Or Child Care."

She was beginning to suspect that he was a racist or a sexist. This was the only course he taught for the nursing department, his major being Biology. There had been comments from the other female students about him, that he questioned their intelligence and made demeaning remarks to them.

"No. I want to be a nurse!"

"I'm sorry to inform you that your chances are non-existent."

She immediately made an appointment with her adviser.

"What should I do, Mr. Emanuel? Can you intercede for me? I know that I can make up the work if he will only give me a chance."

The adviser was a rumpled, middle-aged man who had been trying to give up smoking for several years. He chewed gum constantly, and his office walls were covered with anti-smoking slogans, but his jacket still reeked of cigarette smoke.

"That's a lot of assignments to catch up on, and there's no way you could make up the lab work. The course is very accelerated."

"What do you advise? I'm at my wits end." She was shaking and felt nauseated. All her dreams were disappearing.

"I don't think that you are in any condition to return to your classes. You were injured and almost killed, and it's going to take a while before you are completely healed. My advice? Legally withdraw from all but two of the easiest courses, using a medical excuse. Schedule an appointment with the Dean of Students and review the entire business about the attack, so that he will be on your side when you re-apply to the program. I'll help you with the paperwork. Apply online as soon as applications are accepted, that way, you can sign up for daytime classes with another professor for Anatomy and Physiology."

"But I'll lose so much time! And my student aid will be affected."

"Can you afford to pay for a couple of summer classes?"

She thought of the money she had in the bank. That was earmarked for paying Lakeisha something for staying at her place. She could work part-time, but not at her former profession. Maybe be a salesgirl again.

"I guess I can."

"Get the English and Math courses out of the way. Look at it logically. You're still in rocky shape and can't give your courses all the effort you want to. You'll be forced to settle for lower grades, and you won't get admitted to the program. Katherine, you are going to be a nurse. I guarantee it, but it will tke time."

She felt as though a great weight had dropped off her shoulders. She had been so focused on completing the semester that she hadn't used common sense. He was right. All her energies were going to be directed into getting A's in the two courses she would keep. She would end up with a ton of electives but that would simply make her more educated. She would make it work.

"I have an assignment for you, Lizard." Jack regarded the man seated across the desk from him. He still looked like a schoolteacher, but he had proven to be adept at learning the business, even offering admirable suggestions for efficiency, but there hadn't been any elimination work so far, and he sensed that the man was becoming restive. Then, DeShaun Brown had called and asked if he had a good hit man. His employee had been arrested and put in the slammer, and it didn't look at though he was coming out in the near future.

"Stupid! Forgot all I taught him. Crazy shit head! I really need a good man and soon!"

"You may borrow my new employee. I haven't used him in that capacity, but I have heard that he did quality work at his last place of business. He prefers to be addressed as an eco- terrorist, not a hit man."

"I don't care if he wants to be called Stevie Wonder, as long as he can get the job done."

"I'll send him over."

"You will report to DeShaun Brown. My secretary will give you his address. This will be an elimination assignment."

"Fine. Do you know what the population of the world is at the moment? Seven-point-four billion. Thirty-seven percent are either Chinese or Indian." Lizard's normally bland eyes glittered. "I so want to play my part in controlling the future of the planet."

"I'm sure that you do, but I don't think that Mr. Brown has any Chinese or Indian targets in mind."

"I'll do what I have to for the moment."

"Mr. Brown will be pleased."

The storefront was empty, obscure, very dirty and suffused with the bitter smell of old newspapers, rats and ancientness. The front windows, illuminated only by the fading afternoon light, looked out on a depressing street with no sidewalk traffic, with boarded-up houses, trees that had broken branches and gray trunks. Lizard waited patiently for his prey. DeShaun had described the man that he was to meet: one of his agency collectors who was keeping some of the profits for himself. The same old story. It rarely varied. He had witnessed it in city after city. Even lieutenants and sub-bosses were not immune. Lizard had made many of them part of his mission. This man who was to be eliminated was little more than a runner, but one with big ideas.

A small, swaggering black man, dressed in a purple coat with a brown velvet collar, walked confidently into the dimly-lit room. He was ready to command the situation.

"Calvin's here. You Gizzard? Stupid name. Why I have to turn over the profits to you? You a stranger."

"It's Lizard. DeShaun Brown told you that I was a recent hire. It's a new chain of command. You will get used to it."

"I don't like it, but I ain't the boss. You be the first whitey he ever hired, far as I know."

"True."

The small man reached into his coat and drew out a thick envelope which he handed to Lizard.

The eco-terrorist took the package and stuffed it in his pocket. "I'll see you next week. Same place."

"Yeah, sure. If that's the way Brown wants it." He turned and walked towards the grimy door.

Before he could open it, Lizard stepped up behind him, drew out a thin garotte, slipped it over the man's head in a graceful motion and pulled it tight. It cut into the man's throat as he waved his arms about before sinking to the floor. His tongue protruded and his face started to turn purple. Lizard exerted a little more pressure, bending over him until there was no movement. He waited a few minutes, then straightened up from the inert form. Releasing the thin wire, he pocketed it carefully.

"One more for the earth," he whispered, as he left the store.

Ellie and Martin were having dinner at a lake shore restaurant where customers were treated to the sight of huge waves crashing over the retaining wall between the building and the lake during the warmer weather. It was Martin's favorite place. Frequently featured on TV, especially during a storm, it had an unassuming pine-paneled main room with a separate bar and a patio that was open for business in the summer. The food was basic: fish fries on Friday, roast beef on weck with potato salad, chicken-in-a-basket, tuna casserole, apple pie, cherry pie with ice cream. They drank draft beer while they waited for their orders and enjoyed the view from the windows lining three sides of the room. In February, daylight lasted until about six o'clock, and there was a good view of the frozen expanse as it changed with the slowly darkening light.

"I'm thinking of writing a garden column for the Port City News," Ellie told Martin. "They've approached me about the idea, and I'm considering doing it, but I specified that I would only write about organic gardening. No chemicals, toxic sprays or weed killers."

"When would you start?"

"In the spring. Actually, there's a lot of information that could be covered in the winter, but the column would be off to a running start in April. I would have more time to research the material and pick a theme for each issue. It's a bigger project than you might imagine."

"I think it sounds great. I'll be your most avid reader, especially if your planning on discussing compost. I want to begin building a few bins this spring. Did they get a chance to visit your garden?"

"That was the deciding factor. They were blown away."

"Easy to see why."

Ellie's city garden, on a narrow street lined with very old oaks and sycamores contained no grass. The front yard was small, filled with a vast selection of bulbs. In April and May, daffodils, purple alliums, many varieties of tulips, narcissus, and grape hyacinth bloomed among stones and boulders, lanterns, sculptures, a bench, dwarf evergreens, and a Japanese Maple. The small backyard featured: bird houses and feeders, a pond surrounded by reeds, water plants and rocks, dozens of lilies, irises, Oak Leaf Hydrangeas, and hundreds of other plants that Martin didn't recognize. Tall, rusted obelisks drew the eye upward, and vines clung to painted trellises. A tiny shed that Ellie had painted in blues and yellows held garden tools. Near an assortment of potted plants, a small seating area with three wooden chairs covered in woven cushions and a rustic umbrella table, was situated near the house. He was amazed at how densely the small lot was planted. There were vegetables in tubs: tomatoes, herbs, beans, squash. Although it was still winter and nothing was blooming, she had a stack of photos of the garden at its peak to show them. No wonder the news people wanted her to write a column.

"The editors want to illustrate the debut page with those photos of my garden, and an accounting of how it came to look like it does now, what I've done over the years. They even want pictures of it in winter with the feeders thronged with birds. Good thing that I have before and after pictures. When I bought this place there was nothing in the back yard but a dying walnut tree."

"Aren't they toxic to many plants?"

"Yes. Many yards of soil had to be brought in. Most of my plants are in raised beds."

"I love the idea of the column," Martin commented, as their fish fries were set in front of them.

"Want ketchup?" the waitress asked.

"Definitely."

Martin looked approvingly at Ellie. She was so healthy and attractive. Her black hair was caught back tonight with a scarf, and she wore a loose oatmeal tunic over black slacks. A complicated pendant hung around her neck. Silver bracelets jingled on her wrists. Was Leo right? Should they get married, supposing that she would approve of the idea? He had been to that site once, and felt that he wasn't able to provide a woman with the degree of attention she needed. The job came first. Besides, her son, Mathew, had an excellent relationship with his father, and he didn't want to throw complications into that scene. Ellie seemed comfortable with their present status. He decided that it would not be a good idea to rock the boat. Companionship, weekend sex, dinners-- these things seemed to fill all their needs for the moment. He was happy, happier than he had ever been with a woman.

The night had closed into a velvety purple, and they were waiting for coffee when a strong gust of wind slammed against the windows, and the restaurant lights went out. A confused murmur went up from the patrons sitting in total blackness, until the staff quickly started circulating through the rooms carrying LED lanterns, which they deposited on the tables. Apparently this was not an unusual occurrence.

"Sorry about this, folks," their waitress told them. "Do you still want dessert?"

Martin looked at Ellie.

"I'd hate to leave without some of that famed apple pie,"

"We'll stay," Martin informed their server. "Actually, I like the ambiance." The windows shook as more strong winds hit them. Most of the customers were out in the entrance hall fumbling for their coats.

"It's quite romantic," Ellie observed, gazing fondly at the dimly-lit dining room. "I think I'll have an aperitif."

Outside of the restaurant windows, the lake was now totally dark except for light reflected from the frozen ice.

"As you know only too well, I've always been fascinated by the lake," Martin confessed. "There is so much under that deceptive surface. Did you know that there are hundreds of shipwrecks on the bottom? The last one occurred when a barge named the Argo sank in the western part of the lake loaded with a huge amount of benzene and other chemicals. It happened in 1937, and the coast guard started pumping the chemicals out of the tanker just last year."

"Why now?" Ellie wanted to know.

"An amateur diver just discovered the wreck last summer."

"You mean it had lain on the bottom all those years undiscovered?"

"Yes. It and almost 200,000 gallons of toxic juice."

"Scary. Are there many more down there?"

"Literally hundreds: passenger steamers, barges, wooden schooners, tankers. Before accurate navigational equipment and early storm warning existed a lot of ships went down in heavy seas. Don't forget that this was in the 1800's mostly when the lakes were the main lines of commerce."

"I didn't know about this. Now, I'll see the lake in a new way."

"I love history, especially anything that relates to the lake."

When they finished coffee and dessert, Martin paid the check, and they got their coats and went out into the parking lot. Cops were directing traffic at the darkened intersections on the main road. Martin rolled down his window to talk to one of the men that he knew.

"What happened, Jason?"

"Kid was driving too fast for the road conditions, probably been drinking. There are always icy spots on this section, and he skidded and hit a guardrail, and then a light pole. The car flipped and rolled over the bank. They were lucky it didn't go into the lake. Ambulance came minutes ago and transported them to Suburban. There were three other teens in the car, all injured. What a waste!"

"Lucky they didn't hit another vehicle."

"It's a bitch on the Lake Shore Road. Power is out all the way to the Shoreline Bridge. Must have been a transformer."

Navigating the road was difficult and slow going. Although there were cops at all of the major intersections, there were long stretches of open fields whipped by the wind, snow obscuring the visibility. They passed through small, darkened villages where generators hummed and an occasional candle flickered in a window. Pedestrians clustered on the roadside not sure of where the cars were. The only light came from headlights driving in each direction. Martin honked the horn frequently to advertise their presence, and they finally emerged from the blackness onto the ramp of the Shoreline Bridge, which was illuminated for it's entire length. The city spread out before them glowing with thousands of points of light. The blackout had been local.

"It's really beautiful, isn't it, Martin?"

"I never get tired of seeing the Port City at night. I'm glad that we are staying at your place tonight. I'm a little exhausted by the trip."

"There were a few hair-raising moments when cars were traveling in the wrong lane."

"Some idiots just don't practice safe driving. I'll bet there were a few collisions tonight."

When they arrived at Ellie's house, Martin was lucky to find a parking spot on the street not too far from her house. Like most of the city dwellings, hers had no driveway or garage.

Her son was spending the weekend with his father, and they had the place to themselves. She put her arms around him as they stood in the living room where one light near the fireplace cast a warm aura.

"Do you want a drink?"

"You know what I want," he replied, before they walked into the bedroom.

"That Stevie Wonder guy you loaned me-- he used the hot-wire! Never seen that one done before. I expected bang-bang, but no! No noise, no residue! I am impressed!" DeShaun waved his drink in the air. "I will definitely use him again!"

The monthly meeting of the group was scheduled, as usual, at Hyacinths. The business meeting, with drinks from the bar, had started promptly, and the waiter had taken their dinner orders.

"What's a hot-wire?" Arnie asked.

"It's a garrote," Jack explained. "A hand-held ligature used to strangle one's opponent. Lizard told that he uses the double-loop type that the soldiers in the French Foreign legion made popular. The old Mafia was fond of it also, but it's gone out of favor because assassins love blasting their enemies away. It gives them a feeling of power. With the garrote, you can't see the victim's face because it's done from behind. For some, that takes the thrill away."

"I might be able to use this Lizard in the future," Jake McGill mused. "I like his method—it's clean and quiet."

"Just don't call him a hit man. He gets upset with that name. He prefers to be addressed as a terrorist, specifically an urban eco-terrorist, but just terrorist will do,"

"But he is a hit man."

"You know it, and I know it. We'll let him have his little fantasy. He's nothing like psycho George. Just as normal as could be. You'll like him, and he wants more work."

"Any word on why he left his prior assignments?"

"Only that there was a problem, but then I'm not in communication with any gangs in the other cities."

"I might be able to use him soon," Jake McGill stated. "As a group, we're experiencing a shortage of good hit men, yet the problems keep arising among the lower ranks."

"Shall I send him to you?" Jack asked?

"I'll let you know next week. If things don't straighten out, I will need him. Now, other than this terrorist, what are we here to talk about tonight?"

"There's a new gang in town. I don't know much about its power structure. Maybe one of you might have picked up more information," Jack commented.

"They're in my district!" Arnie Levenson cried, banging his fist on the table. "Moved right in, hoping to sell product to the university students at better rates than I provide. Talk about bold!! Thumbing their nose at me!"

"Who's in charge?" DeShaun wanted to know.

"I don't know!" Arnie protested. "But they're everywhere! In the student union, the parking lots, the dining halls! Runners that look like students—jeans, sweaters, those big, ugly boots! Who knows what's in the product they're selling. It could be bad ingredients, and overdoses are not good for business. Our stuff is safe, reliable. We know our suppliers."

"Can't do nothin' until we know who the man is. Then, you could borrow Jack's hot-wire terrorist and do some erasure."

"I've got people working on it, making buys, pumping for information, but they haven't discovered the head man."

"Gene Lempke could do the groundwork at the university. He's pretty cognizant of the older student role. Isn't that true, Jack?" Arnie asked.

"Actually, he did satisfactory work for me using that cover, so he knows how to carry it off. I would advise you to use him. As ever, time is of the essence. Once you discover who the head man is, you can borrow Lizard. He's eager for more elimination work."

The waiter moved close unobtrusively and began to set steaming plates in front of the four.

"Do you wish more drinks?" he asked.

"Lets get a bottle of wine. Could we have the wine list?" Arnie requested. "I feel like some full-bodied red, maybe a nice Cabernet."

Chapter Sixteen

The detectives were having lunch at Mama Cora's where the proprietor was strolling between the tables playing *All of Me* on his harmonica. His T-shirt today featured Frank Sinatra. He paused at their table to do a few bars before changing to *My Way*.

"How are things going with your daughter?" Martin asked Leo.

"Well, Tina is still angry and confused. She barely speaks to us when we go over to her Aunt Nancy's. Her aunt is keeping her under house arrest for the moment. She's been transferred from the city to the high school in Madison, a smaller, more intimate type of place where the teachers get to know their students and keep in touch with the parents. The grades are better, and she hasn't cut any classes. Through the generosity of her aunt, she's seeing a counselor several times a week."

"Any signs of the Goth fascination returning?" Martin asked.

"No. These middle-class suburban kids aren't into that freakishness, and she doesn't want to stand out. They try to dress well and look more prosperous than they are. Oh, they're addicted to the usual stuff: drugs, alcohol. The overdoses occur as often in Madison as they do in the city."

"Has the counselor discovered any reason for her behavior?"

"He's working on it, but I tell you, we're beginning to see what we were doing wrong. My youngest kid, Gloria, has been inadvertently neglected because of all the attention on Brilliant Rocco and Terrible Tina. She is so nice and asks for so little that we overlooked her! Maria and I feel awful about it, and we are doing our best to make up for lost time. Once a week, we go out to dinner, just the three of us, and we attend all of her school events. She's blossomed."

"Do you think that Tina felt overshadowed by Rocco. After all, he's a tough act to follow."

"Oh, I'm sure of it. I tell you, Marty, you think you're doing the right thing with these kids, and it's just not that simple! It's been an exhausting time for Maria and me. I haven't felt this bad since my former partner was shot."

"You never talked to me about that situation."

"I carried it around for a long time. When something like that happens, you always think that you were in some way responsible, whether you are or not. The guilt! It never leaves. I still wake up in the night thinking about it."

"Do you want to tell me about it? All I knew was that he had been killed. It was right before I came back from department-ordered leave for the incident in the hotel. Battaglia didn't explain anything, just told me I was to be transferred to homicide and partnered with you. I knew that it was a sensitive subject. We never talked about it, and I was still preoccupied with my own problems."

"Briefly—what happened was that we had been called to a homicide on Carolina Street. A lover's quarrel. Some guy had shot his girlfriend. He and a buddy fled in a car. We intercepted them while they were escaping the scene and took off after them. I hate high-speed chases! There's always the worry that some civilian could get in the way and be hurt. Finally, we rammed the punk's car so they stopped, got out and approached them. They were jockeying their vehicle around, trying to get free of ours. The set-up looked suspicious, but you hate to call for backup for just a car chase. The driver rolled down the window, and I proceeded to interrogate him: went by the book, no deviation. He was swearing and yelling at me, the usual names cops get called, so I asked him to step out of the car. You could tell by his eyes that he was high on something. Chet was right behind me. The guy's buddy, in the passenger seat, pulled out a gun and shot at us. He missed me, because I jumped sideways when I saw the weapon, but he hit Chet. My partner went down alike a rock, and the perps managed to free their car and take off. I leaped in my car, radioed for backup, ambulance, the works and went back to Chet, but he was gone. It had been instantaneous. I could never forgive myself."

"Do we ever forgive ourselves? There are hundreds of cops walking around crushed by guilt, and it's about something that was never their fault. What happened to the guy who shot your partner?"

"The two of them were caught a couple of miles away and arrested. The shooter got life without parole. If we had a death penalty in this state, he would have been zapped. The other guy got twenty years for killing his girlfriend."

"You can't re-do that day. Believe me, I know."

"It helps-- talking about it, doesn't make it so heavy."

"Someday, I'll tell you about why I got transferred to homicide."

"I'd like to hear it. Right now, I've got Tina to feel guilty about. I keep saying this, Marty, but you're lucky you don't have kids."

"I'm glad that it's one lesson I will never have to learn."

"You and Elly aren't finally on the wedding track?"

"Things are great the way they are at the moment. Maybe someday, but not now."

Gene sat at a table in a dining hall of the university. He was disgusted. Since his triumph at Port City Community, which had been comparatively simple, he was called upon for any college-based assignments. He hated them. This was not his specialty, hobnobbing with undergraduates. He preferred simple robbery, home invasion, kidnapping within reason, intimidation, particularly of other gang members: straightforward stuff. Now, he had to find the major supplier for an entire university. At Port City, there was one dining hall, so it had been easy to do surveillance on the Jordan women. Here, there were many dining areas serving all kinds of food: vegetarian, kosher, Chinese, Thai: even a food cart in the parking lot. Also snack shacks, breakfast bars, formal dining rooms. How was he going to cover all these venues?

Even in his short time on the job, he noticed many ordinary students who seemed to be engaged in active trading. This meant that whoever was in charge was employing members of the student body as dealers. Makes sense. You could pay them less because they would have no idea of the going rates. The kids weren't even skillful at disguising their activities, which meant the probability of being busted was very high. He had no doubt that there were undercover cops sniffing through the school. Previously, Arnie had stationed accomplished traders throughout the campus who knew how to be discrete and unnoticed, preferably operating on the perimeter: the parking lots, the sports stadium. Now, whoever was messing up Arnie's operation was using students blatantly, and this practice could mean the end of a lucrative business when the cops caught them and cleaned house.

He was on his third dining experience today, enjoying baked chicken pasta, preceded by a burger and fries at the Snack Shack and pastry with coffee in the Koffee Klatch. If he didn't unravel this situation soon, he would be as fat as a hog, and he had always prided himself on being trim.

A student, who looked to be about eighteen, with a scruffy soul patch and the hopeful beginnings of a beard, took a seat at his table.

"Taking trigonometry?" He asked Gene.

Gene shut the Cognitive Psychology book that he had forgotten to return after the Port City job.

"Psychology."

"That looks like an awfully old book. Where did you get it? Not the bookstore."

"I bought it on the net. It's not the required reading text, but it's almost the same, close enough to keep up."

"You taking a full load? Your courses knock you out?"

"Yeah. What are you taking?"

"I'm an English major. Second year."

"Who's your adviser? I have to add an English course next semester, unless I'm too wiped out to take a full load."

"Professor Scottini, but you would be better off talking to your own adviser."

"He's a jerk, and he's never in his office when he's supposed to be."

"Look, if you're tired, I've got stuff that will pep you up," the kid confided.

Gene saw where this was going. It was ridiculously easy to play along.

"Tired all the time," he confessed. "Too many subjects, but what can you do? I want to get the hell out of here as soon as possible and find a job. I got some helpers, but they're pretty bland."

"This is good product. You'll be amazed."

"What is it?"

"It's called Super Boost-- new on the market." The kid was earnest about pushing, but incredibly stupid. No prep work whatsoever. Gene could be a narc, for God's sake, the product sounded like a health drink for doddering senior citizens. Whoever thought up this idiotic scheme?

"You guarantee it?"

"Absolutely." And there, right in full view of everyone in the dining hall, he took out a package and handed it over, quoting the price.

Gene almost fell off his chair. When he got over the shock, he handed over the required sum and stuffed the bag in his jacket.

"If you want more, or a different product, I'll be in here every Tuesday and Wednesday afternoon, and we can negotiate."

Unless you're in the slammer, Gene thought. "Where do you get the stuff?" he asked.

"Can't tell you that," the little league dealer said with a wink, before leaving to make the rounds of the other tables.

I can't believe this, Gene told himself. That kid might as well put up a sign 'Get Your Product Here' and sell it from a tray while walking around the room. Now, this is an easy assignment: take me one day tops to find out who is the main man. Then, it will be up to the terrorist-eliminator, Stevie Wonder, as DeShaun calls him.

After he finished lunch, he walked over to one of many student information kiosks.

"Where do I find Professor Scottini?" he inquired of the pert blond student manning the structure. "I know he's in the English department."

She smiled, exposing fantastic, white teeth. "He's in Marshall-Johnson Hall, room 422. On the right hand drive beyond parking lot F-7."

That's one thing he was going to miss when the job was completed—beautiful female students.

It was a brisk walk, but Gene was determined to fight the excess poundage he was accumulating.

The parking lots were well plowed, and the day was sunny. He felt healthy and optimistic.

When he arrived at Marshall-Johnson Hall, he studied a board in the lobby listing the faculty names and their office numbers. He took an elevator to the fourth floor, no problems with this silent, speedy conveyance, unlike the derelict one's at Port City Community, and preceded to look for room 422. Rounding a corner, he saw a group of students waiting in front of the office. They did not appear to be waiting for academic advisement. They were jumped-up, nervous, checking the corridor suspiciously. None of them carried books. Gene walked past the office, making no eye contact, and knocked on a door farther down the hall. There was no response. He leaned up against the wall as if he was waiting to keep an appointment, not looking at the group at 422. Soon, a man with a dense beard, wearing a corduroy jacket over jeans, opened the door and admitted one of the students to the office. Gene opened his psychology book and watched him while seeming to be reading. I think I've found the source, he marveled. Easiest assignment I've ever had. And it's so obvious!

He waited until the student came out of the room, checking his pocket to be sure that the product was there.

This is beyond amateur! Where are the undercover cops? He closed his book and followed the kid to the elevator where they waited for the car to ascend, and then they boarded it. The student had a suspiciously runny nose and a red face.

Not only runners but also users! Gene was disgusted. That's what happens when everybody decides to go into retail. It's pathetic. Arnie will be pleased to hear this. Now, he can contact the eco-terrorist.

When Martin and Leo returned to the precinct, they were surprised to find Grace Milvern waiting in the reception area.

"Grace, how are you? You look as though you are healing. Come on into the office."

Grace still limped a little and walked tentatively, but her attitude was upbeat, and she was smiling.

Martin had been to see her several times when she was in the hospital, but that had been weeks ago.

Leo went to work at his computer while she sat carefully in the visitor's chair, "I have a lot of news, so I thought that I would stop at the station and bring you up to date."

"I hope that it's all good."

"Very good. I still have my room, and the doctor says that I can return to work in two weeks. My leg will be healed by then. You'll never guess where I'll be working."

"Not the Red Dragon, I hope."

"Russo's! Sal is taking me back. I'll be a waitress again. And Denny is coming to live with me! My parents are overjoyed." She laughed. "He'll be in day care at Small Gifts right around the corner from the restaurant, and after I finish my shift, we'll do fun things. We'll visit playgrounds, the zoo, the waterfront. Everything is going to be great!" She certainly looked better. Her brown hair was curlier, and she was wearing some makeup.

"Grace, do you need any help until you get on your feet? I can spare some money."

"Martin, for a detective, you are fantastic! No, I saved a little when I was at the Chinese place, and I'll be working full time for Sal, so things should be manageable. I appreciate all you've done. I felt so lost and confused when Dennis was murdered, but now things are looking up!"

Martin had almost forgotten about Dennis Milvern, the cause of all the misery. It was amazing what damage one man could cause, before he was forgotten forever.

"Keep in touch, Grace. Let us know how you are doing."

"I will."

After she left, Martin confided to Leo: "Sometimes you feel as though this job is worthwhile."

"Yeah, and other times you wonder what the hell you're doing."

Martin laughed. "Try and be an optimist for a change."

Earlier that day, he and his partner had been called to a multiple homicide on the north side of the city. A man had started shooting at a bus stop where quite a few people were waiting for a bus. Several people had been hit, and the rest started running and screaming. It was pandemonium. Bodies lay on the snow-packed sidewalk, and a dog was running madly in circles. Traffic snarled as cars jumped the red light, fearful of the shooter. One of the drivers had called the emergency number on his cell phone.

When the detectives arrived, the shooter had dashed down the street a few blocks, and pedestrians were leaping into stores to get out of his way. A woman pushing a baby carriage was shrieking and the baby was crying. Martin turned on the siren and took off after the guy in the squad car while Leo called for an ambulance and backup. McCallister nosed the car into the curb half a block in front of the guy, and the two men leaped out with guns drawn. The shooter turned to run in the opposite direction as Leo called: "Stop or I'll shoot!"

The man hesitated for a minute and then dove into a flower shop.

"The owner should have been smart enough to lock the door when he saw what was going on," Leo complained, puffing, as they followed in pursuit.

Inside of the shop, near the door, crushed Daffodils lay in a puddle of water near an overturned pail, their stems broken. The storeowner stood behind the counter with his hands raised, as the gunman held him tightly, his arm around the man's neck.

"I swear to God I'll kill him!" he yelled.

"There are more police coming. There's no way you can get out of here," Martin insisted. "Let the guy go and surrender your weapon!"

"He goes with me!"

The owner was shaking visibly. "Help," he mouthed silently.

More cops arrived on the scene. Martin raised his hand to hold them back from entering the store. He knew that they had to keep talking, hoping to wear the gunman down, make him drop his guard. The hot-house odor of the shop, crammed with floral displays, was making him light-headed.

"He hasn't done anything. Leave him," Leo stated. "You've done enough damage with those people at the bus stop."

"Stupid Bitch!" the shooter said. "She thought I didn't know what was going on."

"Was she one of the people at the stop?" Martin asked in a level tone.

That set the shooter off. He began to rant. "I knew. I followed her on the times she said she was meeting her girlfriends. She was meeting him....."

Oh, God, Martin thought. Another domestic! Is there any other reason for murder these days than drugs or perverted love? We need a negotiator. He's liable to shoot the owner.

Just then the door to the rear of the shop was quietly opened and Kevin Polarski carefully edged into the room, holding his weapon in front of him. "Drop the gun or you're a dead duck!" he yelled.

The man swung around, loosening his grip on the owner, who dived for the floor as his captor fired wildly at Polarski, missing him but shattering the door of a glass cold- storage unit. Leo took aim and shot the guy in the shoulder. The perp dropped his gun and screamed, "I'm hit! I'm hit!" clutching his arm. Martin ran over, yanked his hand down and cuffed him. He read him his rights as he frog- marched him out the door to the waiting cops, who hustled him into the wagon.

"Good thinking, Kevin," he exclaimed.

"I figured that store must have a back entrance, and I could ambush him from the rear."

"It was risky. He might have hit you instead of the flower cooler."

"That's how it goes."

"You OK. Leo?"

"I'm just glad it wasn't a fatality."

"Kevin made a good decision."

"Now, we can go back to the carnage on the sidewalk and see what the team has done about cleaning up things. I swear, I should have been an accountant. My father wanted me to do income tax."

"What, and miss all this fun?"

Chapter Seventeen

Lizard stopped at the door of the English office. He wore a gray generic-type uniform and carried a small tool kit. With his nondescript appearance and glasses, he looked just like a technician. "We're repairing the computers on this floor," he told the secretary. "There's a new virus in circulation and the university wants it removed before the damage is widespread. Could you direct me to room 422?"

"Around the corner on the opposite side of the hall. Will you be checking our office computers also?"

He pulled a small notebook from his pocket and pretended to consult it. "Yes. At the end of the week. Can your office be accessed around two o'clock on Friday?"

"I'll be back from lunch by then. Should I keep using the machine?"

"Keep on with whatever you are doing. We should be able to fix it before it erases any data. Is there anyone in Room 422 at the moment?"

"No, Professor Scottini is teaching his Poetry of the Victorian Era class. I can unlock the door for you."

"It would be better if he was there. I might have some questions. What time does he hold office hours?"

"They're posted on his door."

"Thank you. I'll go check the available times. Could I have your name so that the professor will know I talked to you?"

"No problem, it's Miss Calleri."

Lizard walked around the corner, stopping briefly at 422 to check the office hours, continued down the corridor and got into an elevator. Then, he headed for the parking lot.

The next day, wearing the identical uniform, carrying the tool kit, but with the addition of a handful of keys on a chain around his neck, he rode up to fourth floor and approached the designated room. The keys made him look even more authentic. There was a line of students outside of the door. Lizard scrutinized them discretely. As Gene had noticed they didn't seem to be waiting for advisement. He brushed past them and knocked on the door. It was opened by the bearded professor.

"Did Miss Calleri tell you that the university was checking the computers for a reported virus?" Lizard asked.

"She mentioned something. Do you have to do it now? I'm seeing students." The man frowned, irritably. "These are my office hours."

"The English Department machines have to be done by the end of the week, or you will probably lose valuable data. It's an extremely malignant virus."

"Oh, go ahead. The bureaucracy around this place is incredible! Academics simply don't matter!" He strode to the door and admitted a student. The office was L-shaped, so the two were able to conference privately, while Lizard approached the computer sitting on a desk surrounded by papers and opened his tool kit.

The professor took the student over to the window and spoke to him in a low voice.

"Nathan, be casual as you hand over the money, and I'll give you your package." Lizard could barely hear what was being said, although he had taken the precaution of wearing a sound amplifier. He removed the back from the machine using a tiny screwdriver, and placed it of a chair, totally intent upon his work, as he lifted the garrote from the toolbox.

Scottini walked the student over to the door and let him out. Closing the door, he checked some papers that he took from his pocket and turned to admit another student.

Before he reached the door, Lizard sprang, fast as a Cheetah, with the wire and positioned it around the man's neck. There was no time for the professor to make an outcry, as the terrorist pulled it tight cutting off the air supply of his victim, who fell in a clumsy heap clutching his throat. The incident had only taken a few seconds. Lizard replaced the weapon in the toolbox, stepping carefully around the fallen professor.

"One more for the earth," he whispered, as he exited the office, closing the door firmly behind him.

On the way back to the city, he stopped at a small bar and ordered a glass of port wine and a newspaper to celebrate. The job had been a snap. He preferred using the garrote for elimination purposes, although in the past, he had employed a knife, even a rifle and once he executed by drowning. This method was cleaner. The newspaper was full of accounts of refugees swarming the coasts of distant lands, and soon there would come the climate immigrants, pushed out by changing weather. There was nothing that he could do about those people. He wanted to work only with the ones who deserved to be extinguished. The earth could be so green, so beautiful: forests, fields, animals all in perfect proportion if only the numbers could be kept manageable. He remembered his first elimination. At that time, he was not a specialist but an accountant. In the area where he lived, a beautiful tract of land, many acres of woods and streams had been bought by a developer who had a shady reputation. It was his intent to build four hundred houses with the accompanying infrastructure, after clear-cutting the land. There were articles in the paper each evening about how the project would degrade the environment. Groups of enraged citizens had joined forces to stop it, but the town fathers were turning a deaf-ear to their protests. They cited growth, a reduction in taxes, opportunities for home ownership. The town meetings had turned into shouting matches with the police standing by.

Lizard drove out to the land and observed the many varieties of birds swooping in the mature trees. Gullies and small ponds were abundant. The place was a paradise. He thought about the situation for a long time. Obviously, the town officials were being paid off by the developer.

Ecology had long been a passion of his, and he saw a chance to strike a blow for green justice. He decided to kill the developer. The earth would be better off without him, and it would serve as a lesson to the town administrators. They could be next. He had never used a garrote before, and practiced for a week perfecting his style. Then, he drove over to the complex of offices that the development company owned. A secretary directed him to the president's office after Lizard told her that he was interesting in investing in the company. The office was lavish, paneled in a rare wood, carpeted lushly. The developer rose to greet his visitor, smiling broadly. Lizard pointed out a photo of the proposed acquisition behind the desk and asked if this was a recent project. When the man turned to view the picture, Lizard whipped out his weapon and circled his prey's throat from behind his back. There was no sound, only gagging, as he pulled the garrote tight. The body fell silently to the heavy carpet. Lizard replaced the wire in his pocket and walked confidently out the door, passing the secretary who was busy typing.

That night, he packed his belongings, threw them in the car, and drove to a city in the next state where he became an associate in the Klauder Group. He had found his calling.

He would continue to do his part to save the earth. He left a tip for the bartender and drove back to his apartment.

"I just received this," Martin told Leo, waving a piece of stationary in the air. "It's a letter from Katherine Jordan."

"Is she OK?"

"She writes that she reduced her class load for a semester and soon will be full-time again. Things are going well."

"Is she hooking? Oh, excuse me. That was politically incorrect. Has she returned to her previous career choice?"

"No, she writes that she has a new life as a salesgirl at Downtown Mall in a cheese store and plans on working there until she gets her nursing certificate."

"All your cases seem to want to keep you informed of their progress, Marty."

"It's my brown eyes. Now that it's the end of March, she should be finishing up a semester in a couple of weeks. The colleges don't stay in session long after Easter break. I'm just glad it's worked out for her. She went through hell when that deranged psycho, George Shaunessy, tried to kill her."

"Sounds like she's got a lot of ambition. Maybe nurse Katherine can take care of me when I have a complete breakdown before my kids grow up!"

"Leo, your life is bound to get better. Shall we head for the Juicery? It's my turn to pick the place."

"Not there! There's nothing I can eat in that carrot-cruncher's nightmare. How about Mama Coras?"

"Sorry, I feel like a vegie-burger and a soy shake. I had to be content with mushy noodles and squashed peas yesterday."

"You could have had a prime rib, but no."

"OK, let's compromise on the cafe in the Co-Op. It's got something for everybody."

"What do you think of that strangling over at the university?"

"It's weird, but it's not our case. The suburban police force will have a chance to mess it up. What they know about homicide you can put in your shoe. They will probably call on us when they reach a dead end, no pun intended."

"Isn't that the second one involving ligature? The first was victim was a minor hood in DeShaun Brown's stable."

"Yes. No clues on that one, and I really don't care if the crooks erase each other. Looks like there may be a new hit man in town. This is different method of slaughter than our homegrown felons usually employ. You ready?"

"I'm starved."

"Let's go."

"I never want to see another doll!" Katherine Jordan exclaimed to Lakeisha.

"Thought they were your hobby—your beloved coh-lection. Pay any amount for the right doll." Lakeisha swung the colored beads in her hair.

"That was before that ugly man got shot trying to take the South American one from me. Now, all they mean is death and that idiot, Dennis Milvern."

The Palmer Heights apartment was fairly orderly. Katherine had placed most of her things in a rental storage unit. She had sold the few dolls that were valuable on the Internet, and the rest had been donated to Goodwill.

"I hate this place," she commented as the sound of screeching tires blasted the night.

"Got to live somewhere," Lakeisha responded. "Least there's no gunshots tonight. I was panhandled three times yesterday on the Falcon Street."

"Listen. I have an idea. See what you think of it. In another year, I'll have my nursing degree, and I can get a good job at one of the hospitals. We could go in together and rent a two or three bedroom apartment in a nice section of the city, on a street with trees, shrubs. Being in the Heights is like living in a desert."

"Yeah, but I couldn't contribute as much as you, because managing a fast food place isn't exactly lucrative."

"You've done a lot for me, taking me in, and I want to return the favor."

"I don't know. My boyfriend, Dubois, wants me to have a baby. He's dying for a son, and if I don't give him one someone else will."

"You are crazy! Then you'll have to give up your job! I never saw you as a baby mama!"

"Well, I like Dubois a lot."

"Listen, Lakeisha, don't do it. If we get an apartment it will be a chance for you to get out of the projects. Why would you want to raise a child here? They're talking asbestos removal, the roofs are disintegrating fast and it's dangerous! Your kid will grow up and go to prison!"

The girl bit her nail, thoughtfully. "I grew up around the corner from here, and I never knew any other part of the city."

"Well, now's your chance to see how other people live. Promise me you won't get pregnant."

"I haven't so far. Don't know why, but it hasn't happened."

"Get on some heavy-duty prevention just in case, and if Dubois doesn't want you without a kid, then dump him!"

"Katherine, you are so strong!"

"I have to be."

She was working part-time at the a specialty cheese store in Downtown Mall and men hit on her constantly, just like before. Even her baggy, blue uniform couldn't disguise her sexy shape, and nothing would hide the gorgeous face. Business had increased since she started working there: cutting up wheels of Cheddar, scraping samples of different cheeses from blocks and offering them to the customers. The owner of the franchise had approached her about full-time work, but she had declined.

Easter was coming soon and she would be off from school for two weeks. The mall would be full of silly decorations, and the weather would be warmer. Maybe she could pick up more hours. The money would be nice

"Come on, Lasheika, raise your wine glass and click it with mine! We are going to show everybody!"

Grace placed Denny into one of the battered highchairs that the Arms provided for small children. From what she could see the lunch today was mashed potatoes, salad and meatballs, some of which he could eat. She had a jar of Junior Carrots to supplement the salad. He liked to spit lettuce out. The meatballs could be mashed. She waved to a volunteer that she had become friendly with, and the woman came over.

"Could you watch Denny while I go get our lunch?"

"I'd be glad to. Hi, little guy. What's your name? Mine's Marcia."

Grace went to the serving line and filled her tray, then returned to their seats where she cut up the meat and placed it on a paper plate. Denny picked a piece of it up and smeared it over his mouth.

"I see you got your son back," Jo-Jo commented, stopping at their table. The director looked terrible. His face had a blue cast to it, and he was leaning heavily on a cane.

"We're together again," she informed him, "and it's working out very well."

"Good for you. I'm glad someone is having a success story."

"Trouble at the Arms?"

"There's no end in sight. We had another break-in two nights ago, and one of the freezers was wrecked. Stupid! We don't keep money or drugs in the freezer or anywhere else. This one had only been donated to the place last month by Angelique Food products. It's just malicious!

No clues, of course, not that the police care. And if that were not enough, Herman is going off the deep end again. He plans on leaving the dining hall when he finishes his on-line courses in Culinary Arts, and getting a job at Hyacinths or some other high-class restaurant."

"He doesn't look like a computer literate type or even college material."

"He isn't and he doesn't have a computer. I let him use the one in the office, which is so ancient that it's beyond obsolete. Every day he comes in early and pecks away at it, trying to figure the mechanics out. The program continues for a duration of two years, so it should take him the rest of his life to finish and graduate, taking one subject a semester. Gloria, of course, is doing all the actual work.

Grace spooned some carrots into Denny's open mouth. "What's wrong with that?"

"He has to practice creating the dishes, that's what. We never have the right ingredients in our storeroom, and he gets all frustrated and throws things. Next week they're covering chocolate desserts, and I fear for a total meltdown, no pun intended. Yesterday, he deliberately broke some serving bowls! Smashed them right against the wall. The kitchen is getting to be a dangerous place. And it's all my fault, naturally. He thinks that I should be out drumming up contributions so we can purchase his special foods."

"Couldn't the news do a human interest story about it: cook at soup kitchen seeks to become a renown chef. Send money to help him realize his dreams."

"Oh, God, don't let him hear you say that. He's so temperamental now, and he doesn't need any more encouragement. Even Gloria has about had it with his tantrums. So, you see, things are not too good."

"Well, I have to take Denny home and clean him up for his stint at Small Gifts Child Care. He really likes the place and has adjusted with no problems. Then, I have to get ready for my shift at Russo's. Sal has been so good to me. I'm on the afternoon hour schedule now so Denny can attend day care."

"I'm glad it's working."

"It would never be possible, Jo-Jo, if we couldn't eat at the Arms of Love, and I am grateful."

"We do what we can," the director responded, heaving himself out of the chair. "I have to talk to Gloria's cousin, Clyde. I heard of a job delivering furniture that he might be interested in. He's strong, and he's dying to work. The boss of the furniture company is a friend of mine, so I think he'll hire him. Some people are funny about hiring Indians, but not this man."

Ellie and Martin, in jeans and windbreakers, were walking on the sand at the municipal beach. It was Sunday, almost April, and they planned on having an early lunch after their walk and maybe take in a movie. The beach had been cleaned up, the end of winter being milder than the onset, and the wet, grainy sand crunched under their feet. Enormous stacks of dead branches, tree trunks, window frames, construction supplies, tires and wrecked car parts stood in towering heaps that the city crews had pushed together with tractors and high-lifts. Each year the storms deposited all this flotsam onto the shore. A mass of gulls, motionless and in soldierly rows stood on the sand all facing the same direction, exposing their bodies to the intermittent sun. The beach was littered with a scattering of smashed seashells and piles of shells that were as tiny as a fingernail. What creature were they from? There were millions of them.

"I wonder where they take all this debris?" Ellie said. "I see a few pieces of driftwood that would work in my garden."

"I may take a couple too," Martin responded.

From the beach there was a clear view of buildings and the Shoreline Bridge. The city loomed large and Sunday morning quiet behind empty grain elevators. The lake had partially unfrozen and large chunks of ice were emptying into the river on the far side of the city.

Elliot studied Martin's profile silhouetted against the rough sky. She liked his well-defined nose, the thin face, firm jaw. She was lucky. It seemed to be a perfect relationship. He didn't ask for more of her than she could provide and didn't interfere with her relationship with her son. They seemed well suited to each other. She hoped that things would continue this way for a long time. Her gardening column was taking up most of her interest. The first issue would be coming out next month, and she was excited to see what sort of a response it generated.

"Is your partner in any better shape?"

"I think he's shaking off his depression. He and Maria are going to his bowling banquet next Saturday, and that should cheer him up. His life is his family, and this drama with Tina has taken a lot out of him. His son, Rocco, won another award at Saint Anthony's and looks like a shoo-in for a big scholarship, which makes Tina feel even more insecure. She craves the spotlight, but she doesn't know how to get it other than rebelling. I hope the shrink can straighten her out."

"How did Leo ever get into homicide? It seems like a strange choice."

"Oh, make no mistake, he's an excellent detective. The job wasn't what he thought it would be, but he brings good qualities to the challenge of clearing cases. He'll retire at fifty-five and the two of them will move to Florida. I hear about those plans every day."

"What about you, Martin. Early retirement?"

"I doubt it, but when I do, I'd like to buy a place on the beach and do a lot of wind surfing."

"You can't get enough of the lake, can you?" Ellie laughed.

Martin took her hand. "That and other things, as you well know."

It had been a slow week where homicide was concerned, and he and Leo spent much of their time in the precinct working on reports. They knew, though, that as soon as the good weather arrived, murder would become a seasonal sport, and they would be on the move constantly. Right now, the other departments were busy with robbery, car-jackings, and break-ins. Commissioner Battaglia appeared frequently on television, an indication that the news was slow. Would that man ever retire? He had been hospitalized twice the preceding month. Bleeding ulcers was the rumor.

The wind was picking up, tossing Ellie's black hair about. She bundled it into the hat that she retrieved from her jacket pocket, as Martin stooped to pick up a few stones that interested him. The late morning was losing color, becoming gray. They turned to head back to the car as a fine scrim began to fall between the shore and the waves. It was beginning to snow.

Books by Joan Fitzgerald

Children's Books

The Magic Lunchbox
Not Another Christmas!
Squash by Josh, b'gosh!
There's a Moose in my Juice
The Christmas Pig

Young Adult Novels

The Iris House
Dark Towers
The Long Way Home
Merry-Go-Round

Crime Novels

The Arms of Death
Death in a Cold City

Poetry Books

A Collection. Poems by Joan Fitzgerald

Poetry Chapbooks

Glamour
The Sweet Life